I0589976

In
the
Midnight Garden

Copyright

Copyright © 2026 by Holly Anne
All rights reserved.
No part of this publication may be reproduced, distributed, or transmitted in any form or by any means, including photocopying, recording, or other electronic or mechanical methods, without the prior written permission of the publisher, except as permitted by U.S. copyright law.

No part of this publication will be used to train any part of AI training.

The story, all names, characters, and incidents portrayed in this production are fictitious. No identification with actual persons (living or deceased), places, buildings, and products is intended or should be inferred.

Book Cover by Rena Violet

ISBN:
979-8-9929006-0-6 (Digital e-book)
979-8-9929006-1-3 (paperback)

First Edition: February 2026

To those who screamed into darkness and it answered back
You are not alone.

In
the
Midnight
Garden

HOLLY ANNE

*In the beginning, there was a prince who wanted to die
and a woman who wanted to live . . .*

{Date Illegible}

Hell will break loose tonight—that, I am sure of.

Everything is set for tonight's ball down to the finer details. After I announce my abdication, I shall end it all where it began. All that is left is Narcisa and the council, who, under no circumstances, must discover my plan. My power will not end up in her greedy hands or the council's, for it always belongs to the people.

Already do they struggle too much with shadows of death lurking, with three dead just this week, as some are calling it an epidemic, a plague manifesting in the wake of her death. The court speculation is that she cursed Amaris with her dying words. It's all a hoax to lay blame onto Endovier to incite further division. Propaganda from the demands of the noble, which can't happen if I follow through with it.

The witch promised me the elixir shall ease my soul, so I may see her again—I hope to, if not in this life, then perhaps the next. The witch offered me what I wanted most for a hefty price.

I'd pay whatever I need just to hold her. Even if I am stripped of everything that I am, I can't live without her. Without her, I am nothing, and I've become painfully aware of it as I pen these last few words. It's agony to know she'll never haunt these walls anymore. I'll never hear her quips or taste sweet roses from her lips.

This—this is the only way I will see her again.

The clock strikes the hour, and guests are lingering within the halls, so I must be quick.

This shall be the last show I put on.

One

Stories I read as a child—happy ones filled with magic that had implanted dreams of grandeur—were simply not meant to be.

Childish dreams.

The seamstress tightened the atrocious garment's bodice, nearly knocking me off the pedestal. I glanced at the full-length mirror and suppressed a cough. The dress, a ghastly shade of pink, fitted with capped sleeves and frills, was more of a napkin. Gold trim accented the bodice, and the sleeves made it better if not for the giant bow between the skirt at the waist.

Mama stated this attire was all the rage in France, resembling the style of Marie Antoniette, but I wonder if it was to draw away from my pale glow.

Burning it seemed more appropriate for the occasion.

"Almost there!" the seamstress gritted through teeth as the last gasp from my lungs emerged from its murky depths.

Mama pressed a handkerchief to my palm, a solemn agreement of my condition.

I coughed precisely into the cloth, aware of the intense stares of the ladies of the ton at large.

One wrong move, and it was all over.

Without glancing at the crimson dotting the cloth, I folded it and placed it back into Mama's hand.

"William is going to faint when he gets a look at you!" Miriam said as she took my hands.

I ran my thumb on the soft part of her inner wrist, cherishing my innocent sister's thought. That our situation wasn't dire. That there was more to it than the singular reason I was to be tied to him. That my dreams should be taken and not hers—never hers.

"I dare say that he is going to be one lucky man tomorrow!" She spun me around, much to the displeasure of the modiste forcing me to stare at our reflection.

Despite being sisters, we do not look much alike. Miriam is like a golden flower with a heart-shaped face beautifully framed by long ashy-blonde hair and plump lips the color of a peony in bloom. Blue eyes that shimmer under long lashes have most suitors trapped in her spell with a charming wink and a cheeky smile. None of the suitors nor Mama understands the cunning side behind her looks. Every detail of her appearance, from her dress to her heavy rouge, is an elaborate part of her master plan to get what she wants.

It was a sight to see and something I'd never replicate. Not since I became a means to an end. Her goals, wants, and needs had become my own since we found ourselves in such dire circumstances.

"Oh, Valeria, you look gorgeous! I'm so jealous." She squeezed my shoulder, flashing me her award-winning smile, one that hid more than she'd ever let on.

Better you than me, her smile seemed to say.

Mama gripped her cane, accessing the modiste's work. She nodded. "Better than the dark clothing you seem to wear. Brings out your eyes, darling."

Choking back a laugh, I was met with the stranger in the mirror, with her hair in neatly pinned curls, strands falling into sad dark-green eyes.

They held the weight of dreams, tired from the burden she carried. They darted around the small shop and took in the stark pallor the sickness had exacerbated on her thinning frame. Illness had taken much of my innocence, leaving her round face sunken. The woman in the reflection was a walking corpse.

I forced my glance away.

I won't last the year.

The modiste flitted around the shop, gathering materials and fussing with last-minute touches. "There, miss. Although I can't say this is my finest work, it should do for your special day."

I turned to Mama, her stern expression unreadable in the tight wrinkles of age that had taken much of her youth in the past year after Father's passing given light of our situation.

A tragic story, really. A devastating one if the ladies of the ton found out.

Once upon a time, Boris McCallister was a man of dubious virtue. He had a successful career in managing properties and investing in the newest wonder taking the world by storm.

He married Julia Dryer, a woman from another wealthy family, and had two beautiful daughters. All seemed well as his wealth and success grew exponentially.

But a virtuous man is not without his folly.

Five years ago, Boris had taken to the bottle, much to the surprise and displeasure of his wife, while gambling away their fortunes in the dens so few knew. Further and further, he spiraled into the darkness, which was a complete mystery to his family. Little did they know, his sins would multiply in the form of a bastard and a mistress whose husband was less than pleased by the affair.

The more he drank, the more debt accumulated, and the more desperate he grew to hide it from his family.

Until it was too late.

Father had caught consumption at the beginning of the last year, wasting away quickly with the help of the alcohol permeating his study in his final moments. He often did not leave that room, insisting it would be his tomb. Many a night, I wandered the halls, too sleepless to stay in bed.

Outside of the study one night, I was not the only lonely soul. Behind the door, Father was muttering to himself the old prayers similar to the ones I'd heard in church in languages from my studies. Each line he spoke sounded with such fervor and felt as if the man was afraid for his soul as much as he was of death.

Before summer's breath, he was gone. He left us with debt miles high, a scandal to suppress, and the illness that took him.

The illness that ravaged me.

"Chin up, Valeria. People are watching," Mama whispered, peering over at another young lady getting fitted for her first season. She adjusted the stray hairs falling from the hazard pins, clumps of black hair curled around her fingers. "We must be on our way."

The streets of Endovior were alive and well, with people bustling past us as we made our way to a local tea shop. The sun beamed, the afternoon heat stifling as Mama hastened our pace, flying past ladies and gentlemen darting out of her way.

I clung to Miriam, looping our arms as one as we walked together in swishing skirts.

She hummed a tune, one I had not heard in some years, a sweet lulling melody she'd pluck on her harp.

During simpler times.

I lost myself in the sweet tune, using her more as a crutch than I'd like to admit as the familiar constrict in my chest worsened.

The city's squalor was extra pungent that day in the heat of summer.

I refrained from shielding my nose from the odor and stood closer to Miriam, inhaling her cinnamon perfume.

A large shadow barreled toward us, quick and inhumane, skirting the edge of the crowd and against my peripheral. Black dots floated in my vision, chest heaving as I struggled to keep upright. The silhouette draped in darkness slammed into my shoulder, knocking me off my feet.

I stumbled backward into the man, holding on for dear life and using his trench coat as leverage.

Arms shifted around me before I hit the ground. I felt lightheaded, the crowd blurring around us as the brightness of the day adjusted to the shadow beside me.

I gazed upward to find gold orbs fixed in surprise. Shadows from his hat played against tan skin beneath a mask.

It struck me as odd.

Righting myself, I fluffed out my skirt and ensured my purse had not been open before huffing, "Thanks."

I huddled near Miriam, attempting to keep my distance from this man. He was overly dressed for the hot summer weather, covered head to toe in a long black draping coat and a top hat shielding him from scrutiny.

I scowled, rubbing my sternum to ease a cough bubbling to the surface.

"I'm sorry, miss," the stranger said, their voice coming out more like a growl.

A long wisp the color of moonlight poked out from under his hat as he tipped his hat in greeting and disappeared into the crowd.

"What an odd fellow," Miriam commented. "It's far too warm to be wearing black. He might faint."

I looped my arm in hers, dismissing the encounter. "Come now. I'm sure Mama is furious that we didn't keep up."

When we'd reached the tea shop, I labored in my corset, the swell of my breast heavy as the tightening in my chest threatened to combust my lungs.

It took all my willpower not to double over onto the cobblestone.

Mama scowled, handing me the handkerchief. "We'll get you some herbal tea, but I need you to be careful around these ladies. They are the in of high society, and under no circumstances are we to show them any weakness." Mama leaned in close, her stray gray hairs tickling my nose as she menacingly whispered, "They are not to know that you are sick. If they know, then it is all over."

She pulled away, a smile replacing her scowl. "Shall we?"

"My," Georgia drawled, "you are lovely. William will have his socks knocked off the moment he sees you." She took up the dainty teacup up to her lips, sipping in that drawn-out manner I'd often see in high society.

Her movements were precise and flawless, not a hair or straying glance as she lowered her cup and gave a false smile.

"Although her countenance is quite drawn. Julia, is she well?" Charlotte quipped, her blonde curls bouncing in time to her tapping foot.

Charlotte was young, younger than Georgia and possibly myself. Much of the gossip had pinned her marriage at the very first season she was out.

She had a childlike demure about her many ladies lose well before they are placed on the marriage mart. Her round face and eyes did not help draw her away from the childlike wonder despite a diamond stud on her gloved hand.

Mama smiled. "Oh, heavens no. She is very particular in her diet and has a marvelous skin routine."

Their heads turned in my direction.

I attempted a smile. "Yes. Although the way that you talk, I am more like the vampire of old these days. Who knows, I may be back from the dead soon enough to haunt Endovier."

Mama's stern glare sent a message.

I had crossed the line.

Her gray eyebrow twitched as she rearranged her face back into the placid smile hiding our sins.

The other ladies seemed startled by my answer, their delicate features tense and uncertain while hiding their shock by drowning themselves in tea.

My own tea remained untouched along with the sweets on the platter nearby.

Miriam howled in laughter, "When did you get so funny, sister?"

"William will have his hands full," Gloria said. "Has she met my son yet?"

Son.

I messed with the piece of lace underneath the table. Much of my engagement was arranged with a string of connections I did not understand. Mama was the one to arrange it with the Sharpes, but even then, I was never privy to their conversations. The quickness of it all disturbed me, as it kept reminding me that my life—my choices—were never my own.

It was just this morning I was informed I was to be married in a month to a man I never met.

The news came the same morning I was informed I wouldn't last the season.

Gloria and my mother talked with Charlotte, adding her two cents in marriage advice, fiddling with the large diamond atop her finger.

Chatter kept the shop busy, teacups clinking against their porcelain friends, the lingering aroma of sweets and sandwiches curling in my senses.

I kept my gaze on the pathetic teacup sitting in front of me, unable to drink or eat as the tightness in my chest coiled. I feared if I partake, I'd ruin the ruse. I'd be the reason we are destitute and on the street.

Not that I would live long enough to really see it to fruition.

Miriam grasped my hand from underneath the table and squeezed.

I'm still here.

Half-heartedly, I squeezed back.

"Dear," Mama said. I snapped my attention back to the conversation. She sat her cup down, lips tight. "You haven't had a sip or bite to eat."

I grimaced.

Mama had especially ordered the tea to be the medication the doctor prescribed to ensure I was healthy enough for my wedding.

The lukewarm tea stared back at me mockingly, insisting its sustainability to my miserable life.

"I'm simply not hungry, Mama. Pre-wedding jitters."

The lie formed upon my lips.

Gloria clasped her hands together. "Oh, sweetie, you have nothing to worry about. William will be a good man to you, I am assured."

I nodded, if only to sound interested. "That is a relief to hear, madam."

"You'll be meeting him tomorrow at the Sharpe's estate. It's time that you both got acquainted with each other, seeing that you'll be married."

A shiver of dread pulsated through my body—the momentum in which everything around me was happening terribly too quickly. The world spun, and the patrons in the shop all blurred together as I sat, languid limbs moving too slowly to catch up. They all talked of the potential meeting with William Sharpe in his family home. Their voices faded away.

Even Miriam joined, exclaiming the thought of traveling outside of the city to find herself a love match. She slipped her hand out from mine to talk of things I'd never get to see for myself.

I silently cried out, *I don't want to die.*

Two

The nights were my retreat. A time away from the facade I am meant to play—to be the doll I was brought up to be.

I often lingered in Father's old study. The smell of the musty books and the creaks of the house reminded me of the shifting loneliness eating at my insides from within these placard walls.

I opened the window to the spring air's evening chill. The clatter of hooves and wheels on cobblestone mingled with the hushed whispers of men patrolling the streets.

The window was three stories up, a decent fall and more of a reasonable way out than wasting away.

Quick and simple.

I traced the window ledge with my fingers up onto the shelves to the small piano Father hidden in his study. I tapped lightly on the keys, which were horridly out of tune but playable.

The song came to me, the familiar melody haunting my sleepless dreams ever since Father's death and the disease laid upon me.

As I pushed back on the bench, my fingers quickened the pace to a crescendo trembling—screaming in high trills and echoing off dusty books. Fingers flew as I slammed into the keys the odd tune that had come to me night after night. After coming down to an end into a softness, it took me a moment to realize Miriam was standing at the door fully dressed.

"Couldn't sleep?"

"Mmm. What are you still doing up?"

Miriam winked, softly shutting the door behind her. "Promise you won't tell Mama."

"Tell Mama what?"

Miriam went to the window, whistling out to a passing group of men. With a wink, she hiked up her skirt and draped her leg off the ledge. She pressed her back against the frame, weaving her hands into her golden hair and smiling down on them.

"Oh my, I must have been stricken by that of the green faerie," she lamented down below.

I raised a brow to Miriam, words pressing to my lips, when one of the men called, "Unto the sweet nectar does a goddess drink, mad that she may be to revel in dreams on tis of nights."

Miriam knocked against the window, and a rope and hook made their appearance as she lowered them down.

The man placed a basket of brown bottles onto the hook and waved her on before disappearing into the shadows.

Miriam heaved the basket up, arms trembling. "Don't just stand there, help me."

I took hold of the rope until the bucket was inches from the ledge. Miriam collected the two bottles and placed them onto Father's desk, then stashed the gear into the closet.

I pointed to the bottles. "Miriam, what is this?"

"It's absinthe."

"Absinthe?"

She popped open the cork, placing the bottle under my nose, the strong scent of licorice and spice coating my senses.

I fished out my handkerchief from inside my breast pocket and coughed. "Never heard of it."

Miriam smiled, dancing her way through Father's study, where she fetched glasses and poured the green liquid into the crystal.

"Well, it is delightful, and it is what many call the forbidden aphrodisiac of the self. Claris found a local supplier nearly a month ago. Want some?" Miriam held the glass out aloft and without hesitation.

I did not know much about the forbidden drink, but I did know one thing, if it was forbidden, then it is for a reason. But not without curiosity did I fully intend to tell her no.

I took the glass, the green liquid staring back. "How did you find this?"

Miriam sipped her drink, leaning back on the desk. "One of the gentlemen walked into the tea shop that Mama is so fond of and asked for la fée verte, to which I overheard the man scolding the worker to hide the bottles better. I got interested enough to ask the newsboy about it and agreed to assist in my adventures."

I sipped, the warmth coating my throat and burning its way through to my stomach. Licorice and mint buzzed against my taste buds languidly, intimate and tender upon the flesh.

"I didn't know you were one to partake in such activities."

"Life does get a little dull around here with Mama shuffling you around to these appointments that I ought to have a little fun, don't you think, dear sister?"

"I assure you it is not for my own enjoyment," I muttered into my glass.

"I've also gone to those wrestling matches that the men always go to. Now that was fun! Did you know that they have a whole betting system in place? Simply scandalous to lose so much money on the betting table, but, oh, isn't it just thrilling! I can see why Father was so enticed!"

As I stared out into the endless night, the moon glittered against the faint stars, its roundness within the sky dictating the time in which I had left. No possible time to figure out the meaning of enjoyment, not the way it was nearly six months ago. The box of roses sat out on the ledge was all, but a barren box of dirt had all the time in the world to bloom and see night turn into day until a time it found its way back into the dirt from which it was born.

It had a purpose and a life to find those mysteries and adventures.

To me, I was nothing more than the box of dirt, promised to preserve others.

"Either way," Miriam declared, "Mama is not to know. That would defeat the whole fun of it."

"What about suitors?"

"What about them?"

"Are you not worried about what they might think of your lurid activities?"

Miriam sat her glass down. "Ladies of the ton talk, but the men do not. Besides, whenever I go out, I always make sure that I am disguised as a proper gentleman so as not to draw suspicion," she said with a twitch of her brow, jumping off the table. She tucked the bottles underneath her bodice. Opening the door to the study, she wearily gazed back. "Better get some rest. Tomorrow is going to be a pretty important day."

I drank down the liquor, the cool buzz carting off the burning fire of my lungs with a different fire all the same. "I wouldn't say meeting my husband-to-be is that important." I sighed.

Miriam lingered at the door, returning a half-hearted smile. "I am sure that he is everything you dreamed," she said, shutting the door behind her and taking off down the hall with la fée verte.

Remnants of the drink stained the bottom of the glass in that sickly green hue. Much alike, the glass and I, remnants left within me were waiting to be refilled in whatever made me whole. Unlike it, I'd never have the sweet aphrodisiac to fill me time and time, a blissful escape from the horrors I live in.

The nightmares of living.

Father's grave was in the further part of the cemetery. The overcast sky provided a reprieve from the onslaught of heat, and the cool morning hours offered the kind of solace unfamiliar to me. The orange lilies in my hand bobbed as I walked the path to his gravestone.

The wet grass soaked into my thin dress, darkening its soft pink shade. Even in the somber embrace of the cemetery, I felt the world around me brighten, a welcome sensation against the darkness itching under my skin. When I arrived, I coughed into my handkerchief and laid the flowers at his grave.

"Father, it's been sometime." I sighed. "I hope you know that Mama and Miriam will be fine because of me, and I hate that for them." I sat, the words *Requiescat In Pace* stared back, mocking me with every ounce of my fiber. "If you had just accepted your hubris, I would still have a life to live!"

Venom spewed from my lips, and I unfolded every single grievance I held for the man. The vile and vitriol I hid from others spilled out of me to a deceased man responsible for all our pain and suffering.

For *my* pain and suffering.

"After everything, you're dead, and I'm sure to follow when all I wanted to do was escape, to see the world—perhaps, at one point, play the piano on a grand stage. But now . . . now I'm trapped with no other choice but to dig us out of *your* mess." I picked at the dew-soaked grounds, tearing up blades of grass.

Dirt and water soaked my skirt, digging into my knees, as I flickered to the lilies I left on the stone, the irony of their meaning not lost on me.

I'd planned to leave this summer to travel, to carve out my own path in the world, in spite of Mama's protests. I had everything packed when the storm broke, and in a few short days, my dreams died. Trampled into the ground as our family's legacy was on the brink of collapse with the debt and my illness.

Once my chest felt lighter and all the words trapped within were spilled to dead, I lapsed into silence, listening to crows cawing in the distance.

"Those were quite the words for a dead man. You really didn't hold anything back at all." I snapped my head up to see the stranger from the other day.

He was wearing the trench coat, the brim of the hat lifted enough to see a playful grin cross full lips.

I stood, dusting my hands against my dress. "You heard all of that, yet you are bold enough to approach. Ever heard of privacy when grieving."

The man gestured outwards to the empty cemetery, a silvery band glittering softly against his finger.

"There's no one around, and I was out taking a stroll when I spotted a beauty among the headstones."

"Flattery will only get you so far." I strayed a glance to the path behind him, heat rising to my cheeks.

It'd be troublesome if someone were to catch me talking with a man alone. Yet a part of me wished it to happen to make getting out of my impending circumstance a little easier than running.

Though I simply sighed and prepared to depart. "Pretend you didn't see me. It would be hard to suppress a rumor that I was caught unchaperoned in a cemetery, and I don't want to explain why I was here alone."

"And why *did* you choose to come to a cemetery alone at this hour?" he asked, brows knitted together. A few strands of hair fell loose from a ponytail draped over his shoulder and shifted as he cocked his head. "I can't imagine it was for the company."

A murder of crows cawed at us from a moss-covered angel statue. Their beady eyes trained on us as they squawked with amusement—as if they were laughing.

"It's not something I want to discuss with a stranger. After all, you chose to take a stroll in such a somber place, and I chose to yell at a dead man. Perhaps these are mysteries neither of us shall know of the other."

"Yet you chose to come alone without a chaperone in sight, a little dangerous to do as a young lady. I could easily snatch you up and whisk you away without anyone to know your whereabouts," he pointed out to anyone with a reasonable mind.

Yet I was not reasonable, not since my life had become theirs, with the likelihood of me lying next to Father by winter.

"Please." I leveled my tone, suppressing the urge to speak my intrusive thoughts. "You wouldn't be having a conversation with me if that's what you intended to do, much less declare your intentions. I could very well scream, and someone *will* come running."

The stranger shook his head, a small laugh reverberating in his throat, its velvety warmth out of place for a cemetery. "You are so different from what I had expected."

I stilled, heart thundering in my chest. "I assume you were expecting a grieving mess, unable to string a sentence together without wailing."

The grin faded, the stranger's face falling into a somber expression. "I lost someone long ago, too, so I know how hard it can be to . . . adjust to their absence." The stranger touched the brim of his hat, dragging it down over his eyes.

The unsettling appearance made me think it was a new fashion trend or a new cosmetic surgery to account for his strange appearance. Theories ran in my head. Perhaps a botched surgery was why he hid underneath a coat and hat.

"Sometimes, I come here as well to stalk along the gravestones to not feel so alone." The man stepped closer, towering at least a foot over me.

His broad frame could easily swallow me whole. If I were to die here rather than my slow-crawling fate, perhaps it'll ease Mama and give her some pity points with the ton once the scandal is revealed. Idle thoughts like these often pass through my head, which was why I came here of all places. It appeared only the dead could listen to my despair.

Despite all of this, I wasn't afraid when he took my hand, to be out in the open with someone who was not my betrothed. Although he was not my intended, the small comfort warmed my chilled body as a new strange feeling took hold.

I clutched my chilled fingers to my chest, muttering, "I fear I must be going."

The stranger stepped aside, the motion rustling the tense air between us. "I won't hold you up more than I already have."

I walked down the path, my heels against the stone my only companion, as the early morning sun rose higher, dispelling the last bit of the cool air. Only when I reached the wrought-iron cemetery gates did I glance behind me to find the stranger had disappeared.

Three

According to local gossip, William Sharpe was the most eligible bachelor in the city of Endovier. He spent most of his years courting young, fresh women, only to leave them heartbroken within days of meeting—a playboy if you will. So much so that his mama had to place him on the marriage mart to redeem the Sharpe name.

I wiped my hands on the dress I'd been outfitted, a lamb to the slaughter with a pretty bow. I wore a gaudy pale rose dress with minimum details in the skirt and the bodice.

While the maids dressed me this morning, I avoided the mirror. My outfit covered up the fact I was nothing more than skin and bones touting health in its blush-pink fabric.

I ran my fingers under the hem and over the protruding collarbone many of my other dresses hid.

The drawing room of the Sharpes' home was ornate and extravagant as their own reputation claimed them to be. The walls painted an evergreen color stood as the backdrop to the gold trimmings and paintings dotted along the walls. The artwork was of an unusual design, most of which I'd never seen before in any of the art galleries I'd had the luxury of going to from time to time when Mama wasn't keeping me on a tight leash. A couple portraits of previous Sharpe men hung alongside each other, looking old and dusty, while managing a stern pose.

Not many of the housekeepers snooped through here to see the young woman being fed to the man who was supposed to be the end of me. Instead, they left me to the dull, silent echo chamber and the ticking of the clock.

I focused on the mighty oak doors that stood between my only bid for freedom and who I was supposed to be happy to see.

I jumped to my feet to pace the room as the heaviness pressed into my chest again. I retrieved my handkerchief from my corset, coughed blood into it, and hurriedly stowed it away.

At the center of the room stood a large fireplace made of cool white stones and rugged red bricks. Photographs lined the stone ledge, out of place for such grandeur quarters. The photographs were old stills of black and white, depicting a husband and wife with their young child. The young boy's eyes spoke of the underlying rage spilled from their plicated smiles.

Loud and swiftly, the doors swung open, shoes clicking and echoing on the wooden floors.

I stood with my back to the photographs, the rage of the child burning into my back as I faced the man with the same violent expression hidden behind a false smile.

Smartly dressed, the man wore a suit coat of what should be expected of someone of an illustrious name. Soft blond hair swept back off his forehead, and his suit was a matte gray. He stood out flatly against the room. The finer image of a man of society presented himself immaculately and of what those around wanted me to dream of.

"I do apologize for being late. Something came up, so I must unfortunately take off, but I thought I'd drop in—" His narrow blue pools bore down at mine. "You must be Valeria."

"William Sharpe, I presume," I said, trying to keep my voice light and airy.

Practice pleasing others even if I felt like dying.

William crossed the floor, then took my hand in his and pressed a kiss to it. "You are simply to die for. My mother was right when she said you were a thing of beauty in addition to being the daughter of such a fine man. Although you are looking a bit pale, here, take a seat." William guided me to a chair.

I suppressed the urge to gag, forcing a smile to my lips.

Despite his attentive tone, his eyes continued to rake me for any hidden imperfection.

"Thank you. You are too kind." I glanced over at the door, desperate to take off down the hall and to be rid of such a ridgid choice.

"I know this is all so sudden, but we need to discuss some rules."

"Rules?"

"With my business connections, it's important that we set some boundaries in place. I suppose it's been sometime since there has been a man in the house, and there is a need to take over your father's company as well. It's incredibly important that you play the part of the demure wife."

His words became more muffled the longer he spoke.

It all felt suffocating. Heat bloomed in my chest, the walls closing in on me as the next several months played out for me, beating as a drum against my vision. My stomach clenched at the thought of what my duty was to be before I would expire.

William took a seat next to me. "Our engagement ball is in a month, but I suppose we need to begin our courtship immediately if we are to act like we are in love. Presentation is important, especially given the circumstances. You understand that, don't you?"

I managed a nod, my head spinning.

William went on explaining the "rules" of our upcoming marriage, yet I hardly registered it as his hand slowly encroached onto my thigh.

I dropped my gaze to my leg, to the gaudy signet ring on his pinky tapping away at my lap. Blood bubbled in my lungs, and bile rose, stinging the back of my throat.

I couldn't breathe, my body going rigid, stomach churning as my thoughts raced.

William's words bleated onwards, his touch repulsing me, and all I wanted to do was run. The gilded cage slowly closed in around me as I desperately wanted to scream out.

Instead, I plastered the fake smile I'd been trained to use and nodded.

"How did it go?"

I slammed the carriage door behind me, the traces of William's hand still fresh upon my skin.

Miriam was alone in the carriage, another blessing I'd to be grateful for but still another wandering eye.

I turned to look out the window as the carriage trotted down the street and onward to home—at least home for the next month.

Miriam's curious gaze strained, waiting for an answer I did not want to give.

"Did William cut your tongue out, sister?"

"No, but I fear that he may be a beast all the same," I growled, my lightheadedness fading as the thought of home beckoned.

Even though I began to think of an escape plan that could get me out of this horrid marriage, I realized that, sadly, most wouldn't work.

"Come now. He cannot be all that bad." She smiled innocently and sweetly, and I feared it began to rot my own insides. "You could have chosen the worst on the marriage mart. At least he is a fine man of fine upbringing."

I fisted the fabric of my dress.

I hated it all, the way that many of the "choices" I was given were not choices at all but fabricate disillusionment handed to me on a silver platter to only be dressed up to appear as one. Everyone had done it, Mama, William and his own family—and even Miriam. I struggled to fight the burning hot tears and the choking sob threatening to pour out.

"I can't wait until I find my love match and we are wed," she whispered excitedly to the thick, tension-laced air.

"I think he is far worse than what we have ever thought," I said, grainy and tired. "You still have your freedom, Miriam. Cherish it before it is too late."

"Cherish it? Why, marriage seems so beautiful and wonderful. To love someone with all of your being under the eye of the gods. It seems so magical. It seems so—"

"Hellish to be shackled to a man who cares so little for the person he married. That simple freedoms are dependent on a man where there is a chance that one can end up unhappy more so than if one were to be alone."

Miriam's mouth dropped.

"Valeria, you don't honestly mean that, do you?"

"Miriam, I am starting to think that you do not understand much about the world or what is going on. You speak of love and of such wonders that would be afforded to us, but I am here to tell you that it's not the case. We are broke, I am dying of what killed Father, and I am to be wed to a beast who will surely see that I am in an early grave. These are the hard truths that I must face. I hardly have any time to wonder about love or even the chance to choose for myself."

"You have choices, Val. Mama didn't force you into the match."

I glared, rage boiling in my veins. "No, Mama did not force me into marrying the beast—she practically handed me over to a stranger who essentially did not want me anymore than I wanted him all because we do not have time to secure our livelihood in society. These are things that you do not understand and—I am afraid—you never will have to contend with."

Sniffling, Miriam bit her lip, tears glinting in the corner of her eyes. "I did not know."

"How could you have known?" I said matter-of-factly as my patience for this conversation was nearing an end.

The carriage came to a stop. When the doors of the carriage opened, the driver greeting me as he prepared for us to step out into the late evening air.

"I am Mama's dirty little secret."

I stepped out, taking a hold of his hand, then climb the stairs of our crumbling estate with Miriam at my heels.

"Valeria, wait."

Ignoring Miriam's cries, I trudged on.

The door to the estate opens as Mama stands with arms crossed, a frown adorning her stern face.

"I take it that it went well," she said.

I brushed past her, racing up the steps to my room to be away from the world.

Mama consoled Miriam, speaking in hushed whispers that reminded me of when we were girls. Miriam's cries quieted, disappearing altogether the higher I climbed.

That night, I dreamed of shadows and of blood underneath a hare's moon, of a boy standing alone in a tulip field bathed in ribbons of scarlet glistening under the glow. The boy stretched an arm out to beyond—to the sky—to the gods, raising it high to the moon as a quiet sob filled the night's air.

What have I done?

Four

The party held at the Sharpe Estate was to be a symbol of declaration of our match in the house in which I am to wed. I assumed that Mama and Mrs. Sharpe thought the announcement would deter the curious gaze of the public eye, both for the quickness of the engagement and for the parties involved. The public eye is a formidable foe that'd eat me alive, and that night was no different from the ruse I had held.

The ballroom was a sickly gray color. Guests milled about, caught up in idle chatter and gossip. My skin crawled at the very mention of my name uttered by strangers, casting wary glances pierced through my flesh. Judging as if I was nothing more than live-stock—a commodity to be bought and sold however they pleased. The music couldn't drown out the stifled scream building in my chest.

I bet she is with child and is forcing William's hand. It is the only reason why someone as handsome as him would marry her.

I heard that the McCallister blackmailed the Sharpes, forcing William to marry.

Why is someone as ugly as her marrying him? She looks as if she is going to faint if you so much as breathe on her.

I wrung my hands, scanning the room, praying for someone to see the panic taking hold of my body, praying for someone to come up and to ask if I am all right—to save me from the void of the marriage and the pain building in my chest.

The phantom seared heat on my flesh as if he still had a hold of me.

He will soon.

Face after face, stranger after stranger, I gave up. I resigned myself to the corner of the room, sipping on the champagne flute, its astute buzz of alcohol climbing. My hand shook, and the liquid sloshed over the crystal glass. I choked down the tears ready to burst from the facade I'd practiced since Father's funeral.

I curled my fingers around the flute, turning them a tinge white.

I hated what he'd done, hated Mama for what had to be done, and hated Miriam for being simply what I can not be.

The zing of the alcohol mingling with awful realizations made me lightheaded. The room spun, and the cacophony of music and voices slammed into my head.

I'm trapped.

I was truly and utterly alone.

Air in the room became stifling, the heat setting my innards aflame.

I wiped my hands on another pink dress with trestles that buried me under the bundles of fabrics and tulle—farther from the tiny glimpses of sickly grayish hue.

Sweat beaded my forehead as I struggled to listen to the babbling of one of Mama's friends gushing about my fiancé.

I shrank into myself, hiding under all the fabric as the warmth and heat threatened to suffocate me.

As I tried to steady myself by gripping the table, ragged breaths came out in gasps, and the room tilted. I clutched my bodice, forcing air into my restricted lungs.

The music and the gossip collided with one another in a humdrum of a singular voice. Bile climbed my throat, the sick taste of it coating my mouth as my steadied arm shook.

"Dear," Mama said, "you don't look well. Perhaps you should sit down."

Her lips thinned into a wry, plastered smile reserved for the group as her eyes twinkled with concern. Gazes of the women floated above me, skirts enveloping the tiny corner.

One woman scooped me off the table and walked me toward a sitting chair a few paces from the gathering crowd. Another woman fanned profusely, ruffling away a few black strands stuck to my face and neck. All I saw in their concerned expressions were the sentiments Mama echoed time and time again.

Don't ruin the perfect picture of the ruse you are.

A perfect composure held together by measly frayed threads.

I croaked out, "I need some air," and handed off my drink to a lady in favor of staggering toward the large open balcony overlooking the small gardens below.

I pushed past partygoers congratulating me as though I were a prize horse in a parade before being slaughtered. Smiles—cruel smiles—never once wavered as the balcony archway greeted me and the budding summer air twined itself into my hair and panicked lungs. I rested my head against the pillar of cool stone, resisting the urge to sink onto the granite floor.

The bite of the air left goose bumps along my bare shoulders, and I shivered. The soft perfume of roses drifted from the bushes below, the full moon illuminating the garden in silvery light as soft petals clamored to greet its long-lost lover, only to be restrained by another.

Tears pricked as my chest rose and fell, desperate for air and aching for relief of bloodied release from the building pressure.

I clasped a hand over my mouth and stifled a weak whimper.

"A little chilly, isn't it, Little Dove?"

A few paces from the entry to the gardens was a man stepping softly against the stone with the elegance of a cat, a creature of beauty and oddity. His suit was a decade or two older than the current fashion, a long cape draped over his shoulder flickering with each step coming to rest from the edge of the balcony overhang.

The moonlight cut hard angles into his features, the shadows resembling etchings by careful artists.

I caught myself staring and uttered, "I'm sorry. I'm not supposed to be out here without a chaperone. I just needed some air. Never did I think I'd run into you again."

The strange man gave a low chuckle, long silvery strands falling, with a pair of curious iridescent gold eyes peered behind a black mask at my goose bumps. The man shrugged off his coat, draped it over my shoulders, and cleared his throat. "You'd catch your death out here if you are not too careful."

I quipped back, almost without hesitation, "Perhaps death has already caught up to me."

He leaned against the rail of the balcony, his golden gaze burning with fierce hunger. "Has he, now? What a morbid thought to have as a young lady."

"As opposed to, what, being oblivious of their end?"

The frantic energy from the night bubbled out of me in shocking waves, and I chuckled.

I'd little recourse, as I wasn't sure if it was the alcohol talking, the nerves, or the sheer desperation, but I continued to laugh as thought after thought slammed through my skull with the stranger looking on.

I peered out at him from the corner of my eyes, the thought of him mentioning death in front of me fresh on my ailing mind. "It would be foolish to think I can outrun death. No man can and we are forever to be forgotten by death—in death."

My heart thundered as cloves and spice enveloped the night air, and the odd, familiar sensation bloomed inside my chest.

A cool hand grazed my warm cheek, tucking away a stray strand of dark hair. "Death would treasure a gorgeous creature such as yourself. So enthralled that he'd make any bargain with any gods that'll listen just for you."

I let his hand linger there for a second longer than I'd like, the sensation against my skin tender and warm I wanted to sink further into. Yet the gathering voices of the party and the gravity of the situation pulled me out of my delirium.

I pulled away from the stranger. "That may be a nice sentiment, but I am afraid that death is crueler to humanity than a lover of one. Now, if you'd excuse me, I should be getting back."

I shrugged off the coat, handing it back to him— his gaze ripping into my soul piece by piece and into the act I'd play the rest of my little life.

"What is your name?" he asked.

The whispers reverberated throughout the ballroom, hard to ignore and even harder to fathom that a stranger was here, at a party, without knowing the most notable people for whom the party was thrown.

"You're here at my engagement party, yet you do not know my name?" I scoffed, my fingers playing with the fabric of his coat.

He pinned the coat back over my chilled shoulders as a light smile danced across his lips. "I wanted to hear it from you, Little Dove," he whispered in such a way of temptation.

"Valeria. Valeria McCallister."

"Valeria," he mused, sending a thrill up my spine. He closed the distance between us, extending a hand. "May I have this dance?"

"Dance," I squeaked out, a cough nearly bubbling out. I cleared my throat, forcing it back down into the deep part of my lungs as I steadied my breathing. "I, uh—I don't really dance."

The music swelled from inside, a waltz I surmised, the dance floor awash in skirts and quick movements. From beyond the balcony, my so-called fiancé twirled a girl by the waist and whispered sweet nothings into her ear, his gaze flickering to the balcony.

At the open palm of the strange man's hand, I was struck by the thought. This man could be a trick on my decaying mind and body, or perhaps the gods from long ago were listening to my pleas for control of my own life. Sending this man instead of a way out, I chuckled and took his hand gingerly in mine as he guided us into a waltz.

Out on the balcony, the life of the party dimmed compared to the heat flooding my body. Acutely aware of his ghostly touch from the hand wrapped around my waist and the other that held mine, he spun me in time with the music, and for once, my body was light and free.

We spun and spun, the stranger never taking a stray step or allowing a stray touch between us. As the music died, we stood still, chest to chest, where cloves and spice flooded my senses.

I stared at his lips, amazed at how they quirked back into a grin.

"Seems that the dance has ended, Little Dove."

"So, it seems," I said, hating the longing in my voice.

He dropped my hands, cradling them both. "There's more to life than this. More than what death can offer." He tilted my chin, iridescent eyes searching mine and boring into my soul.

"What do you mean?" I asked, his hands cool against mine, unnaturally cool, as I traced the lines of his palms. Closing my eyes, I pictured him the way a lover would, in an absolute dreamlike status. I opened my eyes only to find him studying me silently as smooth fingers traced along my jaw.

Leaning in, I let the heat of our bodies and his scent envelop me. The urge to see if his lips also tasted of cloves and spice consumed me as everything fell away. My eyes fluttered closed, allowing myself this one curious thought and indulgence.

"What are you doing?" William encroached, a dull blade cutting into the magic of the evening, slow and torturous.

I snapped my eyes open to find the stranger gone, leaving me holding nothing more than air.

My heart deflated at the thought this might have been all an idle, sick dream created by the stress of my impending doom. Except his coat was still wrapped around my shoulders in the same scents of cloves and spice.

"I asked you a question," he pressed. "What are you doing out here—*alone*?"

"Getting fresh air. What else?" I snapped back, fingers curled along the coat reeling in front of the waking dream.

"Don't think I don't know."

"Know what?"

William dropped his charming act. A firm hand wrapped around my arm as he lowered his voice. "You are spoiled goods. That's the rumor, but it is so often that rumors are true enough to ruin a lady of the ton. If it wasn't for the friendship of our mothers, there would be far more questions about the rushed marriage out here, pining for someone as if they weren't the ones that condemned you to hell."

My heart quickened, pulse thumping in my ear.

"Is this speculation, or is there truth to what you speak?" I said, trying to not let the fear show.

Another waltz started up again, and partygoers spun ferociously. Skirts moved in tandem, and jittery laughter spring from drunken lips.

His gaze sharpened to the coat draped around me. William opened his mouth only to close it as voices loitered out in the cool evening air. "Come inside.

The sweetheart toast will be soon." William turned on his heel and disappeared, leaving me on the balcony alone clutching the cloak from a man I'd convinced myself didn't exist.

I prepared to head inside to the stifling sight of the crowd, turning to the gardens one last time to see a shadow watching with keen interest from beyond the bloodred roses.

"Care to explain what that was tonight?" Mama roared inside the drawing room of our estate. "People were mentioning a confrontation outside with half the women swearing that they'd seen you dance with a gentleman."

Exhaustion wore heavy, as did the bruises William left behind against my arm.

I sighed, sinking deep into the cushion. "It was nothing."

Mama paced about the room, slapping her palm against a fan. "This is serious, Valeria. We cannot afford to make mistakes."

"The only mistake is promising my hand to that vile creature without my say," I chirped.

Mama snarled. "Do you know how precarious our situation is?"

"You never let me forget it."

"I'm serious. One wrong move and we'll be on the oust of society. Penniless and out of the street. Do you want to see your Mama a spinster, sewing clothes day to day begging for scraps? Well, do you?!"

"But William Sharpe! There must be someone else!"

"There is no one!" she hissed. "Not one that would ask many questions such as why you have no dowry or the sickly hue of you. Gloria Sharpe is a dear friend of mine and one who is facing the same issue within her own family. There are sacrifices to be made, Valeria."

The fireplace crackled inside the musty, dim room, a fiery glow casting heavy shadows along the walls whispering in. Within the walls lay unspoken agendas and secrets on the precipice to expose us all.

I reclined back into the old chair, blood bubbling from my lungs and into white cloth, staining innocence in an all-familiar color.

"So, I don't have a choice. It was either the sick daughter to be wedded or the one with her life ahead. Doomed one or both, is that all? Is that what I am good for, a pawn!"

Mama's face tightened as she took in a sharp breath. "What your father left behind was a massive debt hidden by a good name. This is the only solution we have to use."

Jaw clenched, I scoffed. "Then, I mean that little to you. You would rather sell me to a heinous man to save our reputation than to ensure I lived to see another day."

"It is not that simple." Mama sighed.

I stood, balling my hands into fists at my side. "I think it is, Mama. You just don't want to see it for what it is."

"And what is it?"

In the many months since the diagnosis, I had planned for the end, but there was always hope that I'd be fine in the end. Enough so that the disdain in Mama's eyes and her scowls when discussing my illness would disappear. That I can walk side by side with Miriam without the constant rising anger and guilt that came with it. That the loneliness ravaging my dreams and bones would be gone the same as morning's light.

"That you love Miriam and the McCallister name more than you love me. That you love them more to ensure I become the dirty little secret—the elaborate ruse that'd end upon my death—and you can go on living your life having saved the family name."

Mama's lips thinned, twitching with the words hanging heavy in the stifling room searing into skin.

I clutched my chest, striding out of the room.

Mama added, "We do not have a choice."

Five

Death thrives within the midnight hours, taking souls longed for release in the dead of night on wings swift as a raven. It was on this night, the evening before my wedding, that Death tried to pry my soul from my frail body. My chest heaved, blood gargling from the depths of my lungs onto the soft cotton. Under the dim candlelight, a crime scene splattered across the sheets—a precursor to my own death.

I groped my nightstand, trying to find the medication to suppress the advancing cough riddling my lungs. Every shuddering breath racked my body as each cough left me more breathless and weaker. Blood—so much blood—spilled upon fresh white sheets.

Breathe in. Cough.

Blood surged out of my chest and past my lips, dripping onto the sheets. My chest aflame, each breath harder to take than the last. It'd be easier to swallow needles. Sour metallic coated my tongue, spilling out of my being, where I was to leave my last dying breath.

Breathe out. Cough—

The pain reprieved for a moment.

My bedroom door flew open, and through watery eyes, I glimpsed the shuffle of frantic people fluttering in trying to get the coughing to quiet.

"Quick, someone get Dr. Blachard," Mama called out.

I curled the sheets around in my fist, and with forehead to the warm fabric, I begged the gods to take me right then and there. To take me from this pain—anything but this pain. As they strapped my body to the bed, I hardly felt anything other than a cool, damp cloth on my head.

"It's going to be alright, Valeria," Mama cried. "This will pass, my dear. Shhh."

Hands cooler than water on a summer's day tickled my burning body.

I don't recall how long this went on for, Mama cooing in my ear and hands scraping my body as the prickling of needles in my lungs lessen. Was it minutes, hours, or an eternity? Slowly, the pain became bearable, and the scene came into sharp focus.

Dr. Blanchard was holding a syringe covered in blood, his balding head looming over.

"We've done as best as we can to relieve the pressure from her lungs, but as you can see, the only fluid we are drawing out is blood. This episode may be the first of many to come, I fear. There may come a time where she will not live past a night of coughing such as this." He dumped the syringe off to one of the maids who scurried out the door, out of sight.

Dr. Blanchard's cold hands pressed down on my chest, and the unsettling pressure nearly forced another bout of coughing. "She appears to be stable, but we should let her rest."

"There is no time to rest," Mama snapped, leading the doctor away from the bedside and out of the room.

I dropped my head to the corner of the mattress, gaze drawn to the cracked-open door from where her shrill voice came.

"She is to be married this evening. There is no way we can cancel an event such as this—gods, what would society have to think if this was the case? No, what she needs is drugs and plenty of it—good ones. Not the herb and nettles you are forcing upon my daughter. I employed to cure her not to guess at what is ailing her."

"Ma'am, I've done all I can with what I know and what I have been taught. Long ago, I suspected that this was the work of consumption, but it has progressed far beyond that—even my best techniques are no match for it."

My exhausted limbs and aching body drifted as I fell into the eerie depth of the darkness. I floated beyond this realm and the next—existing and then not.

Light refracted off the dark curtains of the bedroom, creating shapes and shadows. One took on the shape of a man, tall and cloaked, wisps licking at his heel. Burning gold peered out from inky black, watching to ensure I didn't drift completely into Hades's arms.

For a curious second, I thought of the strange man's words.

There is more to life than this.

When I closed my eyes, iridescent gold smiled back at me, a warming calm to my fraying mind. I sent up a quick prayer to any old ones still listening for one last request, wanting to see the beautiful stranger one last time before the dark came for me.

My tired body relented to the inky void, which surrounded me hungrily. It had all but consumed me when I heard the doctor's last words to Mama.

"It'd be mercy to let her die. Instead, you let her suffer."

I've dreamed the same dream for many nights since I became sick.

I'd first hear the boy with dark raven hair crying in my dream—muttering prayers fervently to the moon. The scene would shift to him, covered in blood and standing in a field of tulips. The petals were sometimes white, other times red. Always, they'd transform into scarlet spider lilies as the scene became washed in blood. Words floated up from the wind muffled against my ears as his sorrow-filled, desperate pleas whisper to me night after night.

Someone help me.

I awoke in a pool of sweat, the vision of the boy fading and the blooming dawn taking his place. Groaning, I threw a pillow over my head to block out the sunlight cresting into windows. Mama, upon hearing I was alive and moving, came in with a steaming cup of herbal tea, the same concoction I'd been drinking for over a year. Not a hint of despair rested on her lined face.

"Drink," she commanded.

Muscles crying out, I forced myself to stretch and sit upright to take the cup. I cradled it, letting the warmth seep into my chilled palms, resisting the urge to look at the bloodstained sheets.

In the commotion of the night, I would not have been surprised if the maids had missed it or if it was intentionally left by Mama as a reminder.

I sipped from my cup. Its familiar taste coated my throat before I quickly finished it, the bitterness lingering.

I kicked the sheets off, draping my legs over the bed and bartering with my own body to cooperate—to yield to me. Using a nightstand as a support, I took tentative steps toward the bustling maids fluttering about.

Mama directed them from the doorway, stepping aside, as a couple of the women brought in a package adorned with a red bow.

"Mama," I croaked, "what is this all about?"

"It's your wedding day!" she beamed. "William sent over a gift and the dress we'd commissioned finally came in."

I weakly nodded, attempting to voice my confusion.

"Hush now, everything will be splendid again, and Miriam will be able to go on to marry as well. Pretty thing that she is, I haven't been able to keep suitors away from her," she mused. She ushered the two maids around the room, swiftly drawing up a bath, smoothing out the wedding dress, and placing it on the hanger.

William gifted me with stacks of books on how to please one's husband and fine jewels I imagined as shackles rather than beautiful sapphires. My heart sank further as they dressed me in silence, adorning the gown with sapphires and putting on finer details until the placid dark circles were all but gone. Blush dotted my sunken cheeks until I resembled more of a clown than a blushing bride.

In the pink dress, sad emeralds gazed back, miserable and dollish.

With the touch of rouge placed upon my lips, I was ready to walk to my death.

Saint Luke Cathedral stood as the heart of the city, guarding it from its enemies and being a sanctuary for the lost and weary. Large bays of stained glass greeted the fading afternoon light, washing the steps leading up to large oak doors in blues and reds. Gothic spires stood high and proud against the setting sun as the procession brought me closer to the beast.

Once, when I was a girl, I'd come to listen to the sermons of Priest Dedalus and hide among the pews. I remembered the smell of musty, dusty summer mornings as I hid up in the storage spaces reading stories, listening to the singing of the choir and bells, pretending I was someone else.

What I would give to be someone else.

"Smile, dear," Mama said.

My lungs burned, and underneath the soft, thin smile, exhaustion wavered with each step I took in the public's eye. Through the door, wedding bells rang ominously as the aisle loomed closer.

The large main chapel space was illuminated by stained glass windows in the same hues as outside, with the largest bay window capturing the last bit of dying light. Time did not exist in this space as guests rose from their seats in the same pews I once sat and sang in as a girl.

Mama took hold of my arm with a death grip and strapped me to her side. "They are all waiting for you, my dear. Just this little bit and you can go peacefully."

"I'm better off dead. This is just cruelty, Mama, and you know it. They'll know eventually you sold me to my death," I said, shaking her arm off me while standing in front of the large doors. I took a shuddering breath as all eyes shifted toward me.

I gripped the flowers, crushing the stems with gloved hands.

William stood at the altar with a smug grin in a rumpled suit. Everything in me demanded I run, but with Mama firmly planted against my side, I began my descent down the aisle to his deepening grin forming into an otherworldly smile, which sent chills through my ill body.

Panic set in.

I focused on taking one step at a time to try and get it over with. Running meant I'd be caught and brought back to where my family is confirmed to be destitute with far-reaching implications. Hiding meant I'd condemn us all to the streets, but I'd be free from William and Mama.

Sweat dripped down my neck and into the bodice of my dress. I was not even halfway down the aisle as the crescendo heightened into the march and the stares of the people began to crack.

I stopped short, my legs refusing to go any farther.

"What's wrong, child?" the priest asked, his wise gaze casting down into my soul, reading it as if I was the scripture in which he knew of.

William grunted, his toe tapping the soft, velvet carpet.

Mama and Miriam covered the exits for me, seated on opposite sides of the aisle.

I shuddered a breath, shuffling my feet along the path and making it up the steps onto the altar.

The priest motioned for the crowd to sit, their faceless stares beaming at the happy couple in front of them.

William grabbed my wrist, nearly sending me into him.

"We are gathered here today to witness the union of Valeria Thorne McCallister and William Duke Sharpe on this happy day. In holy matrimony, do they share their pledge of devotion with one another under the gaze of the mighty gods above us who watches and protects us from all harm."

Blood drummed in my ear, the ringing becoming louder the longer the priest talked, eclipsing and absolute. As the world spun, the church and the faces blurred.

I glanced toward the pews, finding my own shadow watching, awestruck by the events transpiring before me. The expressionless shadow's gaze spoke all that there was to convey, eyes glazed over, sunken deep into her skull. Her body was badly emaciated to the point her clothes were nothing more than a bag on a frail frame.

From the crowd, she mouthed, *Vita et mors.*

Life and *death.*

With my chest constricted against my corset, my own ragged gasps climbed to my ear. I nearly did not catch the words. The anxious gaze of the priest, William's, and the rest of the congregation's pinned me into place.

"I'm sorry, what?" I whispered, shame burning my cheek.

"Do you take William Duke Sharpe to be your lawfully wedded husband, to have to hold until death do you part?" He motioned to a disinterested William.

The words caught in my throat as I tried—no, could not bring myself to say those two little words.

William turned toward the crowd, his words echoing off the walls of the church in a ghastly manner. "She is overcome with such emotion and love for me she cannot speak." He gave the crowd a convincing chuckle, leaning into the small space between us, and whispered, "Say the damn words."

I gritted through my teeth, forcing the words to come. "I-I . . ."

The doors to the church slammed open, and a loud crack of wood against stone boomed into the quiet space. All eyes trailed to the man who stepped forth out of darkness into the dying light of the church's warm embrace.

The figure, cloaked in shadows, approached the altar with ease and arrogance. "I don't have a head for dates, but it appears that I arrived just in time."

His sweet, silvery words turned whispers into silence.

"Who the hell are you?" William said, digging his nails into my wrist, shoving me behind him.

The mysterious man—my stranger—laughed darkly, grinning. "I am the man who has come to take Valeria McCallister as my wife, sir."

54

Six

The cathedral erupted in furious whispers as the newcomer leaned against the front pew, observing the outrage. The man was just as he was the night of the engagement party. The sunlight captured long, silvery hair draped over his black-and-red suit hidden underneath by a cape. Those same golden irises peered out from the mask covering the white lines of his scar as he scanned the room.

"Well"—he stalked toward the altar with a slow, steady gait—"I have an objection to this marriage and I'd like to make myself clear on this matter."

"Who the hell do you think you are waltzing in here and demanding a woman who is about to be married?" William spat. "Valeria is mine."

"You act as if the girl belongs to you." He studied William with a bored look before his fiery gaze landed on me. "Have you asked what she wanted?"

"What she wants is of no concern to the matter at hand," William growled. "What matters is your interruption and rude behavior of declaring Valeria as *your* wife."

"But have you asked her what she wanted?"

"No, of course not. What she wants is of little interest to me for this marriage to be."

Gloria hopped out of the pew, flanked by Mama. "Perhaps we should take this elsewhere, sir. Would you follow me to—"

Ignoring the women, he continued on stalking the altar as if he were a cat and William a mouse. "You have no thought nor bother to ask Valeria what she wants," he added with a sly grin. "Perhaps she doesn't want to marry you? Ever thought of that?"

Whispers from the crowd erupted, and William, red in the face, glared at the stranger. He gripped my wrist like an animal, thrusting me nearly off the altar, then raising my arm high in the air for all to see. "She is mine, do you hear? Her life is mine."

"No, her life belongs to death, and I am here to collect."

Gloria approached William, attempting to alleviate the pressure from my wrist. "Honey, calm down. Let the poor girl go. You're hurting her." She stroked his back in swift motions.

The priest staggered forward, his rosary clutched in his shaking hand. "Be gone, evil beast." He launched himself into prayer, white-knuckling his beaded idol.

"Let us be rational here," Mama said, turning toward the confused crowd. "I am sure this is all a misunderstanding. Everyone, please calm down, and, sir"—Mama gestured to the man—"please see yourself out."

"Mama," I started, twisting out of William's grasp. "Stop."

The man remained stoic, prowling to the stained glass windows at the edge of the church. He flickered up at the images of the gods who bore down on us all, who were judging us all in the events transpiring.

A delicate finger traced upwards to the lines of the images. Shimmering light refracted under his command, twisting colorful strands around his fingers.

"Unto love's curse, I surrender thee a lamb to the slaughter. Find a way to set free your greatest desires."

He whispered the odd phrase softly to himself, almost sounding like a prayer in a holy place in front of the crowd.

William grew further flustered as the gentleman's refusal to leave became more apparent.

William marched over to the man. "From gentleman to gentlemen. I suggest you take your leave before this gets ugly."

The man's gold gaze hardened.

He swept forward and met William where he stood with his arms behind him. "I'll only leave if Valeria wishes it so."

"She wishes to marry me," William growled. "Isn't that right?"

"I didn't ask you, did I?" He flickered to me and nodded. "What do you want, Valeria?"

I hesitated, my mind spinning as my legs threatened to buckle underneath my body.

Chest heaving, I struggled to form any words, shifting to the crowd, then back to the stranger.

William backed away from the man, grabbed my wrist, and pointed toward the priest. "You—marry us this instant. I will not stand for this insolence."

"I-I . . ." I struggled against the bite of pain in my wrist.

"One more word, and I'll have your head on a pike," William threatened. "I will make an example out of you if I must."

"William!" Gloria exclaimed.

She and Mama gathered around us, closing in tight, as William pressed the ring onto my finger.

The stranger sauntered toward the altar leisurely, jaw clenched. "I wouldn't do that if I were you."

"What is a stranger like you going to do about it! She is nothing more than spoiled goods anyhow. What is her value to you?" William barked. To the priest, he demanded, "Say the fucking words."

The priest, still bearing his holy object, clambered down from the altar, much to the displeasure of William, and approached the stranger. "I know what you are and violence in the holy sanctum is strictly forbidden." He flashed the idol into the man's face. "In the name of those revered be—"

The man grabbed the priest, shoving his head aside to reveal his wrinkled neck. Long, ghastly teeth protruded from his soft lips and plunged deep into the priest's flesh, nearly ripping him in two.

In a flash, my dreams became nightmares.

Our congregation gasped, panic rising, with bodies scattering to the fringes of the church and screams echoing in the sanctum.

The man dropped the priest's lifeless body, blood pooling, as empty eyes rolled toward us.

Blood coated the strange beast's mouth, his hands stained crimson as he tilted his head toward the sky to reveal to the nonbelievers the sin he committed for all to witness.

Screams erupted, and the doors of the church were thrown back. Many rushed onto the street, crying out for anyone to save them from the hellish beast inside.

William dragged me toward the back door of the church, only to be faced with the man blocking the exit. "You will not have her! You—you monster!"

With speed so blinding, the man snapped his arm, twisting it as his screams filled the drenched sanctum.

I pressed shaky hands to the wall, a coughing fit bubbling to the surface, needles scraping my insides, while terror further climbed. Bile and blood rose in my throat, my legs finally giving out.

Tears escaped as I wheezed out, "I'm not ready."

With bloodied fingers, the creature tilted my chin, and the terrified reflection of me stared back within his pupils. "Please—I-I—don't want to die." I coughed into my gloved sleeves.

He took my hand and pressed it to his lips, cradling it like before. His mouth opened and then closed.

Miriam ran up behind him and struck him in the chest with the athame, the slick knife sliding into soft flesh.

"Leave my sister alone!" she cried, withdrawing the knife with a sickening squelch.

The man's head fell to the blooming wound under red fabric before he chuckled. Swiftly, he gripped Miriam by the throat, her blue eyes wide and filled with absolute terror.

I trembled, mouth dry, transfixed on Miriam's ashen face. "No, please, let her go. I'll do anything." My voice cracked as the metallic taste coated my mouth. "Just let her go. *Please.*"

He regarded me, then released her.

Miriam scurried next to William, throwing herself onto him. She sobbed into his chest, which he did not react to. He clutched his arm, his muscles tensing, scowling either from pain or anger.

No one dared to come any closer to the stranger and me.

"Come closer," the stranger said.

I obeyed. My legs shook with every step until I was standing inches from him. I braced myself, eyes shut tight, as I expected him to do the same to me as he did the priest, draining me dry upon the altar.

I was startled instead by the touch of careful fingers against my face, tucking a loose strand of black behind my ear and twirling the end of it in front of me. Cloves and spice mingled with the austere stench of death, pressing down on the tightness of my chest.

"Don't be afraid." He leaned in, a hand brushing dark curls back, exposing my neck.

Fingers hovered over pale, delicate flesh, tracing the space, and I imagined he could hear the racing pulse underneath.

"And if I am," I replied shakily.

When soft lips twisted upwards and brought down upon my neck, I stiffened, shuddering a breath against his touch.

I didn't feel the sharp pain I'd pictured or had witnessed in horror. No, the man simply pressed his lips to my flesh and drew back, taking a hold of my chin to meet his sorrow-laced gaze.

"What do you say we make a bargain?"

I shut my eyes, steadying my knees, which threatened to buckle once more in front of the man—a devil in sheep's clothing.

Another cough boiled in my chest, needles prickling my throat as I rasped, "What kind of bargain?"

"Come with me willingly, and I will spare them."

"And if I don't?" I gulped.

The man sighed, dropping my chin to fold his hand in mine and slip William's ring off. "I can easily sweep you away into the folds of darkness in which you may have a chance to outrun death if you so wished it to be. Just as easily as I can slaughter every man, woman, and child."

The man dug into his suit jacket and pulled out a ring wrapped in black thorns with a ruby rose-shaped jewel at the center. After tossing William's gaudy ring aside, he placed it onto my finger and pressed a kiss to my hand. "Choose."

Miriam and Mama huddled together, gazes widened as they hugged one another. It's always been my life for theirs, and this was no different.

"Give me your word."

He dropped my hand. "You have my word."

I shivered as the heavy placement of the ring seared through the gloves. "Then, I accept."

The man turned to leave.

Sirens filled Endovier's night air with the masses screaming inaudible words.

Halfway down the church aisle, he stopped. "I'll be back to collect you. Don't think you can run from me."

He bowed his head and walked out of the church into the failing sunlight as twilight approached.

I crumbled to the ground and coughed up blood onto the stained floor.

"You can't just go with him. That's absurd and unbecoming of a lady." Mama paced the floor of the waiting room in a flurry of panic. She clutched her finest white pearls strung around her neck, continuing to denounce the man—the beast. "For God's sake, he killed the priest and nearly killed your sister."

"But he didn't," I argued from the chaise lounge. I clasped my shaking hands together and dug my nails into the flesh, praying this was a dream.

"He could have, and now he wants you! As if it could not get any worse!"

Miriam sat in an armchair. She stared at the ground, picking at her nail beds, processing her near death.

"I don't have a choice. I either go with him, or you all die."

Mama slapped her fan into her palm. "We must think of another way out!"

"There is not another way, Mama." I wiped my clammy hands onto the dress, noting the speckles of blood dotting the bright rose-pink gown—the blood jewel upon my finger twinkled. "The existence of the man defies every logic, and he will slaughter the entirety of Endovier without fail if I do not follow through."

Out of the tiny room's window, night settled in under the cover of darkness. The sun dipped below the horizon, fading into the black sky as the pale moon rose. I was running out of time.

Beautiful and deadly, his phantom touch etched upon my skin, and soon enough, his fangs would be buried into my neck, draining what was left of my life.

I placed my head in my lap as Mama and Miriam hatched a plot despite the warnings. For the last few months of my life, I'd been told of the impossible, and right then, a new impossible was before me. I should've been repulsed, demanding it was a mistake and fighting to stay here with Mama and Miriam. Yet confusion lay my mind bare as the memory of the graveyard encounter and our dance clashed with the bloodshed I'd witnessed. The crushing weight fell as the hour neared to a close, the quiet contemplation driving me mad in every sense of the word.

When Miriam spoke, it was a welcome reprieve from the thoughts clouding my head.

"Mama, I'd like to speak with Valeria," she said. "Alone."

Mama's worried gaze danced between us, her hand going to her bosom as she slowly nodded. "Yes, of course. I need to find Gloria and straighten this up. I'm sure William is just as upset as well." Mama continued to talk to herself as she exited the small alcove of a room, hatching a futile plot.

Miriam jumped up from the chair toward the window, which served as a mocking timepiece more than a scenic showcase of beauty. "Do you remember the time we climbed the cherry tree and Father was so upset when it was discovered we had done so in our best clothing?"

The memory of that afternoon was a cherished relic, more of a dream than a memory.

"Yes. Where are you going with this?"

She tapped the windowsill, her brows scrunched in concentration and thin lips twisted into a frown. She appeared older, lost in thought and more serious than I'd ever seen her, becoming what I could not.

"You talked your way out of Father punishing us. Father was so mad at us when we climbed down and nearly broke our necks, but you saved our skin. Sweet talking him with such words I had never seen still to this day on how such sweet talking can be done. Perhaps you can talk your way out of this arrangement."

I shook my head. "There is no talking my way out of this."

She bustled forward, taking my hands in hers. "Sister, you must. You must try and get out of this horrid arrangement and come back to us."

I balked at the words. They reverberated against my skull as a tireless joke.

In plain truth, the same truth I hid from her, there was nothing left for me. I was a pawn in Mama's ruse to ensure our futures, and I would've been a ruse for William all the same. None of this could erase the fact I wouldn't last the season.

At least with this choice, I would be swapping one death for another.

I rubbed at her thumb, the softness of hers under the harshness of mine. "He would kill me before he ever gives me the chance to come back even then"—I shuddered—"I'm dying, Miriam. Dying. I will not come back. I can't come back. If I go with this man or stay, I will die either way, and there is no changing that."

"We can find a cure, and there are ways we can—"

"No. There is no other way. At least this way, I can not be a burden to Mama and to you for the funeral expenses or medical expenses. You will not have to worry about having a sister and, instead, start afresh, worrying about other trivial matters such as finding a suitor."

Miriam lowered her face into my lap, crying softly into the stained fabric.

I patted her head just like when we were children.

As her cries quieted, something in her shifted.

She snapped her head up, eyes twinkling with dangerous thoughts. "He is immortal. Perhaps he knows of a way to extend your life. Maybe—maybe you can sweet-talk your way into showing you his secret, and you can come back." She lunged for a hug, squeezing what little life I had out of my body. "Yes, that's it! Ask him to show you his secret and then kill him and come back to us!"

Kill him.

Two little words that seem next to impossible floated within the space.

Miriam, renewed with hope and inspiration, muttered something indiscernible to herself.

"What possessed you to think it would be possible?" I asked.

"I once read it in a book!"

"Miriam, I don't—"

"We are going to need a few stakes and holy water." She stood and paced the floor. "I wonder if we can stake him as he sleeps during the day. Although I am not sure about the whole daylight myth, since he was still walking in the light before the sun was even down."

"Miriam—"

Miriam rambled on further, oblivious. Her movements became more exaggerated, the wheels turning in her mind furiously as her pace quickened.

"Miriam. Miriam, listen to me."

Her gaze snapped to me, fervor blazing high in her eyes.

"That man will kill me before I ever can think of killing him. You need to accept that this is the end of the line for me. There is no coming back from this. Ever."

I spoke softly and slowly, enunciating every syllable with a heavy heart.

It hurt more to see her face fall, the light draining from her eyes.

"No. No, that's not acceptable. You are supposed to be here, and we are supposed to grow old with our husbands and—"

"Miriam, stop. You know as well as I that there was no way I would survive to the end of the year. I know Mama never told you, but the doctor said I was to be dead by winter's end."

"There is hope."

"There is none. I am out of hope, and I am out of time. These are the truths that I have been trying to contend with for half a year, and now these are the truths that you must bear as well." I choked back tears, throat bobbing. "Please, understand."

Tears welled in Miriam's eyes.

"I can't. I won't." Miriam gathered her skirt and ran out of the room.

I dropped onto the soft cushion, exhaustion weighing heavy on my bones. I desperately wanted to close my eyes and awake from this nightmare.

The ring, a sad glimmering reminder of the losses, was tallied upon my heart.

Shuffling footsteps came to the door. It was neither Mama's, William's, or Miriam's, but a new familiar I had since become tied to—its evidence lay itself upon my finger.

"Are you ready?"

The question gutted me with cruel ease.

Curious eyes shifted beyond the doorframe.

I closed my eyes, summoning the courage to say no—to fight back—but found there was none. My will to fight had depleted, and I was, again, stuck with the all-consuming darkness. This time, it would swallow me whole.

I nodded, reaching out to take his extended, calloused hand.

"Shall we, Little Dove."

{Excerpt of a torn letter from an unknown sender}

. . . I will not be rebuked. The throne is mine—his life is mine. I shall have his power—his crown—all of it by any means necessary. If it means playing to the courts and the council, then so be it. I shall make it so he shall never know peace if he continues to reject the alliance.

I will be queen, even if I have to get my hands dirty.

Seven

We rode in silence, the stranger never glancing my way. Instead, he favored the view outside the window. The carriage appeared to be a century old—perhaps even older. Its worn wheels and weathered cabin didn't exactly fill us with confidence for the journey. I'd made the mistake of peering at the window and saw no one driving it.

It felt like hours inside the enclosed space. I stared at my hands, only taking small glimpses outside of the carriage.

The man sat there, legs crossed, staring out into the vast, dense forest, tall evergreens and oak passing us. Even with the night's inky blackness covering the landscape, the moon illuminated the greenery in eerie wonder.

The leery silence ate away at my nerves the longer we rode. There were too many unknowns I was not prepared for, and many had to do with the fiction genre I would have otherwise never dared to read but was sitting before me.

"We are about to cross the border."

I shifted. "Border of what?"

Under dark lashes, gold eyes flickered with amusement. "Castle Briar, my home."

It was slow at first and then it hit all at once, tearing my soul from my body. Bones levitated out of my skin, the buzz tingling chilled limbs. An electrifying heat zapped from cell to cell, and my ears popped, deafening to an nonexistent explosion.

I nearly collapsed and buried my head between my legs to regain my senses. My nails dug into the seat, leaving crescent shapes in their wake.

The burning electricity wreaked havoc until it dissipated into nothingness, and I returned to the familiar jostling pain of the carriage.

"I should have warned you," he said. "It has been quite some time since a mortal crossed the boundary. I often forget the effects that it can have. It's harder to cross when the moon is not at full strength."

The carriage came to a jolted stop, and he leaped out, offering a hand to help me down.

Under the waning moon, the castle was a fortress of ominous beauty, with its tall spires and stone walls standing against the flashing bolts of lighting of a spring storm rolling in. The structure was eerily similar to Saint Luke's Cathedral, as if it were a replica.

All that it was missing was the stained glass imagery of the gods to judge me further into hell.

I'd mistaken it further for a church, if it not for the ghosts dancing around the grounds as we climbed the stone steps. My heart pounded against my ribs, reminding me I was not in a dream.

All of this was real.

I followed a man who feasted on blood and who lived in a castle inhabited by ghosts.

He opened the large wooden door into a space completely different from the sacred church I had wandered into so often as a girl.

A large chandelier hung in the expanse of the space, and two staircases led to a balcony overhang. My heels clicked on the granite floor as the man led me into the middle of the room.

"Ebony!" he called out. "We have a guest."

A cold wind blew, and I shivered, rubbing my arms.

A voice tickled my ear. "I swear if it's another one of those, I'm going to—"

I swung around.

"My, my! She is gorgeous!"

A white apparition of a woman's face appeared first, and a sharp nose and shadows where her eyes should have been pressed closely to my face.

I yelped, jumping back, the urge to cough nearly on the tip of my tongue as my chest tightened. "Who are you?"

When she smiled, her white lips curled up toward her hollow eye sockets.

"I am Ebony Whitten. I am the keeper of Castle Briar while Master is away."

The strange man cleared his throat, snapping both mine and Ebony's attention. "There are a few rules you must abide by during your stay. One is that you are free to explore the grounds as you like except for the west wing."

"What's in the west wing?" I asked, stumbling into him as he stopped mid-stride.

He turned, brows furrowed. "The west wing is forbidden. End of story." He paused. "The second rule is that you are to dine with me every night and without fail. During which you are to guess my name—my true name. If you guess correctly, you win your freedom."

"And if I don't?" I asked, the ring a glinting reminder.

The man from the cemetery and the ball—that was a dream, a sweet, pleasant one I'd courted of my own accord. The man before me was the devil, a beast who'd take my life with one press of his mouth against my neck, snapping me in two like a rag doll.

The stranger began his ascent along the grand staircase and trailed along the banister, appearing lost in thought, his eyes downcast as long strands obscured his face. His lips were curled into a heinous smile as he leaned over the rail and said two simple words.

"You die."

I was quickly shuffled into a room by Ebony. I avoided looking into the dark orbs where her eyes were, both to be polite and to not fry my mind further by trying to figure out how she sees without them. She drifted through the endless hallway, guiding us down rows of doors. The section's musty smell was apparent, as were the spiderweb-draped crevices and dust. Stone walls kept the place cool to the point of freezing, and I had to refrain from tearing my dress in two to provide at least a little comfort.

Ebony stopped outside a door, producing a key. "I'll leave you to get settled. The wardrobe is stocked with dresses from the last guest who had stayed here, although your options may be limited compared to what you are used to. I'll see to it that we get you the proper clothing in the coming days."

"The last guest?"

Ebony nodded. "Yes, Master does not receive many visitors especially of the womanly kind."

"How long ago did someone stay here?"

Ebony avoided eye contact and shoved the door open. "A long time ago."

The space was grand, too lavish for a simple bedroom. A four-post bed stood in the center with sheets that yearned for someone to stay in its warm embrace. Velvet curtains draped a large window that looked out to a courtyard below of rows of lush roses and a maze.

Ebony went to the armoire in the corner of the room and pulled out a royal purple gown. The bodice was trimmed with black lace and velvet, complemented by a touch of lace along the heart-shaped collar dipping farther than mine. The skirt was less full than some of the gowns I have worn, moth-eaten black tulle filling it out in a soft silhouette.

My heart skipped a beat. The thought of wearing it and revealing my thinning frame did not settle well.

"Supper will be shortly, so I'll leave you to change and fetch you later, miss."

I drifted down the bloodstained fabric and shook my head as Ebony stopped short, her dark gaze darkening.

"Is everything alright?"

I stifled the cough building in my throat, searching desperately for the handkerchief, only to come up empty. Nodding, I feigned a simple to the familiar tingle of needles. "Yes, just a bit tired. That's all."

She tilted her head, a long scar serrated against her neck as flesh moved while she muttered to herself, "Hmmm, that's odd. I've never seen that with a living folk before."

"Seen what?"

Her head snapped back up. "Oh, nothing at all. But are you alright? It must have been a hectic day."

I nodded. "Yes, quite." I frowned, brows knitted.

As much as I did not want to show the strange man my ailing body, I also did not want to wear the blood-soaked gown a moment longer. The gown was ruined—that much, I understood—and blood and dirt from the carriage clung to the sad pink. Yet it was the only evidence I had of everything that has happened and of my old life.

You can still come home.

A bloodied cough turned into a gargled laugh as Miriam's last words played over in my head. Ebony's concerned gaze fixed on me as she placed a chilled hand to my back while I doubled over, blood spilling on my lips.

"Something funny, miss?"

I gave her a sly smile, scarlet illness evident to Ebony as the crude hilarity of my situation heightened. "I just remembered I am still in my wedding dress."

Dearest Mother,

The country of Amaris is one of unusualness that I am unsure of since arriving here. The wolves howl late into the night and the mountains sing to the stars and moon on the cold winter's night. There are many trees, tall and thick, that go on for miles in any direction you choose. Different from the scorching sand, mountains and blazing sun of home. I am still unsure as to the purpose on which you have sent me here. The king and queen have been gracious to me since arriving, offering kind words and astute attention to the different needs of myself and Nia to make us comfortable but those sitting on their court are another story.

It is clear that there is tension that my arrival has caused, especially with another woman whom Prince {REDACTED} had been previously betrothed to before the arrangement had been made. I am sure you do not wish to hear of such petty court drama, but there are concerns that I must convey. I hear the whispers among the court and the awful insults about my blood—our country—would do to the Crown. They speak of such violent action that we'd be better off dead. I am not sure why you sent me here, Mother, but I often fear in the deepest part of the night that one of the—the people of the court—would see me off to my death.

Mother, I'm afraid and so alone here. To make matters worse, I have yet to meet the man that is to be my husband. He is a recluse. From what I have heard, he is often away from court. Yet when I inquired further as to what he does away from court, no one knew. I could be marrying someone who dallies in forbidden establishments or other seedy establishments.

The only reprieve I have here is the lush rose gardens that the grounds have. I often find myself wandering the maze, getting lost in the fragrance of crimson blossoms. There is a boy that I run into, sitting there hidden in the far back alcove of the maze. Always with a grim expression he wears— how can one be so grim in such a beautiful place, Mother. The next time I see him, I ought to explain that one cannot wear such an expression among exquisite blooms.

Perhaps I may find a friend here in the den of wolves.

With love,
Cecilia

I

Eight

The beast, who does not eat or drink in any human sense of the word, sat across the long oak table, twirling a glass between slender fingers.

"You're late," he said.

Ebony floated toward him, sweeping white across the spread of food against the dark cloth table, then disappeared into the wall. The dining area, like the rest of the castle, was grand, with beautiful wood-working circling beams to meet the ceiling's great mosaic. A man receiving a crown bowed to the ground in a show of piety with nothing but dark hair shadowing his face. A simple man, an angel compared to the figure wrapped in shadows behind him—the figure cloaked in darkness had only their skeleton hands outstretched with a gold crown to crown him as the world behind them burned.

I pulled back the chair. "If I knew there was a specific time to be down, I'd have prepared myself sooner."

"I see you changed out of that god-awful gown," he remarked before slowly sipping from the wine glass as burning gold peered up from its rim.

"It was covered in blood," I said, frowning.

The glass before me filled with a fine red liquid within its crystal. I held it up to my nose to inspect it.

I'd be damned if I drank blood or anything suspicious from this household without knowing what I was consuming. Perhaps it is how he is to kill me, by lulling my senses into a false sense of security.

I took a small sip and sighed in relief as the soft tang of alcohol calmed my frayed nerves.

"I'm not going to kill you, if that is what you are worried about—especially over dinner. That would be too easy and less entertaining that way, anyhow." He smirked.

"No, I suppose you would have killed me well before now. You probably could sink your fangs in at any point? More entertaining that way, I suppose. The thrill of the possibility of when!"

He rested his head on his hands, chuckling low and softly. "You are not as mousey as I took you for, Little Dove. Instead, you are a fire that is ready to burn everything in its path. Interesting, very interesting indeed."

Before I got another word out, a plate of food appeared before me of roasted duck simmered in a red sauce over a bed of soft potatoes. My mouth watered at the sight, stomach groaning in sheer anticipation. I had not eaten anything other than the tea from that morning, and in the commotion of everything, I had forgotten.

I picked up my fork and knife, maintaining my composure to still be the lady I was brought up to be. One bite of the duck and I nearly lost it as the meat melted on my tongue.

I devoured the meal in slow, adept bites, trying to remember the last time I ate so well. With the piling debt, most of the money had been diverted to staving off collectors, leaving little for significant luxuries such as the meal before me. I tried to keep my composure, shoveling bite after bite.

All the while, my host looked on with amusement, twirling the memorizing scarlet liquid about the twinkling crystal.

Suspicious at the prospect of what or who was in the glass, I set the fork down onto the table cloth, my appetite vanishing at the sight of the staining red streaks.

"Did you not enjoy Bartov's cooking?" he asked. "He is a very good chef, from what I heard, both in life and in death." He drummed his fingers along the table, remaining steady and unmoving.

"It was delicious, but—"

"But what?"

With my gaze lowered to the plate, I fiddled with the ring, sorting the barrage of thoughts cascading through my own fickle mind. "You said I had to guess your name to win my freedom."

"Yes."

"If I guess wrong, then I die."

He nodded. "Correct again."

"So, why should I even try and guess your name if I am to die if I guess wrong?" I asked.

My mystery host tipped his head as a mischievous smile graced his lips, a calculating predator toying with his prey, awaiting the kill to tear me apart both body and soul. One way or another, this castle was to be my tomb—and him, my executioner.

"Explain it to me."

I rubbed my hand along the smooth silk fabric. There was still much I was unsure of, especially if I were to stay alive and not end up like the priest. The idea of freedom tethered my wary nerves together. I needed to buy time and find a way to stay alive.

Find the beast name and a cure for my ailment— not an impossible task.

Not at all.

"Why?" he said.

"You kidnapped me from my wedding, and now you tell me I must guess your name to be free of you. There must be a catch." I scraped my fork against the fine china.

He cleared his throat, offering his glass out to the air to be refilled. "No catch."

"There must be. What sane person kidnaps some-one on their wedding day?"

"Perhaps I am not a sane man." He smirked. "I simply want what I want, and I take what I please. Besides, it was not as if you enjoyed the arrangement. You looked as if you were ready to run."

"So, it is a pity that I am here."

The graveyard encounter, night in the garden—all before I learned what he was, had repeated in my mind. I envisioned over the course of what it would've been like to taste those soft, delicate lips. Yet the embarrassment plagued me as much as the fear of the man.

I held my hand, the ring glinting under candle-light. "Pity is it that I wear your ring and now shall suffer at your whims."

"Not pity, no—never pity."

"Then, why? Why me and not—"

The pressure in my chest mounted. Groping for the cloth napkin, I affixed it to my lips. With my head spinning from the pressure, the world came into focus when I spotted a familiar handkerchief from the corner of my eyes.

The man held it firmly between pale, slender fin-gers, dried blood upon the pink fabric as evidence of the illness. One that could not be avoided.

Burnt gold studied me as I snatched the cloth. "Where did you get that?" I wheezed, body tensing once more despite the ache.

The cough became harder to choke it down as another fit erupted. I pushed away from the table, the cloth firmly pressed as fresh blood splattered onto it. I panted as my lungs relented once more to force air through them.

I stumbled back, black spots danced in my vision. The ground tilted until I was falling. The warm embrace of arms caught me, and the intense aroma draped me until the sharpness of his face angled to mine.

"How long have you been sick?" he rasped.

I pushed him away, struggling to get to my feet as the next fit came. The man grabbed my wrist, the blood on my palm in plain view.

"I asked you a question, Valeria." Grip tightening, he darted between the blood and my startled face, pulling me close against his chest. "How long!"

"You're hurting me," I croaked.

Ebony floated through, white and willowy, encircling us. Gentle and careful, she said, "Master, you're scaring the young woman. I am sure she'd be willing to answer your question if you let her." Ebony placed a chilling hand on my wrist, a cold phantom touch seeping into the searing heat of his grip.

The man sighed, tension releasing from my wrist as his hold slackened enough where he held me with curled fingers. My own body betrayed me, and heat burned across my cheeks as he leaned in.

"So, care to be truthful, Little Dove?"

"A while," I whispered. "At worst, I won't last the season. At best, it's torment. So, please—let it go."

His gaze softened, taking those curled fingers against my wrist and bringing my palm upwards.

"What are you doing!" I fought, his tongue lapping up the blood stained upon my palm in even strokes.

A chill crept up my spine as his tongue left my palm wet but clean of crimson.

"Master!" Ebony chastised, swirling about us. "That is uncalled for!"

I retracted my hand, cradling it to my chest, trying to keep my breathing even.

"There," he said, placing his hands behind him and licking his lips. "Would you like to guess my name tonight?"

I shook my head. "No, I'd like to go to my room! Good night, demon!" I stomped off.

Fatigue washed over me, my body becoming heavier with every step I took toward the door. The ache in my lungs wheezed against my chest as another fit threatened to run loose.

I got no more than to the door when he said, "Silas."

I stopped, fingers grazing the handle of the door. "Excuse me?"

"Silas. You may call me Silas. It is not my true name, but it is a name you may refer to me rather than 'demon' or 'beast'."

I stared for a moment, the name settling over the air between us as the beast.

Silas, my captor, placed his hand into his pocket and cocking his hip, awaiting my answer.

I nodded, turning back to the door. "Good night, Silas."

I found the heaviest item in the room and barricaded it along the door, the armoire my only defense against the beast—not that it'd help much.

I was not going to take my chances with Silas or any other creature.

I went to the window and locked it. After grabbing a nearby chair, I shoved it under the handles, shaking it for good measure.

Once the room was secured enough, I laid back onto the bed, cradling my hand—the feeling of his tongue still fresh upon my skin. With my mind a mess, my body was just as confused between the fear and the budding fascination. I shook my head, dislodging any and every thought of the man.

The darkness called to me. With the pull of the pillows of soft satin against my back, the exhaustion from the day was sweet, inviting, and warm. All I had to do was close my eyes and fall.

Forget sleeping soundly. Leaving myself defenseless in an unknown place wasn't an option.

I jolted from the bed, stripping the comforter off from it. Grabbing a pillow, I dragged myself into the bathtub. I was not going to make it easy for the monsters in the night to make me their midnight snack, and having an extra door to barricade myself in was better than being out in the open.

Pitless black eyes waved in front of my plan. "What are you doing?" Ebony questioned, poking her head through the wall.

"Ebony! Don't sneak up on me!" I cleared my throat of the blood gargling upwards to the tickle of my lungs and clutched the soft down comforter. "I was going to sleep in there."

Ebony raised a translucent eyebrow, placing her hands on her nonexistent hips. "There is a perfectly good bed there."

"I know."

"Must you make this difficult?" She sighed. "If you are worried about the other guests in the castle, I can assure you that they'd been instructed not to bother you."

"And Silas?" Cold hands took the soft comforter from mine as Ebony shuffled me toward the bed despite protests. She remade the bed in record time, fluffing the pillows with unusual detail I found difficult for someone who was opaque at best.

Smoothing out the creases, she softly added, "The master is not all bad. He has just been alone for too long." Ebony pursed her lips together. "I can assure you he means no harm and will treat you as a guest. He is out of practice with having guests, so it might take some time for him to adjust, but you are not a prisoner if that is your concern."

She clasped her hands, bowing her head. "If there is anything you need, do let me know!"

I whirled around and hastily said, "Wait! What else should I know?"

Black pools flickered to the willowy orbs bouncing outside the open door. Whispered conversations were just out of reach as Ebony delivered her bone chilling advice to uphold during my time at Castle Briar.

"Take care to not wander the halls at night. There are beings far scarier than the master that haunt these halls."

The coughing returned within the night with such relentless force. I leaned over the bed, spitting out blood bubbling within my chest. I groaned, heaving myself to the bathroom to rid myself of the mess. I turned on the facet to only find disappointment.

Of course there was no water in a haunted castle.

Clutching my dry throat, I crept to the bedroom. The armoire was pressed close to the door but not enough to where the door was easily accessible to someone of slim stature. Peeking out the door, I noticed an eerie quiet had lain itself over the hall before I snuck out. I wandered down the corridor, flickering candlelight guiding my way toward the kitchen.

I stopped in my tracks.

I had no bloody idea where the kitchen was, and clearly, it was not as if I was at home. Sighing in defeat, turning on my heels, I decided to toughen out the murderous scratchiness when a dim light at the end of the hall and faint voices beckoned me.

Shuddered behind the cracked door on the other end of the hall, I leaned against the wall and begged a closer peek inside.

"Master, are you sure of this girl?" Ebony floated down in front of the large bookcase, a duster in hand, gracefully dancing around Silas, whose face was buried in stacks of paper. "She could complicate things."

"I could not leave her there. If you saw what I have, you'd have gone mad. She was to marry a man who had killed two other women before deciding to marry her. It was atrocious. I smelled the blood on him before I even got close enough to find out the kind of man he was. Atrocious."

Silas's voice was thick and without remorse, muffled from beyond the stack.

"Is that all?"

"She . . . she resembled her."

"I thought so." Ebony giggled. From the crack, she served Silas a glass of the red liquid, mouth knitted into a frown as she flitted about the room, straightening books and other items. "There is much that is at risk. If she is to stay here, we will need to keep an eye on her. The other residents would be interested in the living and with the strange occurrences that have been plaguing recently—I worry."

With his glass in hand, Silas took to pacing about the room, brows tight as he slipped a palm into his pocket. "The castle residents are the least of my problems."

"Ah, yes, the infinite darkness of your work. How many is that now?"

"Thirty-three this month, and it continues to grow. An infestation that has overrun the grounds. It's already rooted itself into the human populace. It's been difficult to control the pest without weeding out the source," Silas growled. "The rampant occurrences have left me with little time to search."

"Don't be discouraged. Perhaps, with the girl, there may be a chance."

"Perhaps." Silas sat in an elegant chair. In one hand was his glass of red liquid, in the other a book he had thumbed through. He tossed the book onto the nearby table as the clock chimed the hour. "Whether she is or isn't—time is not on either side."

Ebony's form flickered. "Have faith. Perhaps the gods are listening."

Silas laughed dryly. "They haven't listened since the day they cursed me." He leaned forward, dropping his elbows to his knees, and rubbed his face, the light of the fire playing with the shadows upon stone flesh.

Ebony draped a translucent arm around his shoulder. "Cheer up. I'm sure that—" The voids of her eyes whipped to the door with thinned scrutiny. "We're being watched."

I tumbled back from the door, quietly retreating down the hallway to my room. My feet skittered faster against the floorboards. From the shadows, a dark mass bubbled—inky black tendrils reached for me, never getting past the opened, lit door. Thousands of red eyes stared back from the dark depths, shifting. Waiting.

I froze as a choppy, distorted animalistic growling sounded from the bowels of the castle, scraping against stone.

Hell . . . oooo, darrrllingg—come closer.

I slipped through the crack of the door, locked it quickly behind me, and pushed the armoire closer to block out the growling purrs from the other side. I stripped the sheets from the bed and dove into the tub.

What frightened me the most was not the inky liquid mass but Silas, who had seen my retreat and the sorrow that coated them.

Dearest Rueben,

I am sure you are aware of the situation at present. Never did I imagine certain players on the board who move against us in securing a foothold in the monarchy. There is a 'complication' we must address before we can continue with any talks of securing the throne. For one, I need more information on this Princess of Endovier is and what it is she wants with the Prince. The quicker we remove her from the board, the easier we can enact our plan.

I must not put too much into writing. Meet me at Flore in the village at noon tomorrow for there is much to discuss.

Narcisa Marius Nicholae

Nine

The doorknob rattled, waking me from the fitful sleep plaguing me.

"Miss, are you alright?" Ebony called from the other side.

I cracked my eyes open, adjusting to the darkness of the bathroom. I sat up, groaning, popping several points in my body as the aching from the last couple of days dulled. I opened the door and jumped back.

Ebony's dark eyes were leveled at the very spot I emerged from, holding out a tiny ornate vial in her translucent hands. Red ominous liquid swished against the ridged crystal. I almost did not want to inquire what it was.

"Master sent me to make sure that you were well after last night. His express instruction was to take it in a timely manner." She handed the vial to me, the glass cool against my warm skin. Ebony danced among the posts of the bed, the white sheath dress flaring out from her. "There may be a point during the day where you won't be able to see me, but trust I am here and will do my best to ensure you are comfortable."

She floated down onto the bare bed, fluttered her dark lashes, grinning sheepishly as if her very nature didn't warrant the explanation.

I examined the vial. It looked similar to the higher end medication I had been prescribed early on before we had to look to other methods once the money was out and we had to put everything on credit. But I knew better than to trust blindly in this place.

I lowered the vial, tucking it into my palm. "What about Silas? Where would he be during the day?"

"Master is busy during those hours, and you must not disturb him. You are only required to dine with him during the evening hours, and for now, that is all the direction he wishes to give at this time."

"Oh," I said, heart sinking. I sat at the edge of the bed, comprehending a few truths that became more unreal not by the day but by the very hour the longer I went on knowing such a man and the ghosts he carried.

Ebony floated up from the bed to the window, disappearing, then reappearing into the dark corner of the room, her form flickering as an old lamp does. "I can leave you to dress if you like. As I have mentioned, we will work on getting a proper wardrobe that you require, but the dresses from our previous guest should suffice." With a wave of her hand, the armoire shifted back to its original spot, and the doors flung open.

A dress of crimson accented in black lace floated toward me.

I ran a hand over the beautiful satin organza fabric. Despite centuries-old the fashion, it was apparent the woman who had stayed in this room had gorgeous taste.

I glanced up, ready to thank Ebony, only to find no one there. The vial sparkled in my palm, crimson glass flanked between gold fringes.

There was something Silas and Ebony was hiding, that much I was sure about. But what exactly, tumbled against my head in the same way the liquid knocked against the glass. What I did know was to trust my own instincts.

I tossed the vial into the nightstand, slamming the drawer closed, then dressed quickly. First order of business was to get a better grasp on my situation, and that involved nerves of steel and daylight.

I ate alone at the massive table surrounded by beautiful artwork I could not fully appreciate the night before. I pushed around a bowl of porridge, taking in many statues and vases. A priceless collection that belonged in a museum and not in a rotting castle. I avoided the empty chair at the end of the table, sitting there in silence with me, mocking its own emptiness.

Once finished, I took to exploring the place I was unwillingly to call home. I walked the long corridors to the room.

Large bookshelves touching the mosaic ceiling greeted me warmly, wrapping itself around the vastness. I ran my head along the wood of the desk, papers aged yellow strewn about in handwriting either illegible or in an entirely different language.

Musk and a touch of spice covered the books. Despite the shelves only being touched by one living thing, they were immaculate and free of dust thanks to Ebony.

I ran a finger along the spines of the books. I would've loved to spend the entire day in this little room alone, but I needed to know what lay in the rest of the castle before I could settle, especially the areas in which are of special interests.

I moved on into the bowels, finding room after room of crumbling elegance in disrepair over the last few centuries. None were of any particular interest, as most were receiving rooms or bedrooms no one had stayed in for a number of years. Down the grand staircase, sunlight streamed through the large windows, illuminating the chilled bones of the castle.

The echoes of my heels on the marbled floors reverberated into the hushed space. I heaved the door open, taking special care to glance behind to see that no one was stopping me. Silas didn't rush down the stairs, demanding I be locked away in a faraway tower alone. Nor did the ghosts or Ebony stop me as I pulled the door open and graced the warmth of the day's rays.

Down the steps, green shrubbery lined the property with white buds hiding themselves from the height of the day. I came upon the rose garden my room overlooked. Roses of crimson curled their petals toward the sky with such brilliance. I took one by the stem and breathed in its sweet scent, a remembrance of the ignorance stored itself away into the dark recesses of my heart. For there is no other way if I were to survive the beast.

Stone benches peered out into the garden basked in the warmth of the sun, the cool rock against my back as I sat and admired the beauty before me. The garden afforded one vantage point, overlooking a small village to the east of the castle. Tiny houses dotted the landscape, standing against the thick fog permeating the road and surrounding fauna. I trotted to the iron gates towering in reach of the little village, careful to not trip over my dress.

There were no locks or chains that kept me in.

Or kept me from going out.

I glanced back, expecting to see someone—anyone to stop me from making a grand escape down to the village. But no one came out.

The castle sighed in resignation as I pushed the heavy gate open and stumbled into the fog. I trudged down the path, the fog thicker the closer I got. A river boarded the town with its dark, murky depth as I crossed over a rickety bridge. One wrong step, and I'd be swept under the current below.

I passed by crumbling buildings of red clay bricks and thatched roofs. Several buildings were missing pieces of bricks and were on the brink of collapse. Decay hung heavy in the air, tickling my lungs the closer to the center of town I walked.

I covered my mouth and coughed into my handkerchief, continuing further into the deserted village. The cobblestone path gave way to the town square where a large fountain gurgled softly in the spring light. The market was in full swing, with many somber townsfolk haggled for goods or services.

Not too far off from the hustle and bustle of the market was a funeral procession somber march through the town square silenced some of the transactions. Six men carried a wooden coffin as a crowd clothed in black followed the casket, singing hushed hymns. Women cried out, wailing to the sky, their song crescendoing as the drummers rolled their drumstick, kicking in time to the mourners' march. Those in the market turned their attention and bowed their heads low, paying respects to the newly dead.

"Tragic, isn't it? Makes it the fifth funeral held this month." A woman in a simple blue dress and an apron walked up beside me, her basket nudging my side. An icy blue smiled from underneath a purple cloak. "I haven't seen you around these parts before."

"I moved here recently."

I lied, avoiding her intense gaze.

She hummed a tune. "Interesting, seeing as no one just 'moves' here. I see you're married." When I shifted my hand out of sight, hiding the ring, the woman's lips thinned. "I'd be careful where you say you are from. Most do not take kindly to outsiders, especially not now. They very well may pin what's been happening on you."

The procession's drummers grew faint as they crested over the hill and into the cemetery. The market returned to its business, haggling and bartering with sunken faces, and the anxiety of death flushed against their necks.

"What's been happening here?" I asked, hesitating to add, *"Is Silas responsible?"*

Wary of listening ears and prying eyes of those in the market privy enough to see the guilty secret, I held upon my finger.

The woman grabbed my arm, guided us into an alley, and whispered, "Many of us believe that evil lives in the castle upon the hill. There have been many deaths since its appearance, and several townsfolk have seen the beast prowling the grounds only to disappear from the scenes into the shadows."

Shadows.

I thought back to the previous night, the inky black mass, and the thousands of red eyes peering from its dark depth. Horror and nightmare incarnate snaking its tendrils toward me, its voice still curled around my ear.

I shuddered. "When you say appearance, do you mean that the castle has not always been there before?"

The woman nodded. "It appeared on the hill less than a century ago. One night, a storm rolled through—divine punishment from the gods I presume for what was to follow. Lighting struck the hill, a clap of thunder appeared, and then it was there, born from forlorn darkness with nothing to explain its abrupt appearance. From then on, people have been drained of blood, dying, or dead within a few days of being bitten. It has gotten worse over the last decades, with the population slowly decreasing either from dying or moving far away. Although those that choose to live beyond the town are never heard from again."

She paused, eyebrows raised in suspicion. "That is why no one simply moves here."

I shook off her hand. "I was kidnapped from my wedding and watched evil tear apart an entire person. It was awful." I trembled.

To learn I was not the only victim—that there was more suffering terrified and enraged me. There must have been some way to survive, to not be consumed by him or any of the shadows lurking in the castle and maybe . . . maybe save more than myself from this hell.

"If the beast in the castle is responsible, why not try and capture or kill him?" I said, a plan forming against the churning tide of thoughts.

If there were more of us, perhaps there was a chance to kill him. There had to be something I could do before being consumed whole by my captor.

"The beast cannot be captured, and we cannot storm the castle nor pass through the fog. Turning instead, in circles just to wind back down the road." She shifted, scanning the dank alley for listening shadows. "There are reasons he is called Death Incarnate. Many cannot escape him."

Quick, shallow breaths escaped from my lips, my chest burning as I collapsed in on myself in that tiny alley. I was trapped there, living with Silas with the high chance of dying by his hand and screaming out to no one when he takes my life.

"What can I do?"

In that dank alley, hot, wet tears stuck to my cheeks.

I wiped my face, rubbing profusely as the stranger pulled out a handkerchief and patted my cheek.

Her expression darkened before the corner of her lips curled into a smile.

"Maybe we can help each other?" She brushed a strand of ash hair away from her face.

I perked up. "How?"

From her basket, she pulled out a scrap of paper and wrote quickly in curling script. "Come to this address on the edge of town tomorrow, and I'll explain." She held my hand, and hope thrummed from her capable hands through mine.

My heart ached as the small part of me thought of Miriam back in Endovier walking the streets, begging for scraps—or worse, being married to William Sharpe.

We strolled back out to the town center, to the bustling of the market in full swing under the late afternoon's light.

The woman swung her basket around her, her dress swaying in the breeze. "I should introduce myself especially since we'll become more acquainted even with the circumstances." She held out her hand. "My name is Ayla Wallace."

I shook her hand. "Pleasure, I'm Valeria McCallister."

Ayla smiled. "I hope to see you again soon."

The unease shuffled along with me as the cobblestone path turned to gravel with the castle looming ahead.

I clutched the note, the black ink a lifeline to the growing anxiety threatening to suffocate me.

In the middle of the four-way intersection, the illusion of choices brought me to this point where one path led to the castle. To the man who will keep me as a doll or a pet until he grows bored and tosses my husk into the dark recesses of the crumpling fortress. Another led to the village who were as much of a victim as I was, trapped in cycles of death, unable to get out, unable to climb the hill and push the iron gates open to rid themselves of the nightmare.

The other two paths led into the thick embankment of fog encasing the castle. The ominous structure loomed over the land, and the air stilled, howling and wailing of death audible from the grounds. The gates were as I had left them, wide open, a sign my captor could've still been blind to my absence. The sun began to dip on the horizon, whispering goodbye to the day.

I trailed the fog-covered road, heading not forward but into the thick embankment.

I had come through a road. If I would've walked far enough, I could've hitchhiked back to Endovier. When I got back, perhaps I could start working to support Miriam and Mama. It may not be glamorous, but it was better than marrying a man I hated.

Or one that would kill me.

The fog obscured everything within five inches of my outstretched hand, rolling waves over the tall grass and gravel road. With nothing ahead and nothing behind, I stumbled forward, the fog licking at my heels, begging me to wander forever as caresses my body.

When I emerged from the fog, I nearly fell to my knees.

I stared in disbelief as Castle Briar stared me in the face.

I had walked in circles.

"No. No. NO. NO."

I charged in the other direction to find I had emerged at the same exact point, right in front of the castle. Disoriented, I sank to the ground, the gravel biting into my knees as fog swirled around.

There was no way out.

I was trapped.

I avoided the predatory glint striding forward, hands in his pocket as the last of the light slowly drifted off to sleep. I didn't look at the tears and bloodstained rocks. Each sob rocked its way through my belly and into my chest.

Death breathed in my ear, seductive and chilling, "Going somewhere, Little Dove?"

Dearest Mother,

I've been spending a lot of my time in the palace gardens. It's gorgeous with blooms so crimson they bleed in the sunlight. What is more special is the garden at night. Have you ever heard of a Moonflower? It's quite special, a beautiful flower that soaks up moonlight with its white petals. It only blooms at night, a rare sight to see among the angel trumpets and morning glories.

My stranger sits there a lot, smiling up at the blooms as he cultivates them. I followed him out there one night and saw him sifting through the garden, his hands covered in earth wearing nothing more than dirt-stained blouses and trousers as he tended to the flower beds.

All I see of the stranger is his long dark hair pulled up high and the silhouette of him, but I can never see his face. He always disappears before I can get a better view or the courage to talk to him.

Although in his place, a red rose always greets me.

Oh, Mother, I haven't seen the man I am betrothed to, and it's been well over two months since I have arrived at this strange place. I've asked their Majesties about their son, and neither of them knew of his whereabouts.

He is as elusive as a snake. Even the snakes are better at being open. What if he is a monster, Mother? What if he is simply hideous, and we're being tricked into this alliance?

I know there is a lot riding on the alliance, but it is difficult to uphold if there is no person to uphold such an alliance with.

No one wants to speak on the matter about the prince with me—more like no one wishes to speak with me at all.

Oh, Mother, it is quite lonely without you or Father. I even miss Beau, the little tyke that he is. There is so much I miss about home from the way the clouds brush the mountains to the howling of the wind on the cold winter's nights.

They do not have mountains here, did you know? They have miles and miles of tall evergreen woods. Even though I am restricted to the grounds of the castle, I sometimes wander into the woods, to get a better lay of the land.

There was a time, Mother, I was lost for hours, that my dear stranger came to the rescue and assisted in getting back to the grounds without the notice of any guards.

Quite clever, he is.

Yet I still do not know his name nor do I know what he looks like and it's driving me mad, Mother.

He is like a phantom I cannot quite catch, and yet he is the only semblance of hope I have within these walls.

Before I sign this letter, I suppose I should tell you that, in a few months' time, there is to be a grand ball.

Please, come and bring Papa and Beau
with you as well. I miss you all so dearly.

With Love,
Cecilia

Ten

"Eventful day, Little Dove," Silas remarked, head resting on his hand. He smirked, taking occasional sips from his wine, glass filled with blood of a presumed innocent, his plate empty despite the feast on the table.

Disgust filled me.

Forcing a smile, I said, "You could say that."

I sliced into the lamb cutlet, forcing my face to remain stoic despite how glorious the food tasted. Even Eden had its darkness, whereas the devil appeared as a snake. Mine was a cunning demon with the looks of a man.

"You never told me that there was a town. Am I to assume that I am to be restricted to the castle grounds?" I remarked.

"No, you are not restricted to the castle. However, I'd be careful in the company you keep there. Many of them do not take kindly to strangers."

"Or murderers," I muttered before taking a bite and relishing the taste. "They say you prey upon the town, gorging on blood and plaguing them with death after death. Quite the story, don't you think?"

Silas cocked his head, sharp features defined under the low candlelight. Shadows played across his cheek, dancing upon his masks, gold eyes narrowed. "Is that so?"

I pointed my fork at him. "They were even so bold to name you as the Death Incarnate. Imagine that. It's curious, though, they consider you a plague on their town, considering you as a disease rather than a killer." I envisioned my fork stabbing into his flesh just as my statements crawled under his skin.

Silas sipped, twisting his lips into a scowl, and stretched his glass out. Ebony floated by with a pitcher, filling it with the dark elixir. "Aren't you curious as to why you cannot leave on any of the roads besides the castle and the town?" I placed my fork down. "You must be curious, and I imagine you are *dying* to know."

He enunciated death as if in delight at the suffering he causes in others.

"The thought has crossed my mind." I sipped my wine, appearing disinterested. I was curious about the mystery behind the fog and even to the fact that all the roads lead back to the castle. That was a fact. If I am to leave this place with my life intact. "I imagine you did not want your little pet to go so soon, huh.

Seeing as your blood supply is dwindling, you have resorted to kidnap—"

He disappeared from the other end of the table, and the cold touch of death whispered across my neck.

I didn't move, aware of fingers caressing the soft skin, brushing dark strands away. I shuddered, willing my body to move to no avail as his breath tickled my ear. "I could've tasted you long before now. But I haven't. Why do you think that is?"

My heart pounded against my rib cage, thumping louder as Silas traced his finger against my neck. I elected for silence, pursing my lips together, and bit the inside of my cheek as his mouth lowered to my ear.

"The only reason I haven't has been out of kindness and respect. Do you wish to test me? Because I could always . . ."

Silas's voice was so hypnotic and deep I didn't realize I was yielding my neck to him until his smile brushed my skin.

I fluttered my eyes closed, groping the tablecloth to the cool metal. I waited for the burning pain, for his lips to spill my blood. Silas tenderly kissed the soft spot. Goose bumps raised along my skin. I should've been disgusted. I should not have wanted to touch him. I resisted the urge to weave my fingers through soft strands and let his lips part to sink into my flesh.

I brought the knife to his chest, throwing my entire weight into stabbing it in. Blood bloomed on his white blouse, Silas staggering back, clutching the knife. Long white strands fell gracefully across his face as he peered down at the blade. "So, it seems my wife has a habit of stabbing her husband."

Silas threw it aside, the clattering coming to a stop out of reach.

"I am not *your* wife," I snarled.

Silas slammed me against the wall, hand wrapped around my wrist, his other at my waist. He hovered over my neck, bloodlust flickering behind his mask. "The ring on your hand says otherwise."

I pushed Silas away.

Truly diabolic—I kept my itching hand at my side, as slapping the vampire would not be the way to go. Body flushed head to toe, embarrassment surged through me.

As I clenched my teeth together, I gritted out, "I'm going to bed." I stormed out of the dining room, heels stomping against the tile.

He called from the doorway, "Valeria, do you not want to guess my name?"

I marched down the hallway, passing ghost residents less than thrilled when I stomped through their bodies rather than move around them.

I gripped the door, screaming, "No, you prick!" into the void, and slammed it closed.

I awoke to the boom of the main castle doors and to the dark room filtered by the soft moonlight. Drenched in sweat, I shucked the covers off, feet hitting the cold floor.

What could have made such a noise at this hour?

I opened the door and slinked down the hallway as the dawn crept across the horizon and into the castle. The structure echoed the harsh steps off its dark walls, and a cool wind blew in from the early morning, the scent of blood twining sharply with the dying summer.

"Ebony!" Silas strode across the main floor, his cape flapping behind him. Under the pale rays, his suit was covered in blood. "Dammit, Ebony!"

Ebony appeared, swirling about the main floor as a white wisp, her white dress billowing as she floated over Silas. "Shush, you're waking up the dead!" Ebony hissed. Dark pools peeked past Silas to the foyer covered with a thin blood trail. "You really did it this time."

"I had to. They are getting harder to handle the more unstable things become." Silas tossed the coat, slugging up the stairs.

I scrambled back into my room, leaving the door ajar enough to see him walk past. Heels clicked along the long corridor, then disappeared. I crept out of my room, tiptoeing down the hall before coming to rest outside the library study. Muffled clattering of bottles and Silas's grunts came from behind the thick oak doors. Ebony's soft, sweet voice shifted with worry, words inaudible, but her tone fluctuating as Silas's grunts became worse.

As I pressed my ear against the door, the only word I could make out was *cursed*. The word had an implication—this, I was sure of.

Silas's voice wavered with intensity, accompanied by shattering glass. Footsteps came to the door, and I scurried back to my room.

I shut the door behind me and rushed into bed before pulling the covers over me.

Moments later, the bedroom door creaked open. I feigned sleep, moving my chest against the terrifying ache and shifting my forehead closer to the cool stone wall.

The floorboards creaked underfoot, approaching the bed until I was sure he loomed over me. I didn't dare to acknowledge my fright. To do so could've very well been a death sentence. Instead, I continued to fake sleep, maintaining those deep, consistent breaths. The space next to me dipped as if the person had taken up residence in watching me sleep. I did not dare look or touch. I kept my eyes firmly closed and let my imagination wander as I prayed they would leave. The pressure lessened after a while, but the burning acuteness of suspicious eyes still lay upon my sleeping form.

I'd stayed like that for what seemed to be an eternity until sleep beckoned, and I slowly drifted off to the plane in between sleep and wakefulness.

When I awoke to the fullness of the morning sun, Silas was gone.

Book after book, I shifted through the stacks and found little to nothing on Silas other than less-than-credible vampire lore. For one, Silas walked in sunlight, when the sun wasn't at its highest. Two, he didn't seem to have an aversion to garlic, seeing as it was in a few of the dishes for the last couple of nights. Three, I do not assume a church would have me believe that a crucifix or any religious idol would affect him. Which left me with little idea of what he was and how to deal with him.

I groaned, tossing the book onto the growing pile before me. I went to the lower shelf I had been pulling from, trying to find a simple title. My finger traced the ancient spines of the books, wiping dust off a few. I doubt Silas had enough time in the world to finger through all of these volumes.

Europe's Mythology.

History of the Dark Ages.

The Meaning Behind the Veil.

After pulling out a book, I flipped it to a random page, rolling my eyes. I didn't know why I expected my answer to be here among his stacks. I shoved the book back when I was met with resistance. Moving others out of the way, I tried to find the source when a small leather-bound book fell out of the small crevice.

The leather-bound book lay on the dusty floor. Wound around it was a single thick strap from its worn cover.

Carefully, I turned it over, afraid it would fall apart. The book was delicate, its thinning worn spots and strap holding the little book together. I undid the tie, greeted by dust as I opened the first page. The page covered with scrawls of cursive were faint and illegible.

Great, I found nothing again.

I turned the page, finding bold traceable script as if the writer was trying to capture much more than simple words.

I am the – I will not be afraid, not after ––. I fear if I do not write my story then I will be nothing more –. –be a puppet to the wills ––– a war, to be able to show how strong our country is––I told them no.

I told them no-not since –.

Look –– I'm writing this on the eve–

"What are you reading there?"

Silas lurked at the doorway, dressed down since the last few appearances and more importantly—not covered in blood. His simple blouse showed off the subtle tanned skin underneath the thin fabric, and midnight trousers accentuated his lean figure. Loose strands of his hair hung around his mask. The black straps tight around his head did little to hide the faint scar—and his annoyance.

It was broad daylight, and he wasn't sleeping in a coffin. Just what was this man?

"I don't think I told you that you could rifle through my possessions, Little Dove."

"Since when did reading become a crime?" I retorted. I closed the book, cradling it into the crook of my arm. "You did give me free rein to explore unless you meant anywhere else but here." I took out another book, barely skimming the cover of it, and settled in with the collection of books in his chair.

I was surprised to see pictures of plants staring back at me.

"You decided to read up on plants, hm." Silas leaned over me, amusement high upon his brow. He placed a hand onto my shoulder, jolting such fleeting images flashing in front of me.

Grass. A large oak tree. A boy with raven hair.

Don't you wish you could be anyone else?

I shifted in the chair, images disappearing as fast as they had appeared. "I wanted to learn a few remedies." I drew out the handkerchief, letting the tickle in my lungs die on the pristine cloth. I rubbed my chest, avoiding the scrutiny in his pale gaze.

Silas crossed the room, propping a leg up over the arm of the chair across from me.

"I am guessing you are stubborn and did not drink the vial I gave you," he said.

I raised a brow, slinking down into the cushion with the book. "So, should I have drunk the mysterious liquid and died then—is that it?"

Since Ebony brought the vial, I had not looked at it since stashing it in the drawer. I don't care if it guarantees me a cure to my illness because I did not trust him enough to consume it. For all I know, Castle Briar wanted to kill me, and I wouldn't let it.

"What is it that you so graciously want to drink? Herbal medicine? Blood from a sacred cow? Perhaps a crushed up red beetle?" I asked.

"My, do we have quite the imagination." He laughed. "No, it's none of those."

"Then, what is it? Why should I trust it?"

Silas's smiled thinned. "I am death, as you have mentioned. Why should you trust death?"

Having enough of his lousy company, I gathered the books in one hand and my skirt with another, taking myself away from this man—and the impure thoughts plaguing me. Quick movements flashed beyond the course of my vision, and I collided with Silas, who blocked my path out.

"I'm trying to help. You should be grateful," he said.

"I don't need it," I hissed.

I strode past him, ignoring my own body's protest of the electrifying thrill and the unrelenting dread dancing upon my skin. Lungs grating from the dust, I buckled over, the metallic cough coming out of nowhere. Books scattered across the hallway, and I gasped for air and fumbled for my handkerchief.

Silas played coy. "Sounds like you have this handled, then."

I glared back.

Silas leaned against the doorframe with a smirk, as if he was enjoying the show. The slow death I was consumed by.

I picked up the books, my gaze refocusing on the plant-covered one.

"Yes, no need for your remedy or whatever. I am perfectly able to find my own solution without the use of you. Thank you. Now, if you please, I'd like to read in peace." I gathered my skirt and walked off.

When I reached my room, I spun to see Silas bowing to me. "Very well, your grace. Whatever suits your fancy, but sooner or later, herbs are only going to do so much to prevent your death."

I spat, "I'd rather die than drink anything from you!" I slammed the door, tossing the books onto the bed, and sank into the soft mattress, groaning. Once the pain in my chest subsided and the heat upon my cheeks had cooled, I sat up and inventoried the books.

I propped an elbow and flipped through the herbalism book, soaking up the tiny paragraphs about various plants and their uses. The images of the hand-painted herbs along the yellow page appeared to be delicately done with fine detail. I shook my head, reading the same paragraph over and over as my vision blurred. I slammed it closed, another tickle in my throat creeping up, bubbling, then inflating into a cough.

How long *can* I last?

The longer I was alive, the more exhausted I became. Lungs ached to breathe normally, and my body continuously strained against the efforts as I grew weaker with each passing day on this Earth. I lay against the bed, heavy eyelids betraying me as I curled up among the downy comforter.

I wanted to remember a time when the cough wasn't there. Where the shame of scrubbing or hiding the blood from others did not fill my ever-waking thoughts. Most of all, I wanted to remember a time when I wasn't so scared of dying.

I drifted off, unable to cling on to wakefulness, aware I had not put the armoire against the door. Truthfully, it wouldn't stop Silas—not even a little—from barging in. I was defenseless in this castle, and he easily could take my life if he so wished.

My thoughts drifted to the vial and the mysterious contents its glass walls harbored. Why was he persistent in trying to get me to drink that? If it is that simple to be cured, what would be the catch? As sleep came, I thought of the boy from the vision standing among the summer sweet grass as the sun's warm, bright rays sweeps across his skin and mine.

In another life, don't you wish we were different?

Finding Ayla's home did not take me as long as I had initially thought. Taking the path on the outskirts of the town, I came across the little cottage. The babbling brook's crystal-clear water funneled into a large wheel appeared to power the grinding machines inside. The yard of the house was covered with tulips of reds and yellows in full bloom despite the deepening chill of autumn.

I clutched my wrap and knocked.

The door swung open, Ayla barreling out. "You came!" she screeched, hugging me tight enough my lungs nearly ended up on the back of her dress. "Come in, come in. Do you want some tea? I have a kettle on." She ushered me inside the cozy, quaint space.

The inside was considerably small, with a long table taking up the majority of the room filled with herbs and spices. Its aroma permeated as if I were standing in the exotic stall at the market on a crisp morning. A fire burned in a brick laid over, and flames licked at the iron kettle suspended above. Various herbs hung over a caged window, the sun baking them as a rainbow stream through spinning stained glass cylinders. The windmill I saw outside spun into a makeshift hydraulic press, cogs turning as the metal grinded behind a closed door.

The floor creaked as I stepped inside. I was struck with a memory of Miriam and me playing hide-and-seek when we were children. I had gotten trapped in the attic for sometime as Miriam sought me out, only to give up halfway. Miriam never told me the game was over and had forgotten about me for several hours.

"I'm sorry for the mess," Ayla said, brushing aside herbs on her table. "I was not really prepared to have company over so soon, and I was in the middle of drying some herbs." Ayla swept dried herbs into an infuser.

Honey and lavender steam floated up from two mugs, the scent permeating the spiced air as she poured hot water.

I took a cup, and the steam blasted my face with warmth. "This smells wonderful." I sipped, the sweetness and softness of the lavender easing my tight body as I let out a breath of relief.

I wandered to Ayla's dainty hands wrapped around her mug to a silver band adorned with blue jewels. The ring was on her right ring finger, which made me think she was married and shared her little cottage with someone.

I tried not to think of the other option that may be the truth to the matter.

"Your ring is gorgeous," I said.

Ayla stretched out her hand, the ring glittering. "Thank you. I know what you are thinking. I am married and such." She took a small sip from her mug, a perfect precursory pause. "It was a family heirloom once upon a time ago. I was engaged, but it didn't end well, so I wear it to remind me what I have lost and what I must gain."

I shifted the mug, thinking about the sentiment. I wiggled my finger where my own ring lay. I wore it out of fear, unsure of what Silas would do if he found I refused to wear it. "You must have had a pretty rough life, then?"

"It's not all bad. Just today, I was in the middle of filling an order for a family. The mother was blessed with a child in autumn's cycle who has become sickly in recent months. The family is worried that the child won't survive to see its first-year mark. I suspect cholera, as the majority of this town has had it in some form or another. But even then, death haunts this town as much as the fog sticks." As she sipped her tea indignantly, her eyebrows scrunched in focus as she stared into the cup. "I fear my skill may not be enough, especially if the monster on the hill still terrorized us."

I perked my ears. "Actually, that is part of my reason why I came here today. What do you know of the monster? Is there a way to kill it?"

Ayla clicked her band against the ceramic mug, the soft ting mixed in with the soft grinding of several of the machines in her space. She brushed a strand away from her face. "There is a legend, one I am inclined to believe. There is an ancient ash tree that is said to have mystical properties to ward off the supernatural and especially of the night-walking kind."

I picked at the bed of my nail, stabbing my fingernails into the bed and letting the blood and pain be a reminder of the nightmare I was to endure. "Where does one find the ash tree?"

Ayla stood, collecting the mugs and depositing them into the sink. "The tree no longer exists. It burned down about the same time the castle came to be."

"Which means that this Death Incarnate will continue to prey on people." I sighed, hanging my head in my hands.

The crushing weight of the world kept building on my shoulders. I kept waiting for it to falter and collapse in the same way that my hope had.

The soft gargled water coming from the sink filled the space. Fire crackled from the fireplace as Ayla hummed a tune eerily and hauntingly beautiful.

I sat there and listened, the melody familiar to one that reminded me of home.

"What am I going to do? There's no hope of killing this man," I whispered into the hopeless void.

I wanted freedom from both death that plagued my lungs and the death I was living with who, in one split second, could drain my life from me. I wanted to see the world in its beauty and push myself to the limit without cause or worry about funds.

I wanted a life.

"Not necessarily." Ayla strode over to the counter and dove into the cupboards. Moments later, she tossed me a sachet. "Go ahead, open it."

I undid the straps to see gray ash. "This is . . ."

"The remaining ash from the ash tree that was burned," she said.

"How did you even get it?"

"Not easily. That is what I'll say about it. Sprinkle the ash onto a blade and shove it deep into his chest. That should kill him."

"*Should*?" I closed the sachet, skeptical. "I don't know this is—"

Blood gargled from my throat, and I hacked it up onto the table, blushing in shame.

"My guess is this is not the first attack you've had." Ayla scooted a napkin my way, and I murmured a *thanks*, cleaning up the mess.

I nodded. "The doctors don't have any idea what it is. At first, they assumed it was consumption, but as it progressed, my symptoms deviated with the same prognosis. I'm not expected to last the year."

Ayla took the napkin and tossed it into the fireplace. The fabric disappeared in mere moments, the same way I would not if I were to go into this plan.

"I might just have the thing to at least ease the coughing spells."

Ayla flew to the countertop filled with her dry herbs, arms moving in time to an invisible beat as she mixed and ground. She pushed up the sleeves of her dress, then dumped the mixture from the mortar into a sachet. With her movements precise, it was memorizing to watch as she flew across the small space.

She handed another satchel to me, the heady scent coming from the bag. "Take a sprinkle of this when there is a cough attack. It's not a cure-all, but it should ease the symptoms more so than whatever your doctor had been prescribing. I have seen this type of disease before, the kind that is ravishing your body. Unfortunately, there are not a lot of remedies."

I held the black wool satchel, a few thoughts coming to mind on the life I wanted to cultivate. "Do you mind if I come back—if I came back to learn from you until I—until I . . ."

She nodded, drumming her nails against the wood of the table. "Yes, I think I like that very much."

I rubbed my thumbs against the two satchels. The ash satchel's bright outer shell hid the true danger it could inflict.

"How much of the ash is needed onto a blade?"

Ayla's smile faltered. "A sprinkle upon a silver blade should do the trick. With that said, you only have one shot to kill him."

I almost did not want to know the answer to the question weighing on my mind since walking into the cottage.

"And if I don't?" I stuffed the satchels into my dress pocket, preparing to leave.

Ayla walked me to the door, her voice a soft whisper. "Let us hope that it does not come to that."

Eleven

"Is something wrong, Little Dove?" Silas cooed from the other end of the table, his wine glass in plain sight.

There had been a few iterations of the plan I thought through, and either option was not entirely a good plan, but with the ash sachet hidden in my pocket, I only had one shot. Since I sat, his wine glass had been empty. "I don't think I've ever seen you so quiet."

I dragged the fork across the plate, pushing around sad carrot slices. Time had been hard to keep track of, but after gauging my monthly cycle, it had been nearly a month since the wedding. I held off trying to do anything with powder since the day with Ayla, and still, it burned me to use it.

I shifted, the feeling of the steel bracing my hip. "I just have a lot to think about, that's all." I placed my fork down onto the tablecloth.

He lifted his chin and chuckled. "Like, what, making plans of escaping or perhaps concocting ways to send me to my maker?"

I took up my glass, swirling the wine before sipping. Anxiety ate at my nerves, and the unsettlement of the wine did not help much. I thought of the mother and the child who were at death's door because of the man before us—before me. If I didn't try today, when would I do the one thing those down in the village could not?

I shook my head, forcing every ounce of courage I can muster, and straightened myself in my seat. "Actually, I was thinking of something far more interesting and involving a lot less-layers. Quite frankly, I have been unoccupied as of late and thoroughly bored."

I attempted to add sultriness to my voice, the same way I had seen Miriam pull in men with the same soft sweetness of a wicked tongue.

I drained my glass and gave him a quirk of a smile, then held it to the heavens. He motioned to the air, and red wine filled not only my glass but his.

"Tell me, how shall I *alleviate* your boredom?" Silas sarcastically replied.

I sipped from my glass, staring into those liquid golden eyes. "Tell me a story."

"What kind of story, Little Dove?"

My feet carried me down to the other end of the table, the soft heel clicking in time to the thumping of my heart and the sloshing of my glass.

I perched at the corner of the table, skirting the edge. I fanned my hand from the folds of my skirt to his thigh where his hand rested. The silver band of vines twisted into themselves on top of his finger—the pair to mine.

Silas's gaze roamed, palms strained against his thigh and around his glass.

I moved a silver strand out of his face, fingers grazing the scar peeking out from under his mask, the ridge line transcending a valley of pain.

Silas snatched my wrist, growling, "I wouldn't do that if I were you."

I faltered, surprised by his tight tone.

Silas relaxed his grip, falling back into his chair posture stiff, rubbing at the inner lines of my palm. The sharpness of his face softened, traveling million miles away to the past of great horrors marring his existence and face. It was odd seeing him as just a simple man who had lived a torturous existence.

"How did you get those scars?" I softly asked.

Goose bumps raised along my skin, the blade biting into it. The longer I prolonged this, the more guilt I felt. I tried to harden my resolve by thinking of the villagers and the child who was sick from the darkness plaguing them in the form of man.

Pain and regret flashed in his gaze. "If it is a story you want, then it's one you shall get. There was a time in which I was not like this. It was a happier time back then. I remembered playing among the roses. My mother would also chastise me for wanting to get lost rather than to attend to my duty. It was on one of these occasions in which I came across an interesting woman among the roses.

"I had seen her there before, watching and pacing the maze of the garden. Now and then, we'd share glimpses, and I'd always made sure to hide my face, as I did not want her to see me any differently than a boy in the garden. Back then, I was ignorant of the politics of the court or even what was going on in my own backyard. At that moment, all I cared about was she was lovelier than the blooms. She had been crying when I surprised her. I did not tell her who I was but rather provided her with some comfort. Little did I know that she was the woman I was to marry to ensure an alliance."

Silas paused, closed his eyes, and tilted his head to the sky. "We did not know who we were to each other, and yet there we were, oblivious to the problems of our countries. We fell in love shortly, but it was not long after when both countries were thrown into chaos with murders—it became difficult for us to go on as we were. War was called for, and with the loss of my Father, I was the only person standing between hell and paradise."

Shadows crossed his face, the past haunting him and wearing down the beast. It was hard not to have sympathy for the man that was. My heart tugged at the prospect of what he had been through, the loss of many people in a short amount of time.

"What happened next?" I held his cold hand, letting it come to rest on my skirt.

The blade against my thigh seared into my flesh. Knots rolled through my stomach, as I was sure he can feel the anxiety eating me away.

No matter what, I could not let him persuade me away from my goal. I had to—I needed to do this if not for me but for the true victims involved in the monster's reign of terror. No matter what, he was still a monster and an evil being that took life.

"The countries went to war," Silas said. "An assassin had been paid to kill me. I walked away with this scar and my life—they did not. That had been one of many attempts."

"And the woman?"

Silas hesitated. "It's not something I wished to discuss further."

"Cat got your tongue." I chuckled, touching a finger to his nose to act coy.

I needed to find a way to get me close enough to him to slip the knife out and stab him. At this juncture, my options were colluding with the enemy.

Picking at my nail bed again, I succumbed to thought. Words tumbled out as if they had been trapped in a dream.

"Hatred and love are an interesting combination and one that goes hand in hand. Perhaps in your other life, you were fighting for a lover's honor or for vengeance. So powerful, it scorned the land, and lives were upended." I reached for him, tracing his chin, forever frozen in time. "A great war fought by great houses, and yet there you were, loving your enemy in all of this. A tragic love with tragic consequences."

Silas gripped my wrist. Images played through him as his face melted away. It was the boy, and his face was hidden behind a glittering white masquerade mask lit by love and joy. The image spun, as a familiar ballroom swirled around us in glorious color. His laughter whispered, while soft phantom lips traced the lines of my neck. Hands cradled the boy's face, leaning in as anticipation soared and met with the flurry of desire.

I am yours until we are nothing but dust.

Dust to dust, darling. We are nothing but immortal.

"Valeria?"

Silas's voice snapped the images in my head off, the laughter of the boy fading until it no longer existed. Until *he* no longer existed. Much to my displeasure, the thoughts and feelings from the image lingered, shadowing the growing anxiety. Hands were on his face, and I was no longer on the table.

Instead, I straddled him with only a hair's breadth between us to share and lips close enough to taste.

"Are you alright, Little Dove?"

I flickered between his gaze and his lips. The burning knife at my thigh was starting to become restricting underneath my dress. I traced his soft lips, and Silas stiffened under my touch, clutching the arm of the chair as his other hand cradled mine.

For my mission, this is all for my mission, I repeated to myself.

"Valeria, I—"

I pressed my lips to his, and his hand grabbed my waist as his mouth opened to me. Fire cascaded into me, injecting directing into my skin as flames licked down my body. Silas's hands explored, devouring my skin in fine sin. I wove my fingers through soft strands, tangling them beneath my touch as Silas groaned.

Silas's lips quirked under mine as a finger traces lazily across my thigh, stroking it higher just under the knife strap. A soft moan escaped my lips as I balled my fist into his blouse and tried to regain control of my thoughts.

"Sweet, *sweet* Valeria."

Shivering, I broke the kiss. "Apologies—got over excited." I placed a finger to his lips, getting up from his lap and depositing myself onto the table, fluffing out my skirt.

I had one shot and one shot only.

His lips quivered. "Eager, are we? And here I thought you hated me." He stood, towering over only to descend again. His lips crashed against mine with power and need as a frenzy drew us further into the abyss.

I resisted the urge, the very thought, my resolve slowly breaking the lower his mouth pressed against my body.

I wanted more.

Silas's lips traced the bony edges of my collarbone. His fist, from the thickness of my hair, fell out of the bun as he cradled my neck. His other hand was at my back, bracing me, restricting me from receding onto the table. Silas kissed me with a deep fury threatening to consume us both, breaths moving in tandem as we fought for control over one another.

He pulled away, hovering near my neck, peppering tender kisses. I tilted my head as a moan escaped my lips before a tight gasp took over, pleasure and pain. My fingers scraped at the knife, Silas distracted as he kissed along my body.

I unsheathed the blade, bringing it over his back, fingers shaking against the grip.

For the villagers—for the children. I had to. I *needed* to do it.

Silas bit down at my neck, and pleasure ebbed and flowed in blissful awareness. My resolve began to shake, and the knife came to rest against my side.

I couldn't do it. Perhaps I am just a selfish girl.

I gazed out of the corner of my eyes, sharp edges dripped crimson.

Silas tugged his lips back, wetness coating them. Flickering out across scarlet mouth, his pale pink tongue licked my blood off them.

I pushed him away, sending him barreling into the chair.

Silas stared up in bewilderment, his mouth red as the metallic scent lingered.

Among a beast, my own virtue was questioned in a place I knew I could not be selfish—I wanted to be, yet staring at Silas's inhumane eyes was an indication I couldn't be.

A shaky hand went to my neck, and I drew it back to see crimson glaring at me.

How long until he kills you?

"Monster," I breathed. I stifled the emotion, adjusting my bodice and shielding movement to tuck the knife back in. I clutched my neck, trying to regain composure and my own dignity. "You are nothing but a monster."

"Valeria." He started to plead and then stopped, face twisting in disgust. His lips curled into a snarl. "If I am a monster, then what does that make you? You came in here practically throwing yourself onto me, and you claim me to be the monster."

"You—you—"

My chest threw itself into a coughing fit of blood spurting from my lips and onto his blouse.

Silas launched into action, sweeping me up and biting his flesh. "Drink."

I pushed his hand away, struggling to get my feet under me.

I hated the effect he had on me, hated the fact I wasted my opportunity to kill him—to be of use to the people in the village. To not be the selfish woman I am.

I needed to give my life to the greater good. If I was to die soon, I didn't have the time to be selfish.

"Perhaps it is best that I am reminded of what you are," I whispered.

I was nearly out of the door when Silas gripped my shoulder and spun me around, my face meeting his chest. Power surged from him, nails biting into my flesh. Iridescent gold cast down upon me, fury and rage bubbling between the surface.

"Would you like to guess my name?"

"I think beast suits you best," I said, keeping the knife close under the folds of my skirt.

135

Excerpt from illegible journal:

-evening of death and destruction. Father is dead, and I cannot even bring myself to write about her. Narcisa believes it to be a message between our two countries, but I believe it to be a ploy to start a war that no one wants. I am to be crowned in mere days and then after marrying Narcisa to seal our alliance. I fear I must start at the beginning if I am to understand how this could have gone so wrong in so many ways.

The troubles started nearly a decade ago when I was all but a boy. Father was embroiled in a costly war with an empire that no longer exists. He never gave many details, but he had several magic folk employed to temper the defenses. Magic to fight magic he said, but it was at a cost, a high cost. Amaris is broke, too broke to feed its own people with too many upheavals and epidemics have broken out. Father never saw the devastation in those villages, the smell of death lingering even among the living. I walked those villages as soon as I was able to comprehend the damage, but even then, it was too late.

The war had taken much from us—it had taken much from me. I still remember the taste of her lips in which there can be no other. No matter the state of our countries—I will not let them decide our fate, but now, it's too late.

All of this was too late.

I was a dutiful son and stood ready to do anything to protect my country and the lives that inhabit it. I knew that I had little choice of the matter—that I could change my fate. I was to be crowned King with Narcisa as my queen, yet I was unsure of what I wanted.

It wasn't until I met her that I finally understood what it means to want—to desire a life you could not have. I write this—

HE

Twelve

I squinted at the writing underneath the candle-light, rubbing my tired eyes. Anxiety knotted through my stomach, and shame burned in my cheek.

I kissed him. In return, he had bitten me, partaking in my own blood. My fingers touched the bandage. Ebony patched me up after the stunt in the dining room, insisting I'd get blood all over the fine fabrics.

"This is not a hospital," she said, her ghostly fingers applying the adhesive to the spot. "But this should do. Try not to get hurt too often here. We don't have many medical supplies, seeing as the inhabitants are dead or *undead*." She chuckled.

Ebony had been diligent in wrapping me up, being the only source of comfort.

"How did you ever become trapped here?" I said, trying to divert my attention away from the fading warmth and the faint ghostly touches not coming from the spirit dressing my wounds.

"I was a nurse sometime in the summer of 1806, taking care of down-and-out folks of the village. I am not sure what it is like where you are from, but those streets are not kind to those whose luck has run out." She cut another strip of tape, cold fingers pressing down on the spot of my neck. "There seemed to be a lot of mangled children that came in, blood in every which way. I lost a few of them to their injuries and a few others to infection."

"So, when did you come to the castle? I thought that this place would be older than a few decades," I asked in place of the question burning through my head.

She thought for a moment. "Silas picked me up from the back alley after I had been jumped by a patient I'd treated. Patched me up and everything, insisted I drink from him, but I refused. I came here when the fever set in from the infection and I knew I was on death's doorstep."

I contemplated for a moment, lost in thought, and held my tongue as questions swirled. "You died here?"

Ebony finished patching my neck, her dark eyes heavy with sorrow. "Master is kind and not the villain that you claim him to be, nor the bloodthirsty vampire the town believes. He is simply a man. A man who has lost everything."

I gruffed, "He does not appear to have lost every-thing. He lives here as an immortal being watching the rest of us grow old."

She gave a wryly smile. "But at what cost? A cost in which none of us will have to pay in this life or the next. He is alone, watching everyone around him move on."

There was a time when I was not like this.

Ebony left me to ponder these words, to curse silence and solitude. I flipped through the journal from the library. The ferocious scribbled writing across the page gave me some indication of whoever it was may have been in distress, desperate to try and capture his words before something bad happened.

Before something got to him.

I rubbed at my face, eyelids drooping. I slid the book onto the nightstand and took the bit of the herbal remedy Ayla prescribed as directed, letting the icy chill settle into my chest to ease the ache. I placed the satchel of herbs back onto the small table, picking up the knife from under my dress and held the blade into my hand. I came so close, only to fail. The next time—the next time I needed to make sure I did not fail.

I tucked the knife under my pillow, blowing out the lights and succumbing to the dark.

Shadows lurked in the corner of the room, watching and waiting as a wolf does when on the hunt—for the opportunity to strike down vulnerable prey. Terror seized my body and soul, chest tightening as a heavy weight pressed down. Snarling teeth tore into my flesh, ripping muscles and sinew until I was but a bloodied corpse. Whether a dream or reality, all there was is blood, splattered against the wall, the bed sheets, and staining my soul. I'm held down, chest rushing and falling, becoming heavier as ragged gasps filled my ears as a plea for air.

Valeria. Oh, Valeria—such easy prey.

The shadows whispered to me, beckoning to follow into its twisted dark depth of the underworld. A sweet song pulsated, and my own body fought to retain control with the icy grip burning cold against flesh.

I wasn't ready, not now.

The embrace was dark, cold, and familiar. Its shadow threatened to consume or tear me apart. I snapped my eyes open as snarling jaws crawled up the bed, snapping into a faceless grin accompanied by a distant, cruel laughter. It flicked out a forked tongue, licking its maw intermittently, the metallic scent of blood clinging to its breath as a claw pinned me to the bed.

You're mine.

A scream erupted from my lips, rubbing my throat dry and raw with the taste of blood. It was too much, the overwhelming agony tearing to pieces upon the chamber bed.

"Stop, stop!" I screamed, sobbing.

"Valeria! Valeria, open your eyes."

It was still dark, a candle burning softly on the nightstand illuminating enough to see the shadows and the void receding from my mind and the bed. Body shaking, I wrapped the blanket tight around myself, darting to the rest of the room.

In my panic, I nearly missed him.

Silas was holding my shoulders, face hard set as the candle licked at his features. Silver hair draped over his shoulder and tickled my nose. The other item I missed was he was bare from the waist up, pale scars etched across dark skin in the same grotesque manner as the one upon his face. Lean muscles in his arm tensed as he continued to restrain me to the bed, breathing in tandem with me.

I shook his body off, the terror still fresh as the taste of blood and death coated dryly in my throat. "Let me go," I said, gritting my teeth. I glanced toward the armoire and found it hadn't moved. "How the hell did you get in?"

Silas frowned, sliding his hands from the blanket and barricading me to the bed as I attempted to flee. "That is what you're concerned about! You woke up screaming bloody murder, and that is what you are concerned with?"

"Of course that is what I am concerned about! The fact that you got in here without having to use the door is a cause for alarm!" I pushed against the headboard, determined to get away from the weight of his body. I kept my eyes glued to the wall, hoping that if I acted indifferent, he'd leave.

Silas paced about the room and ran his hand through his hair. "I don't know how they got in. None of the barriers were breached, and yet they were able to get this close."

I huddled in the blanket, and the icy chill tingled against my skin, heart still racing. Chest heaving, I groused, "Are these your minions? Did you send them simply because I upset you with the truth? Is that it?"

In quick movements, he climbed onto the bed, cornering me. His face leveled with mine as he growled out, taking a hold of my body, dragging me down the bed. "If you want me to be the monster that I am, so be it. I will be the beast that so many people fear."

I thrashed against him, grabbing at his hair and beating his chest. He pinned me down, his head and mouth dropping to the space between my neck.

"It would be so easy," Silas hissed. "It would be so easy to take your life—to swallow it whole and feel no regret. Isn't that what a true beast is—a monster that feels no pain—no regret that takes and takes and takes."

"Stop . . . don't. I—" I pounded at his chest, and a cough let loose before blood spilled from my lips onto the sheer nightgown—and his bare chest. I took hollow gasps, groping for as much air as I could. Each rile cough brought forth more blood that glistened crudely under candlelight.

Silas released me, and I fumbled my way to the nightstand. The satchel hue blurred as the coughing worsened. I knocked over the items on the side table, herbs flying to the floor. The heavy book alongside the scattered pieces. I collapsed, clutching my abdomen. Blood splattered across the floor as a pool formed over the spilled herbs.

I can't breathe—I can't breathe.

Was this to be the night I would finally die?

Body weightless, I was cradled by soft skin nestled among black fabric draped over my rattling limbs. Eyes prickled with tears, I fisted the fabric, the coughing relinquishing itself at last. I dipped my head to my chest, and the taste of blood heavy and exhaustion wavered with each breath. Silas's body braced mine. He shifted, muttering a soft groan as he held out his wrist, the sheen of dark blood dripping onto his pants. "Drink."

I pushed his hand away, the effort taxing, as it did not budge. "No, I can't."

"Can't or won't? Drink."

"I can't."

"Why do you insist on being so stubborn?" Silas sighed, and the cut on his wrist closed. He took my hand in his, admiring them, squeezing softly. "Do you want to be a walking corpse, is that it? A beautiful walking corpse."

"That's not it." I tucked my head into my knees, recalling Miriam's last words. "It means I have to keep a promise. If I drink and become like you—it means keeping a promise that'll kill me either way."

The thought of going back to the crumbling home, to Mama's judging eyes and Miriam's sweet innocence to the world was a noose I was not ready to tighten. I envied Miriam for Mama's favoritism, the control she had over her own life. She had a choice in what she did. Even away from Endovier, I did not have choices—I was more of a pawn in freeing people from a monster who showed more kindness than I had seen in the last year.

I wetted my lips. "I can't go back to being a pawn, to having my life lived for me."

Since I've met this man, I've been open to a world of contradictions of what should and shouldn't be. Nothing about him made any sense, and it terrified me.

I traced the lines of his callous hand, the warmth of his scent and body melding with mine.

Heat burned in the pit of my stomach and threatened to explode in beautifully disastrous ways. The intense desire drove me to the brink of madness to where dream and reality mashed against each other in horrifying beauty.

Silas stroked my back, easing the ache from the cough as exhaustion plunged me further into wandering thoughts.

I wanted to be selfish. To let this man—this beast ruin me and sully the last bit of innocence I had left to offer. Be the last thing I'd experience on the Earth before death swept me away in their cool embrace. I'd accepted my ruination at this man's hand.

Silas's arm crossed my body, nails slicing into his wrist. Blood welled from the wound as he offered it once more. "Then, drink and live on your own terms. Not because you owe a debt or a promise but because you want to live. To visit places you have never seen, to do things you haven't done and everything else in between. Drink and live, Valeria. *Live.*"

I stared at the blood, and it dripped into my lap as dark red stained the white nightgown. "I won't turn into what you are if I drink this?"

I was childish to ask, taking his wrist with shaky hands. I marveled at how the wound slowly closed, stitching itself back together and, in moments, disappeared.

Silas shook his head. "No, it'll just heal, but I will caution you to be wary for a few hours. With my blood in your system, I don't want you to do anything that may risk causing death."

I met his gaze, and questions swirled about in my head as blood coated us both. I didn't speak them aloud as I brought his wrist to my lips. I licked the wound. It tasted nothing like the blood I have been coughing up for the last year. It tasted of dreams, of hope, and of sweet warmth, as if I'd been basking in the summer sun. I took slow, greedy sips—the world fell away into nothingness, fire surging combusting.

He groaned as his other hand stroked my cheek. "That's it. Gently now."

Silas's voice was a million miles away, flooded by other images—visions of the boy.

In a rose garden under the cover of darkness, a halo of moonlight crowned him, face drawn in seriousness as he reached a hand out, grasping it.

They mean to hurt you.

Hurt me?

I fear for your life, Cecilia. They mean to kill you. This, I am sure.

His eyes dimmed with sadness. In this vision, he wore the same suit, with the white mask nowhere to be found. The scene played out from another perspective as if I was in their head, watching these scenes play out, their hands intertwining with his.

A spectator to the past.

Find the truth, no matter the cost. Save him, Valeria.

Blood splattered the lover's hand, shock written across the boy's face. A guttural, soul-wrenching scream echoed in my head. Crimson dotted the vision.

"Valeria, that's enough. Valeria."

When I'm back in my own body, Silas's arm was wrapped around me, the taste of him on my lips. He was holding me still, chest rising and falling in tandem, and my nails were dug into his arm, tiny half crescent indents mar his skin.

"I-I there was—"

His face nuzzled into my neck as he stroked my hair, a calming touch as my mind shattered to what I witnessed. Blood. So much blood with someone in this vision murdered in front of his—her—my eyes.

Silas whispered, seductive and relaxing, "Shhh, you're safe. Just sleep. I'll be here for you to kill tomorrow morning. Just sleep, Little Dove."

My eyelids fluttered, exhaustion calling as the strength from earlier faded quickly. I tried grasping on to stay conscious enough to dissect these visions. I drifted slowly and then, all at once, I fell limp in his arms to be greeted in sleep by a woman's voice in the depths.

Save him, Valeria. You are almost out of time.

Thirteen

I'd bury myself into the bowl of porridge or into scalding hot coffee if I could. When I awoke the next morning, Silas was gone, along with the mess of blood and herbs. The only convincing evidence of last night not being a dream was the silver knife on the nightstand and Silas's nonchalant note.

I found this~

I focused on part of that night when the knife could have slipped from the bed covers. The more I retraced my thoughts on the matter, the more my cheeks burned. I slapped my face, compelled it was a dream—a hallucination in my lonely, confused mind. It would have explained the visions, hallucinations, and the clean floor, but it did not explain the wound.

Or lack thereof.

I took off the bandage this morning and discovered the marks Silas had left earlier were gone. Not even any faint scars to indicate the skin had been pierced. Overnight, the sickly hue had vanished, and for the first time in a while, my chest no longer ached. Silas's blood had worked wonders, but there were more questions than answers.

Then there was the voice that puzzled me.

Save him.

I stabbed my spoon into the bowl with enough force to almost shatter it in two. The voice was a puzzle that did not make sense nor did the urgency of their message. Save who from what? Save Silas? What did he need to be saved from?—wasn't it the other way around? At this point, I may very well have been crazy or slowly succumbing to isolation.

"Hard morning?" Ebony appeared, her eyes raised in a skeptical manner—or at least I think so. "Or a hard night?"

"I do not wish to divulge about last night." I rubbed my head.

Ebony snickered. "Uh-huh, sure." She held her hand up. "Say no more. Although, if you do wish to talk, I am happy to let you know I can keep a secret from you-know-who if you are worried about that."

I sighed. "No, it's not that. It's—"

"Complicated. Believe me. I know that part perfectly well."

I put the spoon down. There were no words to describe the feeling building in my chest and the confusion in my head. Months were passing by, and the longer I was here, the more confused I became. Silas was a beast—a monster preying on poor, unfortunate souls and destroying innocent lives.

Yet—I had a hard time believing he was at fault. Am I wrong to judge him based on what little evidence was present? Silas had been kind if not a little rough, yet at the end of the day, I hardly knew him.

In all of this time, I had yet to figure out who the man was and the truth behind the name game in which I play night after night. If I wanted my freedom and to return to Endovier, I needed to find what it was he was hiding.

I needed answers.

I drank the rest of my coffee, collected my cloak, and headed toward Ayla's cottage.

"What makes you think that it is the beast that is causing all the deaths in the village?" I asked as we wandered down the street.

The market square was busy in the early afternoon light. People happily bartered with each other—ignoring the darkness looming swiftly over their heads. Children ran through the streets, chasing after one another, squealing with delight. It was as if the village's ignorance kept them blind to the true horrors stalking their neighborhoods at night.

Ayla picked up a squash, turning it over and inspecting the vegetable. "Who else would be causing such atrocities?"

"An illness, perhaps?" I pondered.

Ayla continued her inspection, handing me vegetable after vegetable to be placed in the basket. "Illnesses strike slowly and with cause—the deaths are swift and random. A mother can die in an afternoon, and her babe will remain unaffected despite sharing such a close quarter with one another."

"But how do you know?"

She stopped. "I know because I see the damage the very presence of evil has scourged upon us. You ask any man here, and they will tell you the very same."

I had no right to disagree with her thoughts on the matter. Ayla had lived in this village possibly her whole life. Yet there lay with her the uncertainty of who or what was truly responsible for the deaths at play. None of the conclusions I'd seen or heard directly pointed to Silas.

As if she was reading my mind, Ayla tossed her head back. "Follow me."

Passing the winding road far from the bustling square, we arrived at a shambled shack. Shingles were scattered in pieces along the cobblestone, leaving barren holes on the roof.

Ayla rapped against the door, the hinges shuddering under her knuckles.

A voice called from behind the door, then swung open to the bloodshot eyes of a wrinkled woman. Glassy orbs narrowed and then widened.

"Ayla, child I wasn't expecting you."

"It was an unplanned trip today, Hilda. I was hoping to introduce you to my protege who has been assisting me as of late," Ayla said, gesturing with open arms toward me.

The woman flickered for a moment, lips wrinkled into a smile as she allowed us to enter.

There was not much in the home. A table sat in the corner, held up by three legs, surrounded by chairs missing a rail or two upon the back rest. A bed clothed in ratted sheets was pushed against the wall and in the center, and a brick fireplace with a glimmer of flame lapped up the burnt logs.

Hilda pulled the chairs in close, depositing herself in one of the seats and gesturing to the others. "I may not have much, but what I lack, I make up for in a quaint sense of hospitality, I suppose. Now, Ayla, this is unlike you to take on someone much less bring them here. What is it that you want?"

"Can a woman change it up every now and then?" Ayla quipped. She brushed back her hood, and ash strands bounded loose from their hold, spilling overtop the blue cloak. She tapped her nails against the stool, beckoning me to sit.

And sit, I did, for what Hilda said next did not bode well for what Ayla had brought me here for.

"I suspect you are here for me to tell your young protege why the town is cursed by that beast on the hill. Or the pungent death that festers even among the bright flowers of the youth."

"Well—actually, I . . ."

The words muddled in my brain.

Ayla's stone-hard gaze flickered under the faint flames, and I was stunned into silence. I pursed my lips together and chewed at the inside of my cheek as Hilda stoked the fire.

"Life here wasn't always so morbid and fraught with tragedy. I was just a girl when the castle appeared, seemingly out of a thunderclap. My Ma and Pa, like the rest of the village, thought nothing of it. An 'act of God,' perhaps, they had thought initially as no one knew of the beast that lurked beyond its stone walls. That perhaps it was the act of the devil himself—an abomination to the world."

The fire crackled in agreement as a log cracked in two and joined the likes of the ashes.

Hilda pointed to a pair of black-and-white photographs upon the mantle glided in the last fineries. I imagined she had no heart to sell, even if it meant feeding herself or funding the repairs for her little home. In the photo, the man and a woman posed for the camera, their images having faded with age to where they were nothing more than ghosts among the gilded frames.

"It wasn't until the deaths became hard to bear that we began to realize the true extent of evil. Shadows and nightmares were the first, haunting the children and scaring them to where they no longer slept as they screamed all through the nights their horrible visions. Then came the sudden illness where not a single doctor could cure. With each sickness came the inevitable deaths, and soon, it had become insurmountable. There were no longer enough grave plots dug daily to contain the bodies.

"So much darkness in those days. Many have seen the man fly down on wings of shadows to take the lives of so many people."

"Is that what happened to your parents?" I asked. "Did they—did you see the man?"

Hilda, silent for a moment, stoked the burnt logs with the iron hook. Her gaze lifted to the photo to reminisce about the memory of when they were alive and well and perhaps the tragedy.

Ayla's expression remained flat, never giving away the intentions she had in bringing me here or any motives.

"Yes. They had caught the illness from the dark and shortly succumbed soon after. Not even my sister, a trusted nurse, could treat it. It got her that summer of the same year."

"Could it have been a disease rather than a person?" I blurted.

I kept telling myself I had no right to pass judgment onto her or any of the village people. This was their home, and I was just a stranger to them living with the beast—who'd allowed themselves to be touched by him.

"I think it is best you both leave."

Hilda spoke without reservation.

Ayla stood, bowing to the woman. "We appreciate your hospitality, Hilda." From her cloak, she produced a vial of herbs. "For your ailing joints, take three teaspoons with your afternoon tea, and all should be well."

She grunted, "Remind the child to be wary of the dark."

"What's in the dark?" I asked.

Hilda's crow eyes flickered to the only corner not lit by the starving fire. Shadowy wisps congealed, shifting and moving in tandem to the light just out of reach of it. From the inky black depths came whispers of hell crammed into a singular voice, echoing faintly off the small home.

"Death," Ayla replied.

I walked longer than I should have—unease at the little information I gleaned from the village. Silas was still a mystery and harder to pin as simply a terror. As I left Ayla's, it was clear there was more to the story of Silas and the castle.

I wandered through the fog, aware of the clouds affecting the landscape as well as the confusion in my soul. The fog was a dense ocean of white, obscuring anything it saw fit, and perhaps that's what it was there for. To obscure the truth of Silas—of the castle—and the death plague of the village. To make everything before me obscure and out of reach.

A part of me hoped wandering would ease my mind, to get lost and not face either Ayla or Silas. To be forced to make the choice sooner or later. For some reason or another, I needed to stop being selfish and face the music.

For the first time in a long while, I had a choice *I* could make.

I came to the opening on the opposite side of the path, having looped myself around in circles for an eternity. The castle before me loomed, its magnificent structure touching the sky and reveling in the darkening of the gray clouds, an incoming storm on the prowl. The structure was a testament to the ominous warning barricaded within. Stones from the highest parapet crumbled, falling into the blocked off section of the west wing. The pallor of its walls shimmered in the dying light, and dark ascended onto the land once more, a phantom to forever wander that would succumb to the sea of time, crumbling into ash.

I pushed the wrought-iron gates open and made my way to the grand doors of the castle when the thought emerged.

The castle sighed as if it had been holding its breath.

The nights were synonymous with the horrors of the castle. Every bump, every creak was an imaginary demon appearing to me and only me. The ghosts had all but left me alone to my own thoughts. Even Ebony's constant presence waned toward the evening, tending to her master in his study or the forbidden west wing.

I tossed and turned, sleep evading me as those eyes burned brightly in the back of my skull. Upon the soft cushions of the bed, the stares from those eyes bore into my skin, raking every inch of me in search for a weak point.

I felt more exposed than I had ever been.

A loud slam jarred me out from under the comforter, and I quickly stepped to the door, careful of the soft creaks of the floorboards and the hinges. At first, darkness greeted me, eyes quick to adjust to the light of the moon streaming into the foyer from the stained glass window, casting an eerie glow upon Silas's stumbling form.

Just as the previous night, he was coated from head to toe in blood, shuffling along the steps as it dripped down white strands onto the banister. I cowered behind the door, expecting him to go to his study as he often did during the midnight hour.

This time, he turned left toward the west wing.

Silas halted a few steps, searching behind him for wary eyes. I held my breath, praying he wouldn't seek out my door and scold me. He stayed like that for two heartbeats before turning on his heels and shuffling down the long corridor.

I grabbed the silver knife off the nightstand and followed him.

The walls wailed in response once I crossed the threshold. Voices echoed, seductively calling me to follow Silas in deeper.

I floundered in the dark, the glint reflecting off the blade the only source of light.

"What do you think you are doing?"

I jabbed the blade in the direction of the voice, only to be caught by the wrist by strong hands. Golden orbs glistened menacingly down at either me or the blade.

"Valeria, I asked you a question," Silas said.

"I—uh, saw." I was unsure of the lie I was to tell, at least one that'd be convincing to the man currently covered in blood. "You came in covered in blood, so I decided to follow after you."

The scent of evergreens floated in the dark between us mixing in with spice. The orbs tilted with amusement as he brought my hand to his chest, removing a finger one by one from the hilt. "So, you decided to not only come after me and break the one rule I have in place but with a knife. I have to say I'm impressed by your boldness."

My fingers relinquished their grip on the blade's handle, and I watched as it glinted in the darkness of Silas's hand. Utterly defeated, I expected to be killed—or worse, drained.

"What did I say about the west wing, Valeria?"

His tone was dark and devoid of the humor I had become accustomed to.

When I didn't answer, he took my arm and led me back down the corridor. His grip tightened against my wrist as we walked the long, sweeping expanse of the hallway appearing to twist and turn more. We reached the open foyer, and the extent of Silas's discontentment crossed his stone features.

Silas took a hold of my shoulders, searching wildly for a moment before releasing me and hung his arms over the banister. "What did I say? Never—and I mean *never*—go into the west wing alone. Do you know what could have happened?"

"What is in the west wing that is so bad?"

"Nothing you need to concern yourself with."

"Stop being so secretive! Between you and Ebony, I'm starting to think there is more going on with your curses and my freedom than you are willing to tell me," I said, frustration coating my throat.

My mind had been trying to wrap itself around the village deaths and the man before me—to make the connection of the serial murderer the town despised to the tender man that offered a dance and a chance to live.

"I want to know what you are hiding!"

"I can't tell you. Anyways, I forbid you from going into the west wing!" Silas growled, giving me a hard stare from the banister's edge.

I lowered my gaze, the momentum and adrenaline dissipating as I rubbed at my wrist. I whispered, "You were covered in blood. Can you at least tell me why?"

Silas sighed. "Go to bed, Valeria."

I shuffled off to my bedroom door, a few heartbeats away from the banister and the glowing form of Silas. Before I closed it, I made up my mind.

Whatever Silas was hiding had to be in the west wing.

Darling,

There are so few words in which I can express myself. Tonight will be a night neither of us will ever forget. A beautiful ball, dressed in swirling colors of red and purple upon the ballroom floor—what a sight it will be.

I will be the maiden dressed in the colors of our lovely garden. Since this is a masked affair, I will have a gold mask adorned, so perhaps we can dance without restriction.

If you are unable to get away, perhaps meet me in the garden when the moon reaches its peak. Oh, how lovely. A midnight stroll through the rose garden under the light of the moon. Can you picture it? Perhaps, at last, I shall finally learn your name tonight as you had promised so long ago.

I cannot wait to see you. I love you,

—Cecilia

Raeben,

I request that we deal with the issue as soon as possible. Endovier cannot be given access to any of Amaris's resources. With the two countries already embroiled in ongoing wars with other nations, this alliance will exacerbate if not worsen Amaris's standing.

If you do not do anything about this, then I will have no choice but to take matters into my own hands, seeing as the original arrangement was with my family. I will not stand to be rejected in such a public manner.

Yours Truly,
Narcisa Marius Nicholae

GA

Fourteen

eeks went by, and I stepped into a routine. I'd wake to eat breakfast and exchange a few words with Ebony, who'd move objects to let me know she was there, listening to my thoughts. In the afternoons, I spent time with Ayla at her cottage, making remedies and tending to the sick. In the evenings, Silas would always greet me with a smirk and pose his nightly anticipated question. Every night, without fail, he would disappear into the west wing, hiding his secrets and giving me little opportunities to snoop.

I'd stay awake hours after I had retired for the evening when he would leave the castle to be able to enter the wing. But sleep was unavoidable, and so were the shadows lapping at the edge of the bed, ready to consume me alive as the dreams grew stranger, becoming more vivid and lucid as if it was my own memory.

Save him before it's too late.

The sweet song voice called from beyond the soft scent of roses under a bloodred moon. The boy appeared in these dreams, crying and covered in blood, with shaky hands outstretched to the moon, pleading in hushed whispers.

The monotony kept me busy while awaiting the fateful opportunity. Only when the autumn winds began to roll did that day arrive.

I stared at the letter taped up onto Ayla's door in beautiful, elegantly scrawled lines.

Went to take some medicine to the Grandulf family. Their babe is sick again. Odd thing it is, all these sick babes. Anywho, I will not be home most of today but stop back in tomorrow!

Shutting the wooden doors of the castle, I was struck by how quiet it was in the middle of the day. Not even the ghosts, which I had become accustomed to darting in and out, were silent as a tomb. I climbed the stairs to the second floor and found myself at a crossroad between the west and the east wing.

It was sudden. A chord struck in my body, and my feet were leading to the west wing's hallway. I didn't have time to second guess as I dove into the darkness. The hall wound, shifting with every corner I took. The wing expanded further into the decrepit depths.

The dirty carpet and stained, moth-eaten curtains filtered light through the giant holes of the ornate fabric. Cobweb and dust stretched on in the direction of the winding hallway as door upon door followed me along the way. Not a sound echoed, my footsteps muffled by the softness of the carpet.

The warmth of the fading sun broiled the stench of decay and rot, my hand flying to my face to block the awful scent. The farther I went, the stronger the smell and the knots forming in my stomach became.

Shadows lurked at the edges of my vision, sweeping in curiously close before retreating back into the dark corners. Turn after turn, the light faded away, and the lure of voices crept closer, hooking its claws in me. Darkness skittered past in malice and intrigue. I did not dare to gaze upon it.

Valeria, sweet, damned child. Trapped in endless cycles to taste but not understand. To dream and not know. Follow us, child. Come speak with us. We will show you.

The walls echoed with those voices, crude laughter, hissing riddles, and hushed whispers of a crowded room. Yet not a soul appeared. Living or dead.

I stopped in front of a black oval-point door, and shadows slipped under the threshold as whispers died away behind that door. I placed my ear to the wood, listening to the same tantalizing voices beyond reach.

Valeria. The crowd of voices gathered to a singular voice—a woman. Warm, familiar, and inviting sweetly sang from behind the ominous door, *Valeria, help. I'm trapped here. That awful monster locked me in here in the dark. Help me. Please, open the door.*

Loud bangs knock against the hard wood.

Help me. Please, open the door. Valeria, open the door.

Skeptical, I responded, "Who are you? How did you get in there."

The door balked, slamming against the hinges.

"Help me! He's got me. He's got me."

Without hesitating or with thought, I turned the knob and opened the door to the pitch black.

The darkness peered back with hungry eyes. Millions of them stared in cruel glee.

Feet glued to the spot with a hand still on the knob of the door, I froze, watching tendrils of blackness wrap around my limbs, drawing me in slowly. My heart pulsated against my ribs, and I dug my heels into the ground, stumbling back onto the half-eaten rug.

"No," I howled. "No, no, no, no."

Don't be shy. We shall show you the truth of everything. Soon, you will know the game is played. It's been awfully long since we've been let out.

I was slammed with flashing images, fire searing across skin. The smell of death became stronger as the onslaught of my senses turned chaotic. Laughter echoed in my head as the speed of the images intensified. God, the searing, stinging hot became unbearable. Inches of my skin sliced open, only to be seared back together with intensity, only to be renewed again. Body lying bare to the shadows, my legs buckled underneath me, sprawled out onto the hard floor. Nails scraped my throat, the inside rubbed raw. I was screaming but couldn't hear it. I was left in the dark, in pain, with blood and death pulsating in me. Around me—*killing me* thrumming through my body—head— everywhere.

Make it stop.

Make it stop.

Make it stop.

Make it stop.

Dear gods, *make it stop.* I can't take it—I can't, I can't.

"*Valeria.*" Silas shook me fiercely, nails biting deep into my shoulder. The tang of blood brought me too. "Valeria, come back to me."

I marveled at Silas's face in fine detail, bite-size features to focus on. The curve of his lips speaking inaudible words. The wide terror in his eyes, flecks of gold shimmering in the faint light. Silver hair twisted back into a braid framed sharp angles hidden behind scars and mask unto the shadows. A shaking hand grasped my cheek.

"Valeria. Jesus, I told you to stay the hell out of the west wing."

Outside of the door, I was closed off from the shadows that had nearly consumed me. Their touch still danced on my skin, invading every inch.

I was in Silas's arms.

Outside the door.

I was outside of that door and in Silas's arms—more importantly, intact and not shredded into flesh and blood.

"What was that?" I croaked, fingers at my throat rubbing in soft strokes, fingers that should've been mine but were not.

Wrestling out of his arms, I crawled across the floor, staggering to my feet. Leaning against the wall,

I breathed in a shaky, ragged gasp. Skin raw from the fire of a dying ember, digging my nails into bare arms.

I needed to know I was here—I was in my body and not hers.

I was not her.

The images died, and the cool walls of the castle anchored the chilling fire burning deep inside. I trembled at the faint lines of the shadows tracing my skin, etching their being into my soul. Their whispers caressed my ears, and I could still hear them, though their words were trapped behind a closed door.

We can show you the truth.

"They are the children of darkness, the collector of humanity's worst nightmares. I had sealed the door a long time ago to curb their reign of terror. As you can see, they can be quite terrifying when left to wreak havoc on the mind of humans."

We shall show you how the game is played.

"They spoke to me. Something about a game and the truth."

The words tumbled out, yet they did not materialize, a phantom among the plane in which I was not adrift. I was trapped in this body and still felt I had traveled through time to try to solve the mystery. It was there, on my tongue, a way to save us both from the walls closing in as the days went by. How long before it was too late? How long until there was nothing left of—

Silas's hand was on my shoulder, clove and spice a home to bury myself in. It was in a memory, lost, out of reach of what I had hoped to be the truth. He held it at his damn fingertips, yet there were still riddles.

"You heard their voices?"

"You can't hear them?"

"No, I can't. What did they say?"

"They wanted to show me something, I think. The truth of a game they said they were playing."

Silas paled, his gold eyes widening as his hands chased away the fire from my skin, bringing his forehead to mine, melding his being into mine. In that tender moment, my fears melted away, and I huddled closer upon that floor.

Right then, I needed to be sure I was safe. Even if it was with him, somehow, I felt protected there on the floor with him.

Fingers grazed my cheeks, twisting a singular strand between his index fingers, contemplative and possessive. Silas whispered, "Are you trying to get yourself killed here?"

He scooped me up and hauled me through the twists and turns of the west wing. The dark leaped back from him, as if they were scared or if they were a part of him in some manner or form. Waiting to be controlled, to be beckoned to their great master, carrying their prey to safety. By the time we reached the main hallway, they retreated as Silas stepped into the east wing.

Silas opened the door to my bedroom and deposited me onto the soft mattress and tucked me in. A stray touch lingered across my skin, stoking flames through a torn body.

"I want you to stay here, and please listen this time."

"Then, you should tell me what you are hiding in the west wing," I shot back.

"I can't."

"Why not? You are obviously hiding something from me. You have me guess your name night after night. Your castle is filled with ghosts, the village is plagued by death that, supposedly, you are not responsible for. And now you have shadows beyond a locked door that state you are hiding something. I am not as naive as you think I am."

Silas stilled at the door, muscles tense as he pried it open to the indecision and anguish written upon his face. The numbness of my legs were pins and needles as I fought the blankets wrapped around my body.

"No, you're not," he said.

"Then, tell me!"

"I can't."

"So, now what, you are to go back into the dark recesses of that wing and not give me the answers I desperately want no—need to know all things considering?"

"It's better this way."

"Better!" I scoffed, driving my feet down to the floor and driving myself to him. "Nights on end, you ask me the same bloody question. You come back from gods know where in the dead of night covered in blood yet claim you only drink from the willing. You disappear into the west wing that I am not to go anywhere near with a door of shadows that nearly killed me. I have more questions than answers and you are either avoiding it or hiding them from me."

I beat his chest, my fists balled against the fabric of his shirt. I rested my head on him, and there was not a single heartbeat. Not one.

Silas raised a hand, resting on the back of my head, taking a few hard exhales. His other hand shook at his side, and I did not dare to gaze upward. A beast—a man struggling against the inner demons inside his own mind.

I closed my eyes. The thumbing in my chest grew louder as the terrible decisions I had made pushed me further into danger. My head was muddled and confused by not the man in front of me but of the strangeness of it all.

There was much in this muchness drowning out sanity in which madness had brought me to.

"Say something," I said, my own heart ravished inside my chest.

"You called me a beast, and you choose to believe what others have to say. I also hurt you and I do not want you to get hurt because of me, so this is simply the best I can do." Silas pushed me away, retreating behind the door. "Stay out of the west wing."

Silas swept the door closed, leaving me alone in silence.

May 20, XXXX

I write this date out as a reminder to her. I have written many of my stories in these pages. It was right before the summer. My father had taken ill, and it had been becoming clearer that I, as the crowned prince, would be assuming the throne the close to death he stepped. The weight of the crown becomes hard to bear to where I wish I was a stranger, a faceless man living among them to do whatever it is I desire to do. I sit here writing all of this, and I am still unsure of what it is that I want out of life. The only choice I have is breathing down my neck, telling me it is the only way, the only choice I will ever have in this puny existence that is my life. Now, I have two days left before I am crowned King. I know there are plans to dispose of me. The entire court acts as if I do not know that they disapprove of me. That loving my enemy was the reason for all our woes that she is responsible for her country's actions in which she is not the ruler of.

I still can see her, her fiery red hair among the red roses of the courtyard, with the daylight caressing her skin in ways I could not. At least not in the way that I wanted to.

When we first met, this was where I found her, nestled between the hedges, clipping the bushes with tender lover and care. There among those mazes I fell in love with her and how she gave such tender love to the roses to grow them so well and high. Even then, there was no way we would be able to be together. I was the crowned Prince of Amaris, and she was a princess brought here to unite us yet is not whom I saw in those softer moments mistaking her for the daughter of a gardener and she mistaking me as the same.

The simplicity of her life without the weight of a country to bear to only be concerned with tending to roses. I know I have simplified her life so that there was more to her and to the struggles she faced before we had ever crossed paths. I was right to not underestimate her, as it turns out she was the princess, and I fell harder than I ever did before.

Then, like that, she was gone. Murdered by the same people who wished for war and to ensure that I was trapped to be nothing more than a puppet.

A measly puppet.

Even the Nicholaes are getting antsy with my engagement to Narcisa. They want us to be married within days of my coronations, ones I have disapproved of. There is not much there to persuade their minds further from any other notion than to seal the alliance between our two families in marriage. I am sickened by this barbaric notion and Narcisa has been trying the last few weeks since her death to try and replace her.

"You will come to love me" is what she said at the time.

Narcisa was the reason she may have been dead.

I can't let her know about the fact that the love of my life is dead. She would have had my head if she knew that it was the enemy. "Then we can take care of {REDACTED} to bring prosperity to our countries."

It was hard to sit there in those meetings as my advisors spoke on how the coronation should look or the pending wedding. Narcisa flitters around the castle now, talking at lengths about what will change once she is crowned queen. She controls the meetings; she seems to have found her way into the council meetings conspiring with the nobles in how best to launch an attack after the attempted murder of the prince.

I did not tell them the attempted murder was on the crown Princess of {REDACTED}. If we did not meet in the garden after the party, if I did not send

that note to her—would things have played
out differently. Would she have been alive,
right now? Or would there have been a war
waged against our nation where a choice is
to be made?

    To love or to die.

    R

Fifteen

Day turned to night, and I sat in the seat where, night after night, Silas asked for his name in which I never have a name for him. That night, it seemed different.

His seat was empty.

Vacant.

The food was spread across the table, enough to feed a family of ten. The overwhelming smell of brown sugar wafted from the ham sitting under mountains of roasted potatoes and carrots. The fine china glittered under the faint candle, casting beautiful shadows among the darkness. The shuddering castle gave out a few breaths, the wind howling against the walls as the minutes ticked by. A grandfather clock sounded the hour. I scraped the plate, harsh squeaks under my fork.

Silas was not coming.

I leaned back in my chair. I did not know what I expected after what happened earlier. For him to come and act as if nothing was amiss. The secrets he continued to hide provided the citizens of the village more ammo of the mythic beast he claims he is not.

Frustrated, I took to the evening air.

The clouds from the storm had cleared, and I strolled through the rose gardens with the same storm raging on inside me. A part of me hoped that, among the roses, I would iron my resolve. To be the selfless person everyone holds, to be a daughter full of duty, the friend who is willing to risk their life to kill the beast.

To do what is right.

The right thing to do was to kill Silas.

I can end the hold over the village and to protect innocent lives, then return home where I can salvage a life for Mama and Miriam. The plates alone on that table could pay to sustain us for well over a month, maybe more. With him dead, there would be no use for the items of value and could easily be sold. I was no longer sick, which freed up much of our financial situation to get us back on the road to pay off Father's debt and even get a sizable dowry for Miriam. There were enough trinkets for us to never have to worry about money for the rest of our natural lives. All I had to do was drive a stake through his—

The grandfather clock struck ten inside the cavernous walls of stone.

I stood and walked into the grand hallway, then stopped dead in my tracks.

A ghost hovered clear as day in the middle of the room, head skewed as she mumbled inaudible words to me. Her figure flickered, there and then not, and whispers gathered across the space, booming surrounding me similar to the room.

I shivered.

My heart quickened at the very thought of the room, the yearning to remember those visions. I shook my head. This was not the room. This was a resident who was nothing like those dark tendrils trapped behind a thick oak door in the west wing. A guest that never can leave these haunted hollow halls.

"Cruel thorns took root. The time has come. The time has come. Tick tock, the clock is gone, and soon, the roses will wilt," she sang, low and toneless, fluttering about the room mindlessly and swaying faintly behind curtains of red.

The woman wore a billowy dress of red, matching the roses she fondly glanced to while repeating her eerie tune. Fiery orange curls crowned her head encircled with a ringlet of gold upon it. The woman's sockets were vacant as the empty space in her chest.

I approached slowly. "Are you alright?"

I circled around her, the pale translucent becoming more tangible. She went on to mumble more lines, lines in which I did not hear, hiding behind the dark curtains from the budding moon. Black eyes cast to the ground, twisted and furrowed, displeased in the riddles she spouted. The whispering in the room repeated the same strange lines.

The hairs on the back of my neck stood on end, and I slowly backed away, turning away from the strange scene. With smooth wood under my hand, a chilling cold hand gripped my shoulder. The frigidity seared into my flesh with the kiss of death pressed against my temple.

"You will die. *Here.*"

The woman's slackened face offered no kindness I have come to know nor the curious gaze of the dead. Behind her, an army of spirits stood ready, waiting for the end.

Her mouth stretched into a crude smile, hands snapped to my throat, choking the hot summer warmth with icy cold slicing into me. My back slammed against the rail of the staircase, the wood cracking underneath my body. With eyes bulging out of my skull, the whispering became louder, the crowd shuffling closer to us. The edges of my vision faded into black, and the room jostled from view.

I groped the air, clawing at nonexistent hands to no avail. Nothing I did worked as her grip around my throat tightened, the cold freezing my lungs and vocal chords. I screamed, and only choking sounds came out.

"Help," I choked out, nearing the end, my body going limp.

I felt her rage, all of it within the grip around my neck. Every struggle I provided strain against the muscle in her arms as she fought to stay within this realm. The boundary between life and death was shadowy as I peered into the abyss beyond the veil. Between space and time, death was of comfort as reality faded to black.

I'm yanked back, dropping down onto a solid chest. Warm arms wrapped around my waist, keeping me upright and standing, despite legs wobbling underneath me. The world came back into focus as the ghosts hovered nearby. Face twisted, she clutched her hands, the translucent flesh marred in black.

"Are you alright, Little Dove?"

Fingers trailed to my iced throat, but the burn still marred my skin. I did not know if the fingers were mine. Within a split second, I discovered it was Silas's hand keeping me upright.

I blinked. "She attacked, and I couldn't—couldn't—" I trembled at the faint contact of ghostly hands.

Death had been so close to touch, and yet again, I evaded it once more. For a second time that day, I was nearly killed by specters of his castle, and twice, I had been plucked from danger from the same man.

"You, the one who is damned, come to take from death has been so long told. We warned you and now the time nears in which all is lost. Watch as it crumbles around you, as you slowly fade into obscurity," the ghosts hissed in union with the woman's haunted eyes aflame with fury.

All the spirits' rage continued, swarming around us as they pressed us closer to the stairwell.

The woman cocked her head, lashing forward.

Silas swept behind, taking the blow of her hands wrapped tight around his throat. "Go. Get to your room. Under no circumstances do not leave that room," he yelled, throwing the spirit across the room. Silas ushered me up the staircase, transfixed at the ghosts crowd closing in. "Go, now!"

I sprinted up the staircase, ghostly hands reaching for me—preparing to drag me down to their depths. Howling spirits at my heels, my foot snagged at the end of the hallway near my door. I scrambled up. The icy touch raised goose bumps upon flesh, and I slammed the door behind me.

It's only when I slammed the door that it sank in with my back against the horrors of the castle. Spouting words hardly made any sense. It was woven—stitched together in the fabric of my soul, invisibly strung together by the words of worlds beyond this one.

I sank to the floor, my head in my hands.

Hours had gone by, and I had not moved from the door, still trembling at the thought of leaving from my spot. I cared little for comfort if it meant I'd avoid the specters and the dark tendrils hiding under my bed and in the shadows. My knees were more comfortable for resting my head, and it's where I've been when the knocking reverberated against the wood.

"Valeria. Little Dove, I know you're in there."

Silas's concerned voice came through, and the shadows playing within my room shrank.

I unlatched the door and saw him there, ruffled, with streaks of red claws dragged against his perfect skin, ripped through with scarlet droplets.

"Are you alright?"

I kept the door cracked, hesitating to open it farther. Despite there not being ghosts loitering the hallway, I was not going to take a chance that Silas was an apparition pretending to be the man.

Behind the cracked door, I nodded slowly.

"Okay, that's good." Silas strung his hand through his hair and leaned against the doorframe. "This is the first time that the ghosts of the castle have acted like this. I'm sorry that you had to witness such violence, and I am unsure what to say at this point to—"

"Don't. She practically strangled me, Silas. This is the second time today I was nearly killed and then saved by you. There are too many secrets. None of them or all of them seem to connect to the possible mystery that is your bloody name." I took a breath, taking every piece of me to say what is next. "I need you to stay away from me. If you truly care for me in that frigid heart of yours, stay away."

"Little Dove." Silas's face pressed firmly into the wood, and a husky voice breathed against the frame of the door. "You don't mean that. After all, we have our deal, and you live under my roof. There is no escaping me, Valeria. There is no escape."

I laughed, a crude laugh that it was. The concept of escape had been on my mind since day one, but it became smaller. The thought of freedom was slowly fleeting just as the seasons were. There would be no way out—that much was true, especially not when he was still breathing.

"Escaping you seems more like a fantasy than a reality. No use in keeping up with the charade." I slammed the door in his face and locked the latch.

There, I stayed—in my room, at least.

Shuffling feet would come to the door, then skitter away, leaving a tray of food. Silas's heels clicked at my door each evening, and he never said a word from the other side, nor did he ever knock. Night after night, he stood there for minutes, sometimes hours, outside the door. Listening perhaps to the horrid dreams of inky black shadows and the smell of decay locked behind a wall of secrets of his own doing.

On day three of my isolation, a note was slid under the door alongside breakfast. It had been tucked between the cup of hot coffee and a heaping stack of sugar cakes. I had almost thought of it as a bribe until I unfurled the little scroll.

Come out, or I'll break the door down. Remember our deal, Little Dove.

I promptly tore up the note and threw it into the wastebasket. I had my reasons for not coming out. This had been just one of the few that angered me to make a point of never coming out much less answer the door to him. I'd rather entertain the shadows lurking beyond my bed.

I shuddered, climbing into my bed and peering into inky depths of sightless eyes.

The darkness lurked night after night, more so since the day in the west wing. They sat at the edge of the bed, licking at my feet. I'd thought they were trying to instigate a fearful reaction, but as it continued, it appeared rather they had a taste for my flesh. I'd stay up in the candlelit room, watching them.

I did not sleep those three days.

When I did sleep, the dreams were vivid, the colors brighter with the taste of hope and happiness from a long-forgotten time upon my lips. The boy was dressed in bright blue and gold, their raven locks and silver-dusted freckles reaching divine dimpled cheeks. The boy's face had been stained from bloodied tears with the scene before him, clear and blissful.

The summer fields were filled with tulips swaying to the faint breeze, red dancing under the full golden light of the day as well as white petals hugging the moon. One moment, the boy's head turned toward the sun, soaking up the rays into his gold tan skin, warmed and alive. The next, he'd reach toward the moon. The breeze clawed their hands through the long strands of hair, sometimes raven, other times silver weaving the air.

The dream would end, and I'd awake in my bed, shaken by the thoughts that followed. The shame burned upon my face to the cruel reality.

I was my own downfall.

Maybe in retribution, I withered away in the hovel of the room. Trapped with his secrets under stone rubble.

Day four, Silas barreled into my room, the door hanging off the hinges. Under the cocoon of the blanket, he stood over my bed, clothing skewed with half of his blouse tucked into his trouser, hair tickling the bottom of his belt. He frowned, an expression I had rarely seen on the man, taking a hold of the cocoon and hoisting me over his shoulder.

"Hey, put me down." I kicked, flailed, even taking banged my fist against his back. He did not relent and walked in silence, bounding down hallways and stairs. "Silas, put me down. Now."

"No, Little Dove. I will not." The hand that wrapped around my leg tightened. "You are acting like a child."

"A child!" I thrashed. "If anyone is being a child, it is you. What kind of person barges into another's room and kidnaps them? I am hardly dressed as—"

He slammed me down into the hard chair, the silverware skittering from their proper placement.

I pulled up the blanket tight against my bare shoulders, afraid he could see the camise through the fabric and maybe more.

I shivered, keeping my gaze low and trained on the plate in front of me. Dinner was roast lamb, charred meat served on top of a bed of sweet potato mash. A trail of dark spice liquid seeped into the carrot orange mash, turning it brown, and my mouth watered at the scent. Breakfast trays were always delivered for the last couple of days but never the dinner trays.

Silas strolled to his seat, fingers grazing the white tablecloth. Once seated, he continued to tap away at the surface, filling the space in time to the beat of the clock.

Tik. Thump. Tok. Thump. Tik. Thump. Tok—

"Have I done something to offend you, Little Dove? You think saving you a few times would guarantee a small smile from you or at least an irksome comment," he said, fingers coming to a standstill. "Perhaps you dislike my company?"

"Company? You had me almost killed two times in one day." I scoffed. "I am just doing what is simple and staying out of your way so I don't end up like one of your ghosts."

"If I remember correctly, I did save you both times."

"If you would have told me these dangers, I would not need to be saved."

"I warned you about the west wing. It was not my fault that you decided to break that rule. As for my specter guest, I do apologize if they harmed you."

I picked up the fork and stabbed the meat. "Harmed me? You seriously think that is all that happened. Silas, whatever psychosis is, this castle tried to kill me. Multiple times. And they are all under your direction. You keep proving my point correct."

"And what is that, Little Dove? Is there a so-called point that you are making?"

"A beast in human clothes," I said before calmly taking a bite of the lamb, juices exploding to the delicious fireworks and filling my aching belly.

"You say that, and yet you cannot help but find me attractive."

I coughed as a chunk of lamb tickled my throat. "That is awfully presumptuous of you to think that I think of you in high regard."

"But you are not denying it."

"Denying it. What would there be to deny? The awful truth is I am stuck with you." I cut at the meat, slicing it apart in two, like how the priest had died that day not so long ago. Drained and devoid of life, only to be consumed by another to sustain their own existence. "Or I was tricked into thinking that you actually cared if I lived or died."

Silas leaped from his spot, taking a hold of my chair and dragging me up from the table against the wall. Ragged breaths hovered over my neck. "You think I don't care? I could rip your pretty little throat out without hesitation, but I haven't."

"You keep saying that," I growled. "Yet all I see is a monster before me."

I pulled against his blouse, hot breath kissing my neck and tongue tracing the thin vein along my skin.

I flinched, shutting my eyes tightly, hands gripping the wrapped blanket to keep my dignity. I trembled against him and didn't dare to look up. I gasped, body flushed with warm fingers trailing the thin blanket to my neck.

Silas tilted my chin, eyelids half lidded as he studied me under thick lashes. A hand twirled my dark locks between his fingers as he sighed softly, "I hoped by now you would have seen something different. It appears that I was wrong." He shoved his hand into his pocket and returned to his seat. "Please, eat."

Silas never asked to guess his name that evening.

Sixteen

"**O**kay, you have to grind these herbs together and add oil to the mixture to create the salve," Ayla said, pointing to the various herbs spread out across the worktable. "This is nightingale. It's a particular herb that, when used properly, can help with those inflicted by muscle spasm although too much of it in its herb form can be poisonous."

I ground the herbs while sweat dripped from my forehead. "If used improperly, it can cause the body to shut down?"

She nodded. "Precisely. See, you're getting this!" Ayla clapped her hands together, her smile brightening the gloomy day.

I wiped the sweat from my brow. "Most poisons have an antidote . . ." I tried to remember from our lessons and the books I had read the possible ingredients that can reverse the poisonous process.

"Most do but not nightingale. You are better off giving them lobelia or any herb with particulars to induce them to vomit it up and pray the end comes swiftly."

I placed the mixture into jars laid out across the table, careful not to overfill them one by one. "Lobelia."

The market was a first for me to assist Ayla in selling her tinctures and remedies. Finishing the last of the batches, we placed the items into a large knapsack and set out of the cottage.

Winter had set in, the first snowfall happening less than a few weeks ago. The chill in the air had deepened into the greenery, frosting tips of evergreens with the soft crunch of snow underfoot. I shut the coat tight against my body, placing the sack high on top of my shoulders as we walked the cobblestone path to the center of town.

The coat was another gift from Ebony, who I suspected was guilty about the other day. Most of the ghosts left me alone after the incident, but to say that it did not spook me in the slightest would be a lie. Ebony kept her distance but left trinkets and gifts in her place. Besides Ayla, she had been the closest thing to a confidant in the castle.

Silas had been even more of a recluse since the day he barged into my room. Keeping to the west wing, he stopped coming to supper despite it being his one crucial rule. It'd been an unspoken agreement those last few nights as he swept his glass of wine off the table, giving a small nod before departing. The man was a dark storm of untold destruction in my life. Swiftly there, with little warning, only to disappear and leave disaster in his wake.

Instead of fretting over his mood swings, I had been putting that time into learning the art of healing with Ayla.

Those had been the harder ones to attend since the house visit with the woman. Most of those poor folks had evidence of blood loss that tied Silas to the crime more so than I'd like to admit. I never said anything to Ayla about my time in the castle. She taught me skills that had greatly helped others, but there was a missing piece to me that strained against my chest.

The market was packed, and booths lined the small squares as sellers attracted potential customers. Baked goods, materials made of leather ranging from bags to belts, and other trinkets had been perched on tablecloths. A warm bonfire was lit nearby, bathing the square in a glow and warmth with lights twinkling overhead. Loud laughter of children rang out, who were running through the market as several shoppers haggled. The customers rebuked their offer, going back and forth until they pressed gold coins into the palms of the vendors once deals had been struck.

The glory of the cosmic exchange.

Ayla guided us to our booth, smaller than the rest, which was alright, seeing as we did not offer an extended variety of goods. Setting out the worn jars of herbs and signs she had crafted, we sat up shop on this winter morning. Taking out a lighter stick, she lit the end from the bonfire nearby and stoked a pile of herbs. The scent of vanilla and cloves filled the small space, inviting and warm to the chilled air.

"This should help attract customers. Now some may haggle, but the final offer should never be less than a single gold piece. Although if someone looks as if they need the help, we will reevaluate the pricing. Oftentimes, folks come to need the help but do not have the money to do so, while others prey on the good will of others."

Ayla straightened the cloth, then fanned the smoke higher, creating a dizzy overwhelming smell of the incense. Blue eyes twinkled in sincerity, taking care of her display as she prepared for the flood of customers that beckon to the booth.

As soon as we opened for the rush, there was not a singular moment of rest. One after another, they bought the tinctures and mixtures we had labored for days. Gone in mere moments. True to Ayla's word, there were a few who tried to haggle lower than a single gold piece, fighting the fact that it was expensive for this kind of work.

"This is women's work. Why should it be compensated any higher than Darwin's apothecary down the streets?" an old man grumbled, pulling out the singular gold coin and placing it up on the counter.

Ayla took the coin, replaced it with a bottle of healing salve, and gave the man a polite smile.

The man grunted away, shoving the jar into his shabby gray coat, only to glare at me, eyebrow lifted in suspicion. "Haven't seen you around here before."

"I moved here recently," I said.

"The castle, eh?"

"No, sir."

The man squinted, his wrinkled face scrunching as his gaze raked my insides. "Liar."

I winced, rubbing my hands against the fabric of my dress.

I was not ready for folks to know I was staying under the roof of their enemy and not doing anything about it. I opened my mouth and closed it. I had no idea what to say to this man.

"Sounds as if you got something to say. Perhaps you are the monster that lives on top of that bloody hill," he hissed.

"She is a distant cousin of mine who is staying with me. Now run along, Walter. I have other customers to attend to," Ayla said.

"Such a saint, you are. Taking in the misfortunate ones among this land of evil. I'd take care Ayla, there's much at play recently that I'd hate for you to wind up dead. Such a shame, indeed." The man stared. "Good day." He shuffled off down the cobblestone path and into an alleyway.

Ayla greeted another customer, cool under pressure, while I tried to rub the embarrassment of it all off my face.

People walked past the booth, their gazes drawn to the next shiny object or item to buy. Some spoke excitedly, lifting goods off the table to show others. A child pointed at a small toy, a wooden horse. The little boy broke out into a fit of coughing, buckling over upon the ground.

The mother tugged the little boy's hand until they stopped in front of us. "Excuse me, miss. Do you have a cough remedy? My son, he's been coughing terribly for the last week, and I fear he has the plague."

Ayla nodded to me, signaling I should take the lead keenly watching as I rummaged through the bag, pulling out my own blend I had created.

"Here, take this with a few teaspoons of honey, and it should clear up within a couple days." She took the satchel, holding it close to her chest as she fumbled within her coat for coins.

The boy coughed into his hand, brown pools wide as his attention fixated on me. "Scary woman." He pointed at Ayla and me, placing his other in his mouth. "Bad. Bad. Bad."

"That's enough, sweetie. Here." She placed the coin onto the table. Flushed, she picked her son up, then the satchel in her fist.

The child continued to beat his fists into his mother's side. "She's gonna kill us all. I saw it, Mama," he wailed, pointing to the space between Ayla and me.

The mother cooed into the boy's ear, rocking him in her arms. "He is not normally like this. Thank you, both of you. You are saints, wonderful saints." She walked off down the same cobblestone path, her son coughing into her shoulder.

Ayla neatly adjusted the product on the table, softly humming to herself. "People have their opinions. No matter how hard you try to argue with them, they will hold on to them, even if they are harmful. You'll get used to it. Sooner or later, you will leave that castle, and you will not be the stranger in town."

I wondered if the same held true when it came to Silas. If the townspeople saw what Silas was like outside of the walls of the castle, would they change their minds? Silas has been alone in that castle for an eternity, doing who knows what to these people that rather see his head on a pike than be open to the idea that he was less than the monster they portray him as.

Was he less than the monster that I thought him to be? I was not even sure of my own doubt to truly answer the question. He had his secrets—that was clear, but yet he struck me as someone who did not like hiding them. The man simply was afraid of its discovery and the judgment to follow.

Was he lonely? Perhaps it was the reason he did not know how to act human or understand the particulars of the fears to see. Yes, he had all those ghosts, but does a beast often wish for the presence of a living, breathing person?

The warmth and heartbeat from someone.

Silas hiding the truth from me only made me more curious, especially after my last venture to the west wing. One he did not want me to find, to explain how he or even the castle came to be. Perhaps it was I needed to see to prove that he did, in fact, had something to do with the village deaths.

Perhaps only then I'd be able to use the blade against him and be sure enough I was not damning another soul.

Assisting Ayla in packing up the booth, I was struck with the awful task I had to do. If Silas was unwilling to tell me what was going on in his castle, then it was time that I found out what it was—and stop him.

I paced the room, furious and half out of my mind as blood raced through tired limbs. The clock tilling the midnight hour, and all was quiet in the castle. Silas left early that night after our uneventful supper. It was either this or not at all to find the truth hidden in forbidden depths of the west wing.

He could have been back at any moment, and if I did not seize this opportunity, there would be no other chance—not like this one for who knows how long.

I stormed out of the room wearing nothing but my thin nightgown. I retraced my steps to through the wing, getting closer to the whispering voices growing louder in the winding halls. The corridors had shifted, and even with guidance from the light of the moon, it was eerily dark. I clung to the wall, shuffling step by step past the ominous door, body aching to open it once more to learn of what those voices had been trying to show me. The foggy memory of the burning pain and my own gut told me to keep going deeper into the bowls.

Compared to the other wing and much of the rest of the castle, the west wing was a labyrinth. Twisting and turning in different directions, appearing to not adhere to any structural part of the castle. The walls crumbled in sections, with several bricks missing, shattered below onto the rotting wood and giving way to the moonlight. Moths made their home on the shredded curtains, weaving themselves between the sporadic holes. I batted away the creatures as the rafters overhead creaked.

I crept farther, masking the sound of my steps with the groaning rafters and floorboards. When I rattled the knob of a door, I found it was locked. In fact, they were all locked with the entirety of the dead silent space, the castle holding a bated breath.

The farther I went, the more dismayed I became. I counted thirty doors, and they were all locked. Doubt came in at the thought of finding what it was he was hiding. I didn't even know what I was looking for, but with doors being locked, it was becoming more and more difficult, turning into a fruitless expedition.

I stopped in the middle of the hallway, the corridor split into complete darkness lit by a single flame of a burning candelabra. A ghostly arm held the brass with tender fingers, their face obscured and their pale limbs visible, a glowing beacon into the growing expanse of the dark. I cautiously stepped toward the apparition, and the creaking of a door opening cut through the silence.

"Come," the ghost beckoned.

I followed them into the foreboding room, swallowed whole by it.

In the wandering dark, images bloomed as a bud does into a fetching rose. The moon, hitting its peak, illuminated the space in soft light to a scene right out of fleeting memory. Ghosts, swathed in harrowing translucent fabric, waltzed across the ballroom floor. Upon the balcony, two figures stood peering down at their glittering guests.

The woman from the other day was dressed in crimson, with copper curls adorning her head nestled among a crown of gold. She held the hand and tender gaze of the boy from the visions and dreams. A crown of silver adorned sweeping raven-hair-framed eyes of clear midnight blue, happy and unabashed straying soft fingers against hers. The ball twirled around me as I stepped closer to the shadows of the past.

Soft voices rang out, "For our alliance and to the peace of our great nations."

The woman and the man strode down the steps of the balcony, happiness written not on the pale blank faces of death but of ones of sweet adoring memories, cherished after all these times.

The man twirled her around, sweeping her into a dance, their bodies melding. Their forms shifted and wavered under the faint light, the crowd fading to the echoes of the orchestra strumming their tune. Love and happiness shattered into beautiful, striking chords. The colors of gowns swathed the dance floor in hues of merrymaking all to the familiar harsh tones of delicate fingers crescendoing in glorious faith.

One I knew and yearned to hear and play again.

The lovers twined their way across the ballroom, slowing to a stop to be framed by the catching light. Touching their foreheads against one another, whispering low to each other as the man tucked a single strand of red among the spooling fire of the woman's hair. One could argue they were the only ones in the room despite the faraway cheers.

The scene clipped itself, winding itself to further on in that night as I rose higher into the air, climbing my way to the balcony. The ghosts around the ballroom appeared lax, their vacant eyes chattering among one another in conversations long forgotten to time. The lovers embraced in the dark space, tucked away from prying eyes, unaware of the approaching shadow clutching a knife of silver.

The man's gaze flickered up to the shadow only for it to be too late.

All of it was too late.

I watched as the woman's soft voice shuddered upon the bloodied entrance of the knife, her words lost to time. With the slick release of the knife, the perpetrator dashed into the dark, never followed into the depths of the castle. The man's horror-stricken figure faltered a step or two before catching her falling body and failing against the bodice of the dress to staunch the bleeding. He called out to someone—anyone for help, speaking fervently to his bride.

"Shush, hold on. Please, Cecilia, don't leave me," the man said with a quivering voice as ash tears fell upon his opaque features. "Someone! Help us!"

His pleas were drowned out by the merriment of his guests. Blood pooled at her feet, and the light in her eyes was slow to fade until nothing remained.

In a space lost to the absence of time, he was alone, and I was unable to stop the scene before me. I was removed from the pain, the sheer agony laid upon his feet. His torment appeared to be his to bear. I only watched as the past unfolded on itself.

Midnight eyes pierced through body and soul, cutting into decades—no, centuries—in a blink of an eye.

The man was slow to form his words.

"I am begging you, help me. I'll do anything. I'll bargain with any God, even if it means my own soul."

Throat bobbing, I answered him, tears swimming, knowing I can not change any outcome. "I can't. I can't."

"Why not! You are a witch, are you not?" he asked.

I held my tongue. This was a vision of the past. What matter did my own answer have on this poor man's soul to the anguish which lay bare at his feet.

He held the woman, cradling her head to his chest, as a heart wrenching sob let loose into the crowded space. I stretched out a hand only for it to pass through his iridescent form.

I clutched my chest with the only comfort of the building ache to keep me company.

From the body of the woman, her soul rose, watching with evergreen tears to the man's frustrated cries, calling to her longing soul once more to come back to him.

She, with loving eyes, stared at her corpse before flickering upwards from heavy lashes. "Are you the Angel of Death?" she said softly as if in a daze. "Have you come to take me away?"

With the words caught in my throat, I watched as she floated down the grand staircase. Her expression was solemn and wary, and when those evergreen eyes turned upwards to the landing, they rang with familiarity of the present rather than the past.

"No, perhaps you are merely a watcher of past events. I've been so long dead I almost forgot. I always forget, but sometimes, it is better to forget." She offered a sad smile, her form light and free dancing, no longer restricted by the convention of the living.

I followed her down the steps as the ballroom shifted. "What do you mean by that? Does that mean you can see me?"

She nodded. "I am of a past notion. I am the reason events played out as they did and why they persist. I am an echo, one that exists in this space as punishment for sin."

"If you exist in this space, how did you get to the main part of the castle, and why did you strangle me!" I taunted. "The more I am stuck in the castle, the more I am dragged into hell for the sake of people I hardly know stating they need my help. I am tired of being pushed around, so tell me, what is it that you want from me?"

I chased her to the edge of the ballroom, floating into the next memory without cause or warning.

The scene collided in floating, scrambled images, the ghost of partygoers past in endless loops, donning masks among the shifting shapes. The room restructured itself, expanding and collapsing in a blink of the eye.

The woman danced without care in front of my wandering eyes as I struggled to cling to the one sense of the expanding realities, only to come to a halting stop.

The man—the prince—stood atop of the balcony. Weary midnight eyes surveyed the crowd below with a sorrowful, twisted expression. The prince was accompanied by a woman in a tight crimson dress. From the ballroom, I was only able to make out the basics of details, the sweep of blonde hair and the shadowy smirk of plump ruby lips. How long had it been since Cecilia's death? Who was the woman on the balcony?

Cecilia floated to the pair, taking a hand to stroke the man's cheek as his expression grew more irritated from the unheard words. The mystery woman held a glass of sparkling champagne, and he readily accepted.

"For you see, Valeria, it was I who condemned him," Cecilia confessed. "I condemned him to hell, and there was nothing I could do but watch."

The prince shoved the glass back into the palm of the woman, taking to the stairs. We watched together as he doubled over, clutching his abdomen in sheer pain, sweat beading across his brow. Onlookers stopped in the middle of their dance, gasping at the sight in horror. Screams erupted, and guards rushed to attempt to keep him upright as he twisted and stumbled farther down the stairs. White knuckles held the banister, and his crown skittered to a halting stop at the bottom of the steps. A leering silence fell.

Sputtering coughs erupted from the prince, dripping from his mouth into a pool of blood and staining the granite inlays. He clutched at his chest, struggling to rise only for his strength to fail him, his body coming to rest upon a crimson mirror reflecting back soft, vacant midnight eyes.

The ballroom was still. Not a soul dared to breathe a word, inching closer to the body of the man they once called their ruler. The woman at the top of the balcony sipped from her flute, disappearing into the expanse of the upper floor. The guards ushered in to the body, with one checking the pulse and shaking his head.

"It's no use. He's gone," the guard said.

With a perplexity, I turned to Cecilia, who all but paled at the sight of the prince's lifeless body. "Tell me who did you condemn? Can you tell me their name?"

The buzzing of cicadas trilled in my ear. She watches as the guard turned the body over, laying him onto his back.

The beauty of her translucent form melted away. Soft, tender eyes shifted to vacant, dark pits I was accustomed to from the ghosts of the castles. Her dress aged rapidly, the once bright crimson fabric in a blink of an eye becoming tattered and worn. Moth-eaten holes and smears of blood and dirt stained the once vivid fabric. The train of the dress dragged behind her, the echoes of long-forgotten steps ushered in unwelcomed dread.

"I cannot. It's not time yet for you to know. It's too soon. Too soon to learn the truth of what once was," she forewarned.

"Then why show me all of this?" Again, the scene shifted, collapsing in on itself as the walls caved in around us. "You brought me here to see something. What is it that you want from me!"

The candles lit the ballroom so brightly it began to dim. Then flickered. And then there was darkness. The faint glow of the woman's form was the only light within the expanse of the dark, accompanied by the shrilled agony of bloodied screams.

Dying wails were missing dire information desperately needed to understand this place—to understand the purpose of why I was here. The answer, the only answer I received, was the bloodstained hand outstretched to me.

With a shaky hand, I took it eagerly, letting her guide me in the shadowy depths. Dark wisps curled undertow, the screams echoing from stone walls. The dank air smelled of decay and rot and mingled with the soft scent of the first blooms of sweet, delicious roses.

We stopped at a door cracked a hair, giving way to the brightness and warmth of fire burning within.

She curled her hand in mine, kissing it gently. The cold burned before she released it, departing on cryptic riddles. "You will know when it is time when the hour strikes midnight under the eye of the past."

"And Silas? Your cryptic answers and riddles are not helping me come any closer to saving him as you urged me to. So, I ask again, you unhelpful ghost, you, what do you want with me?" I repeated.

Her dark gaze softened, stroking my face as my mother had once done when I awoke from a bad dream. Perhaps this was all this was. A crude bad dream. And I'd awake in my bed to the sun streaming in the window and Miriam bounding into the room in greeting.

The burning cold reminded me it wasn't that simple.

"You have a gift, one that often is a burden to bear. You are not so different from him." She smiled, her body a faint whisper among dancing candlelight. The space around us cracked, fissured formed with the screaming of the crown blossoming louder, cramming itself into my skull.

Cecilia turned to me, solemn solitude her vow to keep. "Save him. Time is short."

The fissures shattered, the inky black scattering at my feet, and I was back in the hallway of the west wing as if I had never left. I turned to the expanse and discovered an alcove. On the wall, a mural depicted the scene that I'd witnessed. The lovers swooned at the top of the grand balcony only to meet a tragic end. Eeriness stayed with me there, imprinted upon my skin just as the mural was upon my mind. Just as the blood and icy hand held mine in tender care.

I shook my head, leaning against the doorframe, and peered into the room to the scene before my eyes.

Seventeen

Soft bubbling of the pot mixed in with the harshness of tubes clinking together as Silas ground the mortar.

"There," he muttered. "That should be the last of it."

I slinked against the wall, peering into the laboratory. It was quaint, with a charm to it, smaller than the other rooms in the east wing. Books were stacked high upon a large oak table and papers scattered about, similar to Silas's desk. Test tubes, herbs, beakers, and other scientific materials intermingled with the open books, some filled with liquids of colors mirroring the grand stained glass window looming behind him. Plants lined the back walls of various species I often saw at Ayla's cottage clustered around the window.

Within the grand room, a fire crackled from the fireplace, burning bright and hot, illuminating the scene before me. Silas poured liquid after liquid, crushing powders and mixing them into a sweet red fluid. Silas turned behind him to stroke the leaves of lavender and pluck several berries from the plant. He placed them into the mortar, pressing them into a fine juice, slipping it into the liquid and turning it a shade darker than blood.

What was Silas doing in possession of nightingale berries?

I shivered.

I leaned in close, staying within the shadows. Watching as Silas continued to add to the pot propped up by a small inlet flame that burned high against the ceramic. He lifted his head toward the door, yellow eyes shining toward the very spot in which I hid. I whipped my head away from view and held my breath, waiting to the sound of pounding heartbeats. I ventured a single glance to the crack of the door. Silas had moved. He hovered over the fire of the mantle with the cup of dark crimson.

An immortal's somber gaze peered down upon that cup filled with death or life, the gambling of his fare. Silas stretched an arm to the mantle, resting it against the sweeping wood carving downcast to the cup. His knuckles turned white against the stain, and for a moment, I thought it would crack.

Silas raised the glass, toasting to the haunted or the damned or whatever God a creature such as him has to pray to. In one fell swoop, he downed the contents as it trickled along the corner of his mouth in a sickly red hue.

The cracking of the fireplace answered the space in its eerie silence, becoming nothing then everything. Silas coughed, and blood spurted from his lips and onto the carpet. It seeped from his mouth and eyes, a gruesome sight, his crumpled form silently moving with each rupture. Eternity passed, and Silas convulsed upon the ground on all four legs until he collapsed onto the dark hardwood, body twitching with a pool of blood forming under his head.

I placed a hand to my mouth, muffling the scream that built inside my chest. Shock rooted me to the spot as I watched the last breath disappear into the air of the castle walls. Silas lips muttered softly a prayer in a language I recognized but did not know the words to.

Silas killed himself.

The work had been done for me and Silas . . . Silas was dead.

I wanted to laugh, to cry, to scream to the rooftop that the beast—the harborer of evil, was dead.

I sprinted out of the west wing, my legs carrying me through the hushed hallways. I threw open the heavy doors to the clean, crisp night air. As I wrapped my hands around the cold wrought-iron gates, the weight of his death played out over and over in my head. I could not help but let the horrifying smile stretch itself across my lips in such elation.

I was free.

I could try and return to Endovier and carve out a life for myself.

The village was free, and there was nothing stopping humanity from living on in absence from the blood drinker. Yet—the unease settled through my bones. The Earth rumbled under my feet, howling screeching into the night air from within the castle, as stones crumbled from the west section of the castle onto the far grounds.

Briar Castle was collapsing.

I clung to the wrought-iron gates, feet unsteady as the rumble ceased to stop almost quickly as it started. Wind stirred the curtains of the windows, dancing in front of the open door.

I staggered to my feet, to the curious gaze of the castle itself, moaning an evening song of misery. Silas was dead, and the castle filled with ghosts—well, there was not much I could do for them.

I pushed open the iron gates, shuffling forward onto the gravel road. The fog hung heavy in the pre-dawn morning. I took a step, closer to the line of fog lapping my heels. I hesitated at the intersection, fists balled at my sides.

Silas was dead—I saw him kill himself. Freedom was right there, beckoning me to cross the threshold and never return. The ballroom and the ghost of the woman—the one from my dreams and vision flashed before me. The desperation in her vacant eyes and the pleading in his voice rattled in my head.

Silas was nothing to me.

He is nothing to me, I repeated in my head despite the burning truth.

I walked swiftly into the fog, swimming through the thick undercurrents of smoke. The crunch of gravel under my toe accompanied me the farther I went into the embankment. The cloud bank opened into the stormy gray of Castle Briar.

My heart sank as I stared up at the crumbling stone and cawing crows. I was stuck in the in-between Silas had locked me in. Castle Briar was nothing but a haunted house.

The cool air against my skin and the fiery heat in my lungs brought me to the edge of a precipice, one I could not hold from jumping into the cool water below. The castle and its crows stood watch, judging on high as the first flash of lightning cracked across the sky in purple streaks.

I gritted my teeth, choked down my pride, and turned back to the castle.

Damn it all.

The ghosts of the wing left me alone, their watchful gaze boring into the back of my spine the longer I stayed within the castle wall. Silas was where I left him, face down onto the hardwood. The mess of blood was extensive enough to kill a normal man ten times over—this was overkill. Silver hair strewn out across the floor as the blood created a halo around his head. I placed my fingers on his neck, checking his pulse.

Nothing.

I sat back on my heels, dumbfounded. I was not sure what I would have found when I walked back into the castle, but this was not what I had thought I'd find. I hiked the skirt of my dress high onto my thigh to clear the blood. I tucked a strand of my hair, looking at the table of herbs and instruments he'd used. Up on the fireplace, the cup stood as a testament to what it held, to what it had done to Silas. I took it off the mantle, sniffing the cup.

It was potent, the subtle scent of various herbs I'd seen in Ayla's cottage floating through the powerful stench of nightingale. With the idea of an immortal man whose blood was used as a cure-all, using poison did not settle right. I steal another glance at Silas's body, still unmoving and dead. I strummed a finger along the table in which he had prepared the poison, bottles on bottles, their brown opaque glass a window into their obscured contents.

"What were you doing?" I thought aloud.

I lifted one of the bottles, reading the label. *Essence of Rose.*

Such a strange name for an herb and one that I do not know. I'll have to ask Ayla the next time I see her. With Silas dead, I don't think she would have many customers, as the majority of the town's problems seemed to disappear overnight. I lifted my head, his hand outstretched. Slick blood trailed from where his arm had been under his body.

I returned the corpse among its companions and cautiously approached Silas's unmoving body. I lowered my fingers to his neck. Still no pulse. With a closer look, his arm had appeared to have moved from underneath himself, a silver locket clutched in his right hand. I wrangled the locket out of his fist, careful enough to not disturb his body much more than I needed or wanted to.

The locket was circular, the front bearing a crest design that struck me as faintly unusual. I ran my thumb over the image. The gold had faded to a soft rose from time. Two dragon heads eating their tail, Ouroboros style, with twin blades slicing into their long bellies. Their great bat-like wings frame the background in an odd heart shape, with stenciled letters long since faded.

I have a gift for you! Turn around!

It's gorgeous, but are you sure?

Of course it is to remember me by. See, you can put images into the glass casing and carry me with you.

The vision ended abruptly as I kneeled over Silas's body and not staring into the rich blue eyes of the mystery boy who haunts me.

The locket opened in my hand to the graying worn image of a woman, her figure slender and delicate, as if she were a doll. She was regal in beauty, with voluptuous lips stretched high into a stunning smile. A Roman nose scrunched in a few lines marking her face. The mystery woman, the ghost appearing to haunt me and the section of the castle, was vividly alive, smiling into the camera. Eerily, she looked familiar to the image in the reflection that has stared back all my life.

To the left was the blue-eyed boy in the same dark, sweeping raven hair with a silver crown on top of his head. His clear, warm eyes greeted the camera.

I nearly dropped the locket to the floor.

Who was Silas, really? Did he know the couple in a previous life?

I turned to leave.

Blood soaked through the trimmings of my dress and dripped down my arm as I carried the locket to the table to clean and examine closer. Mind wrapped around the mystery before me, I did not notice the slow corpse moving at my feet.

I fell forward, head slammed into the hardwood floor slick in blood. A warm hand grasped my ankle, tugging me back several paces as nails dug into my flesh.

I whipped around to gold orbs, wild and frenzied, with blood trickling from them. From the wide-set mouth, the horror of fangs protruded from faint lips.

Silas's harsh rasp revealed to me only three word before descending into madness.

"Please, help me." Silas's hold shook, nails biting into my ankle and drawing blood.

I tried to shake his hand off, but his nails dug deeper. Warm blood trickled down my legs.

I kicked. I flailed. I fought. "Let go of me!"

His hand flew free, while my leg made contact with his head, sending him back down onto the hardwood floor. Silas grunted, fingers trailing to his mouth. A pale pink tongue flickered out, lapping up the blood trickling down his exposed arm and turning the sleeve of his white blouse red. A mix of horrification and pleasure etched his face as he cleaned his hand of my blood.

Hunched over, wrenching blueish purple fluid all over the hardwood floor, he slammed his fist onto the ground and finished the ugly display. Shuffling his body away from me, he leaned against the stone as firelight danced off the gold of the black sheen mask.

Silas's stare flickered to the locket. "Where did you get that?"

"Clutched in a dead man's fist. Where else do you think I got it?" I said. I found the countertop of the table, hoisting myself up off the floor about twenty paces from Silas, not that it would help much if he wanted more blood. "The other question is how the hell are you alive, and what the hell were you doing that you were using nightingale?"

Silas averted his eyes to the small inlet window, a wistful longing pained expression drawn across. Eyebrows knitted together, he opened and closed his mouth a few times and rubbed at his chin. He shifted to the floor, stilling as if a statue trapped in a memory of mourning. "I have told you that, in order for you to win your freedom, you are to guess my name. A name that keeps me bound to this castle and to my curse. A name I do not even know nor remember it ever being mine."

"I am aware."

"I have been alone for centuries. There had been many before you who died tragically to find the truth or stupid enough to not heed my warning. The curse has made it so I cannot die from old age. It also binds me to the castle, and with each passing year as the stone is worn away, so am I."

I crossed my arms. "So, you thought, what, killing yourself was a better option? I thought you just said you cannot die. Tell me this was not the first time you decided poison was the best choice."

"No." He cleared his throat, chest rising and falling in stagger breaths. "It had been the sixtieth attempt. At first, I tried fire, nasty smell if you can believe that. Bloodletting, that one was an interesting one, severing my own limbs—poor Ebony having to clean all of that up only for me to come back from the brink of death—every medieval torture method one can use to inflict pain. Poison happened to be twentieth on the list, in which there had been many recipes and attempted each with their own nastiness."

My arms kept me from slinking down onto the floor thinking of the different ways he had tried to kill himself. No wonder the town feared him. He was an insane beast and *unkillable*. My thoughts drifted to the knife. Was that even an option? Could it kill him, as Ayla claimed, or was it as much of a shot in the dark as the torture scenarios the man had concocted?

Silas continued to recount about the different poison variations that he had used, his eyes squeezed shut.

Snap. Silas's mask clattered to the ground, stopping him mid-sentence.

I froze, fixed on the long gouge marks visible. "Your mask."

Silas's hand raised to the left side of his face, tracing the deep scars etched into stone. He fumbled for the white mask that lay nearby, securing it flimsily to his head with the broken strap.

"I suggest you stop looking at me like that."

"I'm not."

"You are. Don't lie," he snarled, his fangs protruding. "I hate liars."

I furrowed my brows. "Why would I show empathy to a monster? For one, you nearly took off my leg." I shifted the fabric of my dress to show five small puncture holes, oozing blood and clotting. "Not to mention—bit my neck." I pinned my hair back to show him the two faint puncture marks on my skin. "Tell me, Silas, what reason do I have to lie to you?"

His jaw clenched, glaring at me from across the room. If I had half a mind, I'd stop right there and not provoke him further. Instead, I turned away, turning over the brown bottles into the mortar grinding the herbs into dust. An anti-poison is hard to construct if you do not know what the poison is to begin with, but since I had the audacity to watch, I knew how to treat it. I added water to muddle down the mixture and mugwort to purge the rest of the toxins from his system.

"Yet, knowing all these facts, it is clear I'm a thoroughly confused woman who does not know what she wants in life, death, or anywhere in between. Perhaps it's my confusion in which I have developed such a thing as empathy to a beast—to my captor," I huffed, placing the contents of the mixture in a cup, carrying it to him.

Eyes wide, Silas handled the cup with shaky hands. The bluish hue of death still clung to his tan skin but had started to recede. He inhaled sharply, bringing the cup to his lips, and drank deeply, never once wincing at the taste.

Finished, he set the cup down. "You are by far the stupidest girl I have ever met. Reckless with your own health, your own wellbeing and happiness for others around you. You think of others before you think of yourself." A half-hearted smirk graced his lips. "Even to be reckless enough to save an irredeemable man."

I sat next to him, the warmth of the fire licking at the icy chill of bare skin. I drifted to a time not so long ago, when circumstances were not as they are. A time before Papa died, before Mama wanted to pawn me off for the betterment of Miriam. Before I carried hatred, jealousy, and regret while staring down at my own tombstone erected in secret, yearning for a small sliver of hope.

"When I was a girl, I was told that the world was mine to take—to do what I pleased with. I should have known it was a farce because Father died, leaving us debt and a good name and to top it all off, I was dying from a disease that had no cure. Mama's only recourse was to find a suitable match for me without little question. I had to be selfless for the sake of my family and for Miriam who did not deserve the hatred that brewed. I had to be someone else for the sake of everyone.

"I hated who I was becoming. I hated the thought of my freedom being stripped away from a marriage I had no desire to enter but from a disease that limited who I was, what I could do. I was a doll to my mother, a pretty little doll who would do anything she asked, even if it meant killing to preserve our image to society."

I tilted back. Every thought over the last year slammed against my skull. The night in the drawing room, a distant past where the stark realization was the reality I must live in. Miriam's wild hunger for more as she called out to the men below to partake in the green faerie, talking nothing of dreams—of love.

Miriam's sweet, innocent face was too kind to endure the life I was to hold. Mama's pretentious lies to her so-called friends. The fake smiles, crude laughter, ridiculous lies. I balled my fist into my dress.

I took a sharp inhale, smoothing the fabric out, acutely aware of Silas's tense expression.

He reached over, tracing my arm, stroking calmly. "The cemetery and even the night out on the balcony, I sensed your unhappiness—a flower desperate to bloom out of barren Earth. You looked so much like her."

Silas pointed to the locket, to the woman whose face oddly looked like my own with the same dark-green eyes.

"I did not realize the extent of that unhappiness until I followed William to a brothel after the party. The man beat the life out of a woman, skipping into the darkness without any regret. I had been out of my mind picturing his smug face hovering over your life-less body. I walked in that church to spite the gods. My only concern was hoping I was not too late."

I laughed, short and bitter. "It must have been one hell of a curse for you to spit the gods in a house of worship like that."

"You have no idea. I have been this way for a very long time, so long I'd forgotten everything that it means to be human, and I've grown weary. This"—he lifted the cup—"is how I repent for the sins that I committed in my past and my sins in this life."

"The locket?" I held the locket out in my palm, the weight of it settling into my hand just as the heaviness of my heart began to ache. "You seemed upset when you awoke."

Silas tenderly took the locket. "When I awoke to this life, this was all that I had left. A curse and a clue to who I was before to reclaim my name. Yet, year after year, my mind beats against the rock, withering away until I am nothing more than the beast many call out. Never to know what it was to be human, just a mindless monster needing to sate their thirst."

He held the locket up to the light, the picture of the boy and the girls staring up at us.

"I have seen them," I tentatively said. As I watched his reaction, the words came to me slowly, as I was unsure in how to respond. "Now and again, I see them in visions that never seem to make much sense other than I have seen that boy on many occasions and the girl"—I pointed to her—"she was the one that attacked me the other day. Before I—just now—she wanted to show me a scene from the past."

Silas perked. "What did she show you?"

Cecilia was in the room with me, her worrying tone flooding my senses and dreams until there was nothing, gripping like an animal demanding I listen. Demanding I obey the disembodied voice. In the daylight or under the shadow of darkness, she urged me to follow her simple directions without offering up anything else.

Save him.

"How she died," I said. Tears built the more I stared at the vivid faces of the dead. "How they both died."

Silas watched me for a moment, his fingers tracing circles along my goose bump-riddled flesh, expecting the horrors I'd witnessed—to bring to life the missing piece of a woman he doesn't remember or not clear enough.

"Mm." Silas closed his eyes, leaning back onto the stone, the worn red bricks crumbling to the failings of a broken man.

One who'd give his life to end a curse that has kept him trapped for so long.

Sunlight peeked into the curtain of the inlet window, its warm rays beading through the shared space between us. The sunrise moved over the horizon, the beams reminding me of what was and what had been. A new day, a fresh beginning—life's repetitive cycle.

Sitting in the room with Silas was nothing but the past. It clung to the old castle like vines wanting to exist in something rather than nothing. The sunrise was a future that continually arrived to wipe the slate clean.

"I should get going." I stood to my feet.

In good faith, I knew the darkness harboring underneath my skin, boiling beneath, the desire to push past the box constructed for me for years. Silas described a selfless creature when he could have been further from the truth. I was a selfish girl wanting selfish things I could not possess, not in the lifetime I wanted.

Not when there were other people to think about.

How could I be sure? Who was the true monster?

The more I thought, the more I became confused in the web of secrets woven around me.

I strode to the exit, to the whispering voices greeting me down the hall, an invitation I was to heed. I did so without turning back to the solemn man who had been watching me.

Eighteen

Silas waited for me once I returned to the castle. The sun slowly set, casting a glow upon the dark-gray stones. The rays weaved themselves through the window, a rainbow of color dancing onto the marble floor, illuminating Silas's mischievous smirk.

I shuttered the door closed, lugging the bag higher onto my shoulder. "What's the matter?"

Silas stepped toward me, walking alongside and guiding us up the staircase. "I thought I'd greet you at the door, Little Dove."

I raised a brow.

Silas's dark sleeves were cuffed at the elbow. Streaks of blue and green ran up his arm, smearing it as he wrung them. The same streaks were found painted onto his cheek, and silver hair was tied back, with strands coming loose over his face. A messy angel, glorious to set human eyes on and he appeared so normal—human, even.

At the top of the staircase, Silas cupped my hands, jerking me close. "I want you to see something."

"Sure." I nodded.

Silas guided us to the west wing. The hallways were the same from the last time, yet they appeared to be lighter, not shifting itself as a maze would. The voices were hushed, falling silent as Silas and I went deeper into the wing. The shadows did not even dare to come near him, repulsed by his presence. Or perhaps not hungry for the suffering of an immortal who rarely left.

Silas led us to a door painted in blue and green colors that stained his cheek. The mural, gorgeous as it was, depicted a meadow of red tulips in the great expanse of long, tall grass. A willow tree stood proudly as the focal point of the mural, as its tapered limbs swayed gently in the breeze artfully crafted by skilled fingers. The scene was split between the warm light of the sun kissing the red blooms and the silent guard of the moon.

An odd sensation flooded in, one I could not place, as I stared at the image.

"Do you like it?" he asked.

I nodded. "It's beautiful, a dream—an absolute dream."

Silas knocked on the door thrice, and it creaked open on its own accord. Inside was as magnificent.

I nearly fell to the floor, elation buzzing through my body wildly staring in on the beauty of such a simple space.

A grand piano, sleek black and dusted in gold trim, stood in the center of the space, overwhelming the room in grandeur. The study's collection of books was outmatched by the sheer ones towering toward the ceiling as if it was touching the kingdom of God. A ladder clutched the shelves in reference, beckoning the mighty seeker to delve further into the stacks. The shelves wrapped themselves circularly against an iron staircase that went to the very top. Off to the corner lay a desk, less cluttered than the one Silas had been using in the east wing but not far off. Books stacked close to the desk made it so it blended in with the cherrywood. The mahogany scent mixed with sweet paper, and I almost forgot where I was for a moment.

I ran a finger or two against the white keys of the piano, their notes singing out in crisp clarity. I cautiously played a few bars, watching for Silas's expression. He gave no indication of recognition, much less displeasure in me playing. I tapped another bar or two, thinking back to the night with Miriam and her green faerie men. The pull of the piano was too much, and I soon lost all sense of self, sitting on the bench and diving further into the piece I had committed to memory long ago.

Fingers ached as chords sang in sweet melody. The tune was a sad song turned to triumph under the pounding of keys. The soft melody boomed from my fingertips, filling the space and calling to the spirits to listen. I began to crescendo into the final movement, tapping the ivories with little effort thudding with the trapped force of my heart. Soft tears kissed my cheeks, and I descended into a hush pianissimo, fluttering the keys until the end note hung in quiet solidarity.

I wiped my cheek. "Apologies, I got a little too excited."

"That's alright, Little Dove." Silas ran a hand over the piano, leaning against it wistfully. "I heard that you have been helping the town with illnesses. Coughing, aches, pain, all the basic medicine."

"You disapprove?"

"No, not at all. Ebony simply was telling me that you were studying hard on various plants and herbs. You've become very efficient at coming up with a simple fix to yesterday's conundrum. It's an impressive skill to have."

"Thank you. I must admit I had a teacher who taught me most of what I know. Fills the time, and I can be of better use to the community since I—well, since I—"

"Can't kill me."

I grew abashed. "Yes. Although it is by far the one skill I was to have, I do find it useful to have, but it is not what I had expected for myself."

I strayed a few notes. The ache of the dream of playing in a concert hall has been etched forever into my soul. The gathering crowd clapped as I finished piece after piece like the many other famous pianists. I thought of playing as simple as breathing until everything was put on hold. Like that, my dreams were gone the moment we'd discovered what Father did and what Mama had to do—what I needed to do for the McCallister name.

"Why is it that you are showing me this? If I remember correctly, you said the west wing was off limits."

"I did, and yet you had broken it several times, but I suppose if I was angry this would be an entirely different conversation." Silas slid down onto the bench next to me and pressed a kiss to my hand. I watched as the ruby gems sparkled under dying light as Silas rested upon the black band. "Let's . . . let's start over, shall we. I have been neglectful in my marital duties to you, as I have been so consumed by this curse business. Even though you still think of me as a beast, I am still your husband. As such a declaration, I am gifting you access to this space and my laboratory to use how you like."

He dug into his pocket and produced a set of keys of black obsidian. "The west wing will yield to your command and show you the doors you wish to enter. These will make it so you are not lost."

The beast bowed his head, casting a halo of glow from the evening light. The same beast I had been calling a monster for months bowed his head and released my hand to the piano, the keys clasped in my palms. I did not want to fight the illusion any more than I was of the man set aflame by the dying light with the singular thought eclipsing my senses.

I wanted to touch that light.

"This is lovely," I said, the heavy weight of the keys settled across my lap. "I don't know what to say."

Silas lifted my chin, meeting his soft gaze. "Don't. This is yours to do as you please." He dropped his hand, shuffling out of the bench and standing. "I will see you for dinner in a few hours. I'll send Ebony to fetch you when it's time."

Silas turned, making his exit known, and I, stupid as I was, grabbed his shirt and croaked out, "Wait!"

Face flushed, I was startled by the fact the last time I had been this close was when I attempted to kill him. His lips still seared across my flesh, humming with electricity ready to explode and consume me in a grand blaze.

I choked it all down. "Can you keep me company just for a while?"

Silas cupped my cheek, pressing a light kiss to my head. "I thought you would never ask."

Hours passed in that little room, the clock tolling the hour reminding us the dinner was upon us.

I closed the cover of the piano, and Silas stashed his book away before escorting us down to the dining room where we took up our seats. He was still covered in the blue streaks, his image different from the pulled together man who had greeted me time after time at this table.

I still was in the tan blouse and dark trousers I'd worn to the market on such a chilly afternoon, a stark contrast to many nights. Both were so different from the start of our little relationship. My stomach grumbled, and food materialized out of the veil. Steam rose off a bowl of soup, mingling with the smell of spice that dotted the pool of reddish hue, potatoes and carrots floating with chunks of red meat.

Grabbing my spoon, I dug in, savoring in the warmth and comfort of the stew.

Silas sat back in his chair, his standard wine glass in hand, with his head resting on his fist. "I guess you did not eat while you were in town?"

I swallowed, shaking my head. "I try not to stand out too much. It's harder to explain where I am from if I have to interact with the townspeople."

I left out the part where the weekly markets were the only times I truly interacted with the townspeople, and even then, I was always met with suspicion.

The man from earlier came to mind. I tried not to wince at what would have happened if I had told him the truth. That I dine with what they considered the enemy. The glass perched between Silas's fingers held crimson liquid that sloshed along the sides, streaking down the crystal in thick streaks.

I placed my spoon down onto the table and felt queasy at the very budding question he held in that glass. "Silas, can I ask you something? It's about the townspeople."

I did not want to upset him after the nice evening we shared, but I had to ask it before it burned through me in awful unpleasant ways.

Silas perked, his movements were similar to a cat. Graceful and elegant, leaning back and sipping his wine—or what I wanted to believe was just that. "What would that be, Little Dove?"

"Well—I um—it's—where do you get your blood supply from? You say you don't drink from the towns-people, but there have been many deaths, some of which they think you are responsible for so I—" I fiddled with the rose ring on my finger. "Then there are the nights that you come in covered in blood. I don't know what to think."

His jaw tensed, lips curling in answer. "You want to know if I drink the blood of the townspeople. Honestly, I thought we passed this, Little Dove. I had hoped you were not like them."

"Are you?" I winced at my own words.

I wanted to challenge him. To give me the answers I desperately needed. Silas sat his drink down, eyebrows furrowed. Lips parted and then closed, golden orbs hardening from across the room. Muscles in his arm flexed, his neck straining, jaw clenched with every click of his tongue.

He shook his head. "Does it make a difference?"

"Yes," I whispered.

"I'll ask again." He rubbed his thumb along his index, his face twisting. As if contemplating, constructing possibly. "Does it make a difference to you?"

I wished it didn't. I imagined myself on several occasions pinned against the red backsplash of the wall, my own blood adding to its various hues, mixing with the sky-blue splotches. I'd imagine his fangs bearing down upon my neck, taking with it my life with little effort ebbing from my frail body and flowing into his. The nightmares of dying by his hand, hard to ignore—and even more so when he stumbled into the castle covered in bright crimson.

"Yes," I whispered meekly. I shook my head, straightening in my seat. "You come in covered in blood and still say you are not killing the villagers. As you said, we are married, and as your wife, I want to know what you do out so late that you come back covered in blood."

Silas sighed. "You wouldn't understand."

"I'm your wife, or so you call me," I scolded, not fully understanding the weight of a single word. The red jeweled ring with its black briar band weighed heavily upon my finger. "At least try to make me understand. I want to understand."

In a flash, his seat was empty. I searched the room, time turning into precious moments. My pulse quickened, blood roared with fury. Trembling, I shuffled closer to the door.

"Where do you think you are going?"

I was slammed against the wall, the wind knocked out of my lungs, meeting Silas's wild gaze hovering over my neck as nails dug into my shoulder. The metallic taste coated my tongue, and my breathing hitched. Silas's face twisted, teeth protruding from his upper lip.

"It's not the villagers' blood. It's mine."

Silas pressed his head against my neck, body shaking as icy warmth shivered down my spine. Silvery snow strands tickled my nose as the ache in my chest bloomed, wanting for the touch and conflict.

"Your blood? Silas, why do you say that it is your blood?"

Silas looked up from thick lashes with round eyes as if he were a child who got caught. They fluttered shut as he kissed up the length of my neck before stopping at a sweet and tender spot. "I can hear how your pulse quickens at my slightest touch. I can hear it jump when you are afraid. Your blood sings to me, and I often want to heed that call, but I can't. I can't, Valeria." Silas ran a finger across my neck, listening to the drumming of my heart.

"Silas," I croaked.

His body was warm. The heavy set of his hands rested at the crest of my hips. Lips wandered to the bone of my collar as Silas pressed light kisses to my skin. I kept my palms against the wall, afraid but not of him. No, not of him but of the consequences at play.

"To not hurt you, I have to hurt myself. Hunting down shadows to take the urge out and protect the innocent as much as I can. But it's becoming harder and harder to ignore. I don't want to hurt you, Valeria." Silas shuddered a breath against my neck. "I care for you, and for the first time in a long while, I am afraid of the thirst."

"The blood in the wine glass you drink night after night."

"A poor excuse for a blood substitute that never leaves me fully sated," Silas whispered. "I'd been so careful for so long, and now, there is something valuable to me that I don't want to lose. Not again."

With his breath hot against my skin, I closed my eyes and wrapped my arms around him. Evergreen and spice enveloped us in the tight embrace. Silas trembled. I needed to be sure—to know if he was capable of hurting me. To confirm the confusion tearing me apart between desire and duty.

"It's okay. You won't hurt me, and I—I trust you. If you need to sate your thirst, then do so. I trust you and know you won't bring me any harm. You won't harm me."

I opened my eyes. Silas's muscles strained, quivering as he bared his teeth, grazing my neck. He shuddered, ticking my ear. "I can't. I won't."

That's all he said before he left the hall.

17 May XXXX

All I want to do is die—is that so much to ask? All I want is to be with her, and life is already hard enough. There is to be a ball after my coronation, and I know there is a plan to remove me from the throne. I'd like to see them try.

If I go down, then I will burn Amaris alongside me in the pits of hell for what they did to her.

I will make them pay with their lives.

There is a visitor who has requested an audience with me. They stated they could help, and I am curious to see where this meeting shall lead.

DE

Dear Rueben,

I am writing to you, as we both have mutual concerns with the prince's behavior since the death of Cecilia La Flor. It is clearly evident that he does not intend on furthering the alliance in joining our bloodlines and prefers that we remain sideline to the conflict between Endovier and Amaris. I have a proposal to make of both you and the council in regards to our shared concerns. I'd be happy to discuss this in the chamber at nine tonight while the prince is busy with other matters.
Yours Truly,
Narcisa Marius Nicolae

n

Nineteen

"Is everything alright?" Ayla asked.

We walked through town on our way to a house call she had received. A child had recently gotten sick, and according to Ayla, it was an illness that came on quickly and without mercy. The mother had broken down Ayla's door this morning, begging for assistance, half crazed and fearful.

"The mother had seen into the eyes of death when she spoke of the little one," Ayla stated shortly when I had arrived at the cottage that morning.

I was afraid of what we would find. "Didn't sleep well, that's all," I lied.

I rubbed my arms, the thin cloak doing little to stave out the chill bite of winter. The dark trousers and thick blouse I wore were the warmer choice than the dress Ebony had insisted on. Although they did very little to keep the cold out. In comparison, Ayla dressed in a simple cloak, appearing to be warmer than I was. Ashen strands framed her oval face, ethereal and elegant among the townsfolk we passed. She shifted the brown leather bag, glass clinking together.

She raised an eyebrow. "Is that so? Remind me later to send you back with lavender and chamomile."

I nodded.

Since the snowfall, many people have shuttered themselves away into warm homes waiting for the winter to pass them by. The slush on the unpaved roads piled up with dirty snow prints guided us along the stretch of road through the center of town, while paths splintered off in different directions into alleys and to front doors.

"This is the sixth house visited this month. More specifically, the sixth case of a person exhibiting similar symptoms."

"Is there an epidemic going on?" I asked.

"Perhaps," Ayla hinted. "It's imperative that we find the cause of the illness quickly."

We climbed the steps to a rickety door, the hinges barely hanging on by the bolts. The street the house resided on was on a barely lit road, and the smell of decay hung heavy in the dingy air. Drunken voices came from farther down the road, men stumbling in the dark from a nearby tavern as they joked to one another about their work or women.

Ayla knocked lightly on the door and waited to the sound of stomping and voices answered. The door swung open, and a frail woman appeared, dirt smeared across her face while her hair was wrapped up in a cloth covering her head.

The mother's mouth trembled in greeting as she said, "Come in, she's inside resting. Please come in."

"When was the last time that she had anything to drink or eat?" Ayla asked.

"Two days ago, and she won't take anything."

"What treatments have you tried?"

"I gave her a tonic Bestia prescribed and even the blast herbal tea they sell at that pharmacy down Charlie Street. Nothing has worked to break her fever, and she hasn't been awake for more than two minutes." The mother glanced toward the child, who had barely stirred upon the entrance of guests.

"Why did you not come to me sooner?"

"I was afraid." The woman sobbed into her hands, hiccupping with each breath. "I don't have much to pay for a doctor. I barely have enough to cover the rent and even less for food. Please, I'm begging you. I cannot lose Dehlia."

I stepped through the threshold and understood why Ayla had been worried. The living space was small. A bed was off in the corner of the room with a mattress laying on the ground nearby. The bed had the child curled up underneath mountains of blankets, her face flush from the fever and her breathing shallow. The area was sparse, neat but cramped with a table and chairs in the middle, dresser on the back wall, and the kitchen consisted of one counter and cabinet. It made me wonder how a single person could live here let alone a mother and a child.

Ayla emptied her bag, placing a white cloth onto the table and then placed the jars down. In total, there were about eighteen bottles of varying herbs and a single clear bottle to place whatever she made into. Ayla took out her mortar and pestle, as well as a bottle of syrup, its dark-chocolate-brown liquid sloshing in the bottle.

"Valeria, I need you to grind up the dandelions and elderberries to start. We will try giving her a fever reduction that'll aid in the cough that the poor girl has."

I nodded. "Right." I took my cloak off and worked on the bottles.

Under the dim lighting, I picked up the berries, their skin appearing more black than purple of an elderberry. I examined them more closely, the color never reflecting the purple. I shook my head. It could not have been a mistake that Ayla packed nightingale berries rather than elderberries. Or it was the trick of the light.

I threw the berries into the mortar. The unsettling feeling pounded against my skull in time to the pestle grinding the stone.

Ayla examined the girl, speaking softly. The little girl answered meekly, her voice barely a whisper. She whipped out a stethoscope to listen to her heartbeat, shifting it across the thin fabric of the girl's chemise. "Alright, I need you to lay you back so I can listen to your lungs. Can you do that for me, sweetie?"

The girl nodded weakly.

Ayla took another quiet moment, listening to the girl as I quietly ground the dandelion flower into the black mush. I added liquid to the mixture to where it became a drink rather than syrup.

Ayla withdrew her stethoscope. "Lungs appear to be healthy. Tell me, sweetie, what hurts?"

"My body . . . I feel so tired . . . and the dreams. The awful . . . dreams."

The girl's eyelids were drooping as if she were passing on into the realms of dreams rather than into capable hands.

The mother wrung her hands profusely. "She has been talking nonsense for days about these dreams. She often awakes in the middle of the night screaming bloody murder. As if she was being killed rather than sleeping. It's awful."

Ayla turned back to the girl. "Can you tell me what your dreams are about?"

The girl paused, wheezing with each raspy breath. "There are these shadows . . . . Hungry shadows and they want to eat me. They grab at me as if I am a snack. I am not a snack."

I stopped grinding.

"Eat you?" Ayla pressed.

The girl nodded. "Uh-huh. It's like the mist around the castle. They don't have faces, but I can tell that they have eyes and a mouth, and they are hungry. They want to eat me, and I tell them no. I tell them no, and I scream, and the next thing I know, mother is shaking me awake, telling me to stop screaming."

I was suddenly submerged into icy waters, my hand coming to a stop.

Ayla stood, guiding to the workstation, and she grabbed a bottle of chamomile. "Do you have any hot water?"

The woman sprang into action, going across the tiny space to fill the kettle and then back to the other side where a fireplace sat near the beds. She placed it over the fire as Ayla sprinkled the leaves into a small cup, mixing it with honey.

"This should help with the sleeping problem, but she does have a profound weakness that is hard to explain."

The mother scowled. "It must be the vile thing that lives up there. That would have to explain it. Every physician I have talked to said that they have never seen anything like this and don't even know where to begin." The woman crossed her arms, her gaze on the sleeping child, curled up and fighting sleep as tiny eyes watched the conversation closely. Worry played across the mother's lips, straining, and tightening as her throat bobbed. "Tell me, is *he* responsible?"

Ayla just packed the bottles back into her pack.

Her normal, serene features strung into a contemplative worry.

"I will come by in a fortnight. I have materials back at the cottage that may be of used to ease her symptoms. I am afraid her diagnosis is one I cannot treat, but I can ease." Ayla's eyes darted to me, full of understanding and the message clear.

Silas was to blame.

Ayla said nothing on our way back to the cottage. The quiet ate at me, knowing that, in some way, regardless of the facts, I was responsible for the little girl's slow decline and imminent death.

The moment we entered the quaint cottage, Ayla whipped around in a fury. "Why isn't he dead yet?" Ayla demanded. The firelight bounced off the cottage, dancing across her twisted frown. "I gave you the way out of your entrapment, and he is still not dead."

"How do we know he is the one responsible for these deaths?" I inquired. "Silas said that he—"

"And you honestly believed that monster?" Ayla slammed the table, and herbs flew around the small space. She tapped the table, face darkening, lips twisting into a frown. "The man needs to die. If you can't complete the job, then someone else must in your stead. I can't let him continue to flaunt himself. Things are already dire enough as it is."

"Why can't you do it yourself if you are so sure he is responsible?" I shoved my chilled fingers into my pocket, watching as Ayla paced the length of the cottage.

Ayla wore a nondescript expression, tapping a long thin finger against her chin. "I can't get past the mist. No one can, remember. You somehow can, which makes it your duty to slay him."

"I can't."

"And why not? I don't know if you know, but every day that he continues to live, someone will die. That girl will be dead in a fortnight, and you decided to give the monster humanity."

"I can't. He said he is not—"

"That man is dangerous. He will kill you and suck you dry—you know this. He is the enemy."

"And what if he is not?" I argued, striding forward to meet her dead on. "Since I got here, I have been told what is right and what is wrong. No different from my life back home. I'll ask again, how do you know he is responsible for these deaths?"

"Get out." Ayla finished.

"What?"

Cold eyes steered toward the door, and Ayla had transformed into a different person right there. The softness hardened to stone. She was no longer the kind, patient woman I had come to know but of someone with an unknown vendetta.

"I said get out. Until he kills you or you kill him."

"Ayla . . ." I strode forward, clutching her hand in mind to find it cold and detached.

When an eerie chill spread through my body, I jumped back, staring at the space between us with Ayla, unmoved at what I had witnessed.

"Go. I believe it's best that we finish our discussion for today."

I did what she asked and walked out to the fading winter's light.

My mind tore itself in two on the familiar walk back, the light nearly gone, and the road below me faded under thick trees. Silas had given me his word that he wasn't involved with the matters of the town folks, and Ayla's outburst had me even more confused. Who was I to trust on who it was killing people?

If it truly was not Silas, then who was targeting these people?

Who wanted the little girl dead?

These questions pounded at my skull. I did not notice the change in the path, enveloping the dense forest. The fog became thicker, wrapping itself around my heels. Night was fast approaching and the path difficult to see.

I tripped over a branch, falling onto the dirt. "Great. Absolutely wonderful." I stood, wiping the dirt and snow from my trousers.

Valeria.

I froze, glancing up at the trees, fading into the night with the fog lapping at its stripped trunks. Long limbs stretched toward the twilight, creating shapes and shadows, making my skin crawl. The forest whispered back, giggling among themselves as if conversing with the ominous winds.

In front of me, down the long stretch of the path, stood a wispy shadow similar to the ones hidden in the castle depths. Unlike the children of darkness, the shadow's wiry grin revealed a set of jagged yellow knives.

Valeria, foolish child. You should have killed him when you had the chance.

The black mass darted forward, swiping past me. Stinging pain laced up my arm. I placed my hand to my shoulder, the slick metallic smell flooding my senses, pulse racing at the sight of bright crimson.

Blood dripped from my palm and from the wound on my shoulder. Behind me, an army of shadows rolled over one another, their masses mingled with each other as a pack of wolves excited by the scent of fresh meat.

I bolted down the path, rustling behind me and around me. Chased by death, I ran hard. With my limbs on fire, the shadows sliced into flesh, leaving a blood trail to follow. There was no escape. The harder I ran, the more the shadows slashed into me. Hot tears streamed down my cheeks, the pain mounting, and my limbs became jelly, threatening to fall from under me. I slammed against a boulder, blood sputtering to my lips.

Come now. We just want a play thing. You don't mind, do you?

I slinked to the ground, my vision swimming. The shadows converged into one singular mass and sprang forward to pierce.

"You don't stop, do you?" a voice said.

Silas's pained face winced with blood seeping from the corner of his lips. His stone-hard body covered mine. The scent of blood, thick and nauseating, seeped from blades of wispy shadows pierced through his back. Red-coated silvery tips splattered against pristine white cloth and dripped silently onto the ground and into me.

Silas groaned, "When I say run, do so and don't look back."

I widened, hands clasped over my mouth to prevent the scream from erupting. Silas's body was riddled with thick blades of black, puncturing tan, immortal flesh. Blood pooled at his feet, as the blade released their grip with a sickening muted sound.

"Run!" Silas yelled, facing the imminent threat balling together for a second strike. "Now!" Silas pushed off the boulder, facing the shadows head-on with brute force.

I did what he said, running as fast as I possibly could, daring not to look at the battle behind me.

"Oh my Lord," Ebony gasped.

I slammed the doors behind me, clutching at my shoulder, letting myself fall upon the granite floor. I didn't move—the fight dissipated, and the adrenaline propelling me faded. Utterly exhausted, I closed my eyes to the ache of my limbs and the searing heat of sliced flesh.

"Help me." I gasped, the pain seared itself in waves with every minor movement I threatened to make.

Ebony's wispy self gathered materials and dressed the severe wounds. She sat me up against the banister, moving quickly to stop the bleeding as I tried to make sense of the shifting shadows. It couldn't be a coincidence upon leaving Ayla's that after talking about such shadows I was attacked. But try as I might, I struggled to comprehend what happened in those woods. There was no simple explanation I could come up with that made my doubts dissipate.

Ebony laid a gentle hand upon my shoulder. "This one will need stitches. Would you like something for the pain before I begin?"

I tilted my head to the door, watching it open to the chilly winter's night and to the shadowy figure slowly to approach.

"There you are! Just what on Earth happened out there?" Ebony called to the figure.

The floor under me began to quake, shaking the Earth tenfold to the stone collapsing from higher up. A low growl purred in my ear, and my own eyes fluttered upward to the heavens to see a hole opened to the gray clouds. White shimmering flakes floated down in thick curtains, the storm upon us. The cold swept through in heaving waves as the blizzard bore down, the pure white snow blotting the blood and the tortured scream.

"The shadows, they got to her. I was too late in tracking her down. The *roses*, Ebony. The goddamn roses," Silas growled.

I blinked, his body bracing the cold wind to the garden as red petals joined the snowflakes, slicing the air with cruel beauty.

Cool hands pressed to the wound. "Forget the roses. She needs you. She lost too much blood, and I can only do so much. So, I suggest you do something before you regret it later."

I began to fade, the pain taking its place. Ebony's dark features blinked in for a moment, the blood—my blood appearing on her opaque apron, a steel needle poised in mid-air and then disappeared into the dark. Her voice warped at the sound of crashing and the fiery sting of my shoulder.

Hot tears stung my cheeks and then it all went black.

Twenty

I awoke sometime later, the night air still and dark. Listening to silent beats, I splayed a palm out onto the soft comforter. My hands shook as I raised them to my shoulder to find the smooth cotton bandage in its place did little to soothe the budding, anxious knot. The oddity was not lost on me since I had begun living with an immortal who could fix me up. I replayed the events over in my head and came to the undeniable conclusion.

I'd nearly been killed, and this time, I had to do something.

I threw open the drawer, finding the silver knife and the ash powder. With shaky hands, I tucked the items away, throwing a jacket over the thin nightdress and walked toward the west wing.

The castle was empty, a void that sucked the life out of people, trapping them here to haunt the halls and to house the monster. It was a stain on the landscape, a terror on lives, and it needed to go. The shadows behind me told me such, so I limped through the corridor in search of Silas's bedroom. He had to be there, and I had no other choice but to catch him off guard.

I had to do it.

I needed to do it.

I didn't want to.

The girl's pale hand weakly stretched out to hold Ayla's plays on repeat in my head. The little girl would be dead in a fortnight.

I waited a hair out in the main corridor to see if Ebony or the other ghost would catch wind of my plan. Out on the stairwell, the cold draft from the raging storm blew across the space. I glanced up to the crumbling hole in the ceiling, snow packing the stone and dusting the granite in white.

The pit of my stomach dropped as I stared at what appeared to be a crime scene. The wind howled against any logic in the collapsed ceiling, and the wood rot permeated the icy chill.

The knife shook in my fist, chest rising and falling with quivering gasps. I ignored the searing pain in my shoulder and marched forward. Doors blurred either from the enchantment that bound the castle or from the ghosts. Ebony and the others would be upset their master was dead, but perhaps then she could move on beyond the living.

It would only cost my heart to ensure the suffering does not continue. He may have saved me, but what of the other innocents in the village? Killing him was the only option to stop this.

I just had to believe it. To stop the continuance of pain—perhaps this is what Cecilia had meant by saving him.

Using the two keys on my belt, I stepped forward into the dark corridor and found myself at the door Silas had promised me it would bring me to. I poked my head inside the lab to see if he was working, only to find that it was empty. Moving on, I grew more on edge with each creak and moan. My heart drummed on overtime. The farther I pressed, the more the castle withered.

The hallways shifted, creating new passages, walls crumbling and rotting into dust, and the floors caked in black soot creaked with my weight. The smell of rot was incredibly potent. I covered my nose with my sleeve to no avail. It clung to the living, into the dingy darkness I traveled into. A ghost popped between walls, floating listlessly without paying much attention. I nearly knocked back onto the shredded carpet.

I looked back to the stretch of dark corridor. It filled me with a sense of foreboding. I stood, shaking off the feeling. I had to see this through if not for me but the little girl eaten alive by the shadows of the castle. I shuddered a breath, body vibrating as the blade shook. If I were to run into Silas, I'd be dead.

The hallway ended abruptly to a red door. The door, compared to the rest of the surrounding wood, appeared to be in better condition, smooth and free of the dank rot underfoot. I sent out a silent prayer to anyone who'd listen and grasped the handle, hoping I was right.

Before I lose the nerve to do it.

I gripped the knife, unlocking the door a crack. Peering through it, I noticed the room was drawn in inky blackness, all except for a small candlelight from the bedside table. A form laid upon the bed, not moving at all—not even a single hitch from its chest to signal signs of life. I cautiously entered, my back flat against the wall, shuffling slowly into the space.

Silas's icy drawn face was still, flickering under the light. He appeared dead, pale rigor mortis and all. The four-poster bed was in shambles, the posts collapsed and leaned against the other for support as the fabric draped the bed in shredded cobwebs. The illumination played off his hair, glowing with every flicker draping over the webs. His mask sat on the bedside table, leaving his left face bare. The rest of him was dressed in black, with his hands clasped together onto his stomach. It struck me. This was as if Silas was dressed for death, and this was his tomb.

A beautifully curated tomb for a beast.

My heart skipped a beat. I prayed to whatever gods were listening that he could not hear it as he laid there blissfully unaware. I mustered any courage that was in my body. The same affirmation propelled me forward to the bed, hovering the stake over his chest—his heart.

The knife shook within my palm, and the surety to do such a task vanished with each line I repeated over in my head.

I *need* to do this.

I *have* to do this.

I needed to do this for the little girl, for the people in that town who suffer at his hand. I have to do this for my freedom. The sooner he is dead, the sooner my problems are solved.

The knife trembled in my hand, my own breaths quickening. I forced my arms to drop only to find that they couldn't. Tears stung my eyes. The tip traced the outer part of his blouse. I only need to press it in, so why couldn't I?

One little swift movement, and everything would be done with. I can go and live my life—we all can. I can be selfish at something else—not this.

Lower, come on lower, I chanted to myself. I squeezed my eyes shut, throwing my body into the blow to find it still does not want to obey.

The wind howled in my ear. Blinding pain laced my back, reigniting the wound in my shoulder. A hard grip pinned me in place, snapping my wrist nearly in two against the wall. The knife laid on the ground near the bed.

Silas was no longer in the bed. His body was pressed into me, claws digging into my flesh.

Beautifully wild.

The gold flecks of his eyes were gone, replaced by crimson, mouth twisted, baring his fangs. His pink tongue licked my neck in earnest. The flap of his blouse fluttered freely to see the faint marks still fresh to ooze blood onto the wood floor.

Drip. drip. drip.

"Silas." I shivered, my throat bobbed. "It's me, Valeria."

The red in his eyes intensified with the predator finally taking its place. My heart beat wildly in my chest, adrenaline pulsating through me.

I ducked from under him, sweeping past strong arms for the knife. With the cool blade in hand, I turned to face my assailant.

Silas stalked slowly, his wounds bleeding profusely. "Finally, a sweet, delightful treat to sink my teeth into, and you're here to help me to sate this incredible thirst. What a considerate Little Dove you are."

Silas's chilled words crawled against my skin. The man hours earlier was gone, and what was in his stead was Death Incarnate.

He lunged for me, fingers grazing past. Lunge after lunge, I dodged till the cool stones were against my back, and I was out of places to run. Silas sauntered in close, body tensed as if to restrain himself. His lips hovered briskly over my neck. Sharp nails pinned me in place with his fangs inches from my vein, which pulsated under the tip of the points.

I used all the might I had and pushed us to the floor, bringing the knife to his neck. "Silas, if you don't snap out of it, I'll have no choice but to end you before you end me." I straddled him, pinning his arms with my legs as he snapped at me.

Silas laughed, cruel and distant. "Just a taste. I promise, just a taste."

I knocked his head against the hardwood. "Silas, if you have any humanity left, then show me."

Tears bleared the lack of my senses, falling against the pommel of the knife before silently kissing the monster's cheek.

Silas blinked, the red in his gaze fading back to their golden hue. He rested a shaky hand upon my thigh, the weight of his action resting heavy. He flickered to the blade and then up to me. "It's best if you leave while you can. Who knows how long I have left before I am consumed whole."

I took a few stilling breaths, poised in my duty only I couldn't.

This man tried to kill me, and I couldn't.

I dropped the knife, letting it clatter beside me, the shame burning upon my cheeks. Silas reached forward, pinning me in his place and buried his head into the crevice between my neck and my wounded shoulder.

He shuddered. "The thirst is growing, and today, in the woods—I wasn't strong enough. You were hurt by those things, and all I saw was blood—so much blood."

Silas shifted his head, teeth brushing against my neck. "I was so terribly afraid." Unconsciously, I brushed a hand to his cheek with his hand meeting mine. "I want these gentle hands, these kind eyes, and this . . ." He kissed my hand solemnly as a prayer. "I should not want such a thing, but I do, and a monster like me should not want such things." Silas nuzzled my neck as he rasped, "I'm running out of time."

I wrapped my arms around him, defeated, as he was in the turmoil of my own emotions flaring and fluttering. "If you need to drink to heal those wounds, do so. I won't hold it against you. Show me that you won't hurt me."

"And if I can't restrain myself?" He softly kissed my neck and tenderly brushed aside my hair.

I hugged tighter, reassuring us both in the hurricane of confusion. "Then, I die. Simple as that. Isn't that what marriage is, forged trust from a series of blind risks? If you truly care for me, as you said, then you *will* restrain yourself and drink only what you need to heal."

"Understood." Silas shivered, and I braced for the pain as his teeth plunged deep into my neck.

It burned through my veins, tearing me in two. My life force flooded into him.

I gripped his blouse, nails biting into his back. It was not long before the pain was replaced by the sweet flood of warming electric fire coursing through my veins. Detached from my body, my limbs fell to the floor, limp as Silas clutched me close, showing no signs of stopping. Cloves and spice invaded my nostrils, and I succumbed to the darkness, the efforts of staying conscious straining the deeper I fell.

I wanted to live. I didn't want to die. But in the cloudy haze of the carnal act, I didn't mind so much the possibility of being loved by death.

I moaned, Silas stiffened in response, licking up traces of my blood. The room spun, shattering and fracturing piece by piece, slipping into the space of the past in a time of the present.

The man with raven hair sunned himself out in a field by a lush rose garden. The vision changed to him twirling about a ballroom in a stunning gold mask. The strange familiarity at the tip of my finger, and if I reached far enough, I'd know. I'd know the truth beyond the veil to aid the present.

I barely registered Silas withdrawing from me, burying his head in my chest, and watched it slowly rise and fall with each waning breath. I'm softly carried, body floating listlessly and deposited upon something soft caressing my back. The vision faded, and I found myself in the realm of reality.

For a while, I remained there, floating weightless in ecstasy as Silas stroked my cheek. It comes back to me in pieces, slow at first. The room and the darkness glared beyond the shadows of the bed, my head in Silas's warm lap, his hand resting against my cheek with a gaze of serene light—lacking the hunger that had stained his golden eyes red.

When they returned to their iridescence, gold freckles around the irises, and without his mask, his scar was prominent across the left side, gouged deep into the pale flesh in fading white lines.

I found myself staring at the scar more than I'd like to admit. I turned away, blushing.

"Are you alright, Little Dove?"

I forced my head to move, nodding as I adjusted. "I think so," I managed to say, failing to sit up by myself. I flopped back, and dark spots danced in my vision.

Silas wrapped his arm around my waist, hoisting my body up. The fiber of my body was frayed, strung together with sinew that did not move on my own accord. I blinked, once, twice and thrice—the room spun, the light encompassed my head and the rest of my limbs. My hand traced up my neck, finding two little pin prick marks from his mouth. They were deep, but not deep enough to inflict damage, almost as if his fangs were that of a needle rather than teeth.

I winced at the memory.

In my early diagnosis, Mama had all kinds of doctors try all numerous treatments to make the sickness go away. She lost Father just a few months before when I had started exhibiting symptoms. The first part of those treatments included a needle pressed into my chest to drain the fluid clotting in my lungs. I never knew how effective it was. Mama, after seeing the mess that it took to hold me down long enough to endure the remedy, forbade the doctor from doing it again.

At the time, I thought it was because she did not like to see one of her own in pain. But as my illness progressed, I found that was not the case.

She just hated the screaming.

I pulled my hand back, finding faint blood glistening on my fingertips. The weightlessness of my body found this to be amusing while the grounding aspect, the one that was still wrapped up in Silas, shuddered.

I came to kill him after, and I, once more, yielded my power to him. I failed the little girl, failed the townsfolk who are dependent on me to do something. Yet, here I was, wrapped in the arms of the enemy.

Tears pricked my eyes. I was a despicable human being, and I did not deserve to live. Not while so many are dying. I was no way closer to freeing anyone and instead gave myself up to the beast.

Silas brushed my tears away. "Valeria, talk to me."

"I can't." I trembled. "I should be punished for what I did."

I hated that I was trembling, hated the shame that stained my cheeks as much as I hated the fact that I allowed myself to be fed on, to be vulnerable. My hands had evidence riddled in the faint lines.

"Punished? Little Dove, what for?" Silas softly stroked my cheek, whispering sweetly, "If it's because you almost put a knife through me, I forgive you for that. I'd hardly think less of you, especially due to circumstances."

His voice was light, carefree, as if we did not just share a terrible secret with one another in his own bedchamber.

"It's not that." I leaned back against his chest, finding warm comfort in him. I held his hands, tracing the faint lines of his palm—the calluses of centuries marked upon flesh. There was a man in which these marks were attached to, one who yearned to be understood in the same manner humanity were to be. "I don't understand you at all."

"What is there to understand?"

"I have tried to kill you over the last few months, and still, you regard me without worry. I am by far the last person who should be here. You trust me so willingly, and I hate that."

I traced his heart line. "I promised to kill you, and I became a wimpy assassin in hopes of saving the townsfolk since I knew I was doomed. Now, I can't even be earnestly certain killing you would solve the problems in which they are facing. I promised so much, and yet I am nothing more than a confused woman who is selfish."

The tears began in earnest. I huddled my knees to my chest, hiding my face into the fabric of the thin gown.

Silas perked up, his fingers twirling loose strands. "I do not think you are selfish—confused, possibly, but selfish, no. It is not a sin to know what you want, Valeria. To take a bite out of life in its full glory. Human life is short. Why regret what you desire?" Silas said with such ease it struck my chest, splitting my fraught heart.

I laughed, a pounding headache forming. "This is coming from the immortal who has nothing but time. Tell me the truth, the shadows . . . If they are not yours, then who is controlling them?"

"I do not know," he replied. "It's been an item I have been investigating for some time now since they first snuck their way through the wards." Silas shifted off the bed, pulling me to the head of the bed coming face to face with him. He propped himself up on his elbow, the other brushing my hair as his fingers lingered softly over my skin. Silas relinquished with a sigh, snuggling in close. "Someone from long ago, I fear."

In this moment, there was such serene peace I have never known nor have thought I'd have. My gaze landed on his soft lips, which smirked slightly as if he was taunting me.

"You are not truly responsible for the deaths and the shadows?"

"Correct."

"Then who is, if not you then who?" I contemplated. "Why do they think that you are the one to blame? Don't you care?"

"Of course I care. I am quickly running out of time, and I am nowhere close to breaking the curse over the castle and the town below." Silas paused for a heartbeat or two, returning with a witty grin. "Perhaps it is better that they despise me."

"I am serious, Silas."

"So am I."

"What happens if you never break the curse? What then?"

The more time passed, the more I realized Silas was not much different from me. A man trapped by the fabric of others woven centuries ago.

In the twenty-one years I have lived under the McCallister roof, I never had a chance to think for myself. To allow myself the opportunity to think about my own desires outside of those of my family. Outside of the want—the need to survive and without that constant dread, I did not know who I was.

Silas lightly kissed my hand. "I suppose I'd cease to exist. The town more than likely will disappear alongside me or, if they are lucky, will be free to join the rest of the world. My unwilling hostages' fates remain unknown, simple ghosts of the living in the same way I care for the dead."

I curled beside him, warmth spreading under the thin fabric of the chemise despite the cool stone and the overhead draft.

My heart drummed loud enough to be heard within the quiet space. The soft down pillow comfortable against my head, my eyelids drooped slightly as my vision began to fade. The rhythmic graze of his fingertips was hypnotic, guiding me into what my body wanted—rest.

I wasn't ready to drift, not yet. Another issue pressed against my skull that I had to know before sleep took me, and I was left, yet again, vulnerable.

"Silas, I need you to tell me something. It's about the reason why you want me to guess your name."

He raised his eyebrows. "Yes, Little Dove?"

The vision of the boy came to mind, and the strong connection to Silas was impossible to ignore.

Fighting against sleep, I cupped his face, pressing my lips against his sweet, warm lips. I reveled in the taste of him, the enveloping scent of cloves and spice, the delicate urge to want more. My body craved more despite the fatigue. He moved against me, his hand wrapping around my waist, pulling me up onto him. I straddled his hips, his hands weaving through my dark hair.

I needed to see those visions, to see if they contained a clue to this madness.

To stave off my own madness.

This man, for better or worse, was the reason I was here and not six feet under. To an extent, I owed him my life, but he never asked for it. The prospect of loving a beast was less frightening in these moments without judgment. Perhaps he was right. It was not a sin to desire.

I pulled back, taking a moment to take in his beautiful features before it would disappear. Before the world told me it was wrong. Before I lost all sense of self, plunging into the abyss with him.

"The woman and the man I keep seeing, they have something to do with you, don't they? Your name— your true name is what is keeping you all trapped here in this sublimed space."

His eyes clouded, his hand covering mine. "I have given you everything you need to find the truth. It's up to you to piece them together." Silas pressed a kiss to my forehead.

"Piece together," I breathed before launching into my own worries as a distraction. "You could have killed me tonight, Silas. If you hadn't stopped—if I hadn't." I hesitated to finish, the words twisting in my mouth. "I may have been merely a corpse on your floor."

A smirk crossed his face, nuzzling deeper to rest among my dark waves. "I should have said the same of you, Little Dove. Tell me that, honestly, it was the best you could do, an ambush and a knife." He clicked his tongue. "Honestly, I expected more creativity."

Each press of his kisses along the bare skin of my neck set flames up my flesh, my own breathing hitched, expectant of the sweet kiss and more. To be set aflame until I combust into nothing more than cinder and ash.

Against my neck, he whispered, "Did you not enjoy yourself? To do what I did takes restraint but the effects, as you are aware, are pleasurable."

My toes curled, snagging against the smoothness of the stain fabric. Heat burned my cheeks as the memory of that particular kiss flooded. The intense ecstasy vibrated, and I became delirious with the need of such heady high.

I promptly scolded myself. It was bad enough I had allowed him to taste my blood. It was enough that I was in bed with Silas and another to revel in his illicit touch. One of a monster. Yet I wanted nothing more than to revel in such delight, to let him ruin me with such deliciousness of wandering hands.

I no longer fought against it.

{Date illegible}

The woman came again to the castle today. She offered up a way to ease my suffering to forget the blood of that terrible night—so much blood. What she wants in return is something that I can contend with in this life and after. All in exchange to not see her bloodstained tears close for the final time. To not wish vengeance upon those responsible.

To not look at a rose and only see its thorns.

If I agree to her request, there is no turning back from the path I shall pave. Death would be better than to be without her.

Twenty-One

I pressed numb fingers against my chest, savoring the little warmth radiating from under my cloak. The tavern in which I sat was modest, smelling dank and smoky from the burning pit. Few people sat at the bar, nursing their mugs of ale and sorrows.

I nursed mine with reservation as the turmoil in my mind ebbed and flowed like the inlet I remembered as a kid.

As I stood at the edge of the world, the cool water lapped at my feet as I awaited the tide to pull me out. The calls of seagulls and the salty smell of the sea kissed my skin, balancing on the edge brimming with the possibility of the freefall dive into the seafoam below. Faced with exhilarating death, I'd curled my toes standing at the precipice of it all.

This morning reminded me of that feeling—the thrilling idea of falling into the unknown.

The cobblestone path I once took to Ayla's cottage was diverting, a crossroad into the village and a grim memory of the last time we had spoken. I had entered the village that morning in hopes of finding definitive proof Silas was not the one behind the villager's troubles. Despite the proud attempt, no one wanted to answer questions from a stranger.

The winter sun glistened against the fresh snow, villagers shoveled their abodes and took fire to the larger paths to melt the slush. Upon seeing me, they scurried away into dark corners and into their homes, wary of the passing stranger no longer accompanied by a familiar face.

A somber silence echoed to the long sound of church bells in the distance. They sounded even now inside the tavern where I picked at meaningless conversations from the others around. Salvaging anything I could from the troubles plaguing them or a clue— anything to ease the unrest within my own soul.

The door slammed, and the walls shuddered as the cold blasted in to be greeted with stifling warmth. An older woman knocked her snow-ridden feet against the floor, stalking forward with a limp. A cloak hugged her close, obscuring her face as she approached the bar.

"Ale, sir," the familiar voice called to the bartender. She settled in next to me, dropping the hood back to gray ratted hair flying out from a bun. Hilda's gaze flashed to me. "Fancy meeting you here, child."

She smirked, turning the ale in my stomach sour. "I would have thought you'd be dead by now, living on that hill."

I sighed into my mug. "No, I am still very much alive."

"You sound as if 'twas a bad thing." Hilda rapped her knuckles against the counter. "Mm, suppose death has a way of putting things in perspective, don't you think?"

When I didn't respond, she turned back to her ale and drummed her knuckles against the hardwood. Hushed voices spoke low, trading in secrets and scandals, when all I wanted was to keep mine and find Silas's among the whispers.

More than half a year had passed since the night in the church, and I was no closer to my freedom or figuring out Silas's curse. The shadows and the weird curses appeared to be my only clue, with the black hair boy haunting my every waking thought. The little I knew was his connection to Silas, and even then, he was, well, Silas.

A few months ago, I didn't imagine anything outside of duty and death. Choices that weren't mine to make freely had since presented themselves to me. The fear was making the wrong choice in the face of things I didn't understand.

"I see." Hilda narrowed her eyes, taking a long stave of drink. "Ayla is not with you. Something happened. Perhaps our discussion the last time has caused some . . . doubts."

I shifted in my seat, drumming my fingers against the rough wood. "No, she is not." My mind flashed to Ayla's grim face in the cottage. But I had no proof—no true proof or any evidence of another person who could be behind it. Most of the villagers, just as Ayla was, were convinced it was the man on the hill who was responsible. "We just had a disagreement, that's all."

"Shame," Hilda said. "I thought you were quite the pair. It's been sometime that Ayla has had anyone close, outside of visiting me every now and then. Not since the death of her parents and fiancé. The odd thing is that it was—I saw her mother now and then, eerily similar even for mother and child. Her fiancé, on the other hand, met his unfortunate demise."

"Unfortunate if you mean the entire lot of us thought him guilty and behind the plague." I snapped my head to the bartender.

Hilda waved her hand in dismissal. "Ya'll were chomping at the bit to condemn him. Wasn't he the preacher for a time? I half remembered how many folks of the congregation objected to the town's . . . handling of the matter. Never paying any mind to the oddity of that little shack just out of town."

"Aight, there you go, telling strange tales about the girl," the bartender remarked, pushing two mugs forward. "As if she hasn't done enough, but the rumor mill keeps churning."

"I didn't order another."

"Trust me, dearie, you're going to need it." He huffed with a slap of the towel, tossing it over his shoulder and sauntering off at the call of another patron.

"It ain't just me who thinks it's peculiar she showed up out of nowhere the same time that castle did." Hilda mused into her mugs, taking long drawls before giving a happy gasp and wiped her chin. "Nothing beats some ale on a cold winter's day, dont'cha think?"

"You seemed to know a lot about Ayla and the creature on the hill," I surmised, swirling the mug about and watching the foam froth over the porcelain edge.

The bartender rolled their eyes. "Don't listen to her, sweetheart. It's just the ramblings of an old woman who has a few screws loose."

Hilda waved him off, scowling. "The only reason no one is pointing a finger is her willingness to assist us in our troubles and the tragic end of her fiancé. No one is willing to admit to her face the horrible damage done." She took a sip, then smacked her lips. "Now tell me that you haven't had at least a thought of the unusualness when your grandmama told you about the castle and the fog on the grounds to prevent anyone from getting close or of the fact she's the only one who can seem to cure such a thing."

"Bah! She's done nothing but kindness. She even treated Marius just last week, and he's doing better after catching whatever the blast was from when he got too close to the perimeter of the fog!" the bartender remarked, leaning over the counter to challenge the old woman.

Hilda laughed. "Seems I struck a nerve." The old woman shifted in her seat with glee, seemingly in anticipation. "Oh, yes. Been here quite a while. Almost too long if I have anything to say about it."

"What can you tell me about the creature on the hill?"

The question tumbled from my mouth before I could stuff it back in, and the tavern went still.

The bartender paled, fist balled into a rag stuck into a mug as he, too, listened in close.

Wrinkles turned upwards, her mouth stretched thin, revealing teeth missing in her placid smirk.

"Interesting question. He is quite the enigma even here in such a cursed place. Beautiful to some and monstrous to others, quite the conundrum. Wanted to die so badly, and yet he didn't listen to my instructions carefully."

I frowned. "Wanted to die—how do you know that?"

My heartbeat drummed against my ears loud enough for all to hear.

Ba-dum-ba-dum-ba-dum.

"Hm, strike two, I see." She motioned for the bartender, exchanging wordless glares with the man. The bartender gave in with a sigh, and another mug full of ale appeared. She wrapped bony fingers around the mug. "You had a look about you, a knowing of too much yet too little of the grander picture. I had not seen others possess in quite some time. You're close. I can tell you that. And Ayla has had many assistance over the years, but none seemed to . . . stick around long."

The crackle of the fireplace snapped me out of the trance, as if it were a piece in a grandeur puzzle of a greater mystery. I never asked Ayla out of respect for her and her privacy such as the reason behind the ring she bore, her family, or how she can claim to know so much in a place that knows so little. But with the lump in my throat, perhaps I ought to have, which terrified me more than I'd like to admit.

I chipped away at the ale, the buzz from the alcohol encircling my limbs as the fog descended upon my senses. The tavern seemed to flicker as the residents of the castle do, pale figures draped old harsh woods. Conversations became nothing more than grating whispers I strained to hear over the loud buzzing.

"Have you heard the tale of the prince who wanted to die?" Hilda peeked over, graying hair shifting white. Shadows danced at her fingertips, inching closer hungrily, licking up the dying light. "Of a stranger promising to end his suffering, although he bought more than he wanted. Suffering for so long as we all have—endless, boundless cycles."

The tavern flickered between the realm of the living and the realm of the dead. The men all stopped their conversation and glanced in the direction of the bar, eyes black as coals reflected back. Pale flesh glowed iridescent, peeling back until there was nothing but the cavernous walls appearing through the apparitions. The bartender was reduced to skin and bones, forever poised to clean the rotting wood with nothing more than a disintegrating rag.

I gazed down at the mug in front of me, the ale nothing more than grave dirt and ashes. I spat out gravel, clawing at my tongue to rid the taste of the dead. I stumbled out of my seat, vomiting up gray bile. I heaved until bile stung my throat and my eyes bleared.

"The question should not be about if you heard the tale, no," Hilda croaked.

I slowly turned to see the rotting corpse of the woman.

Maggots slithered out of holes that riddled her decaying flesh, blood dried on two gouges upon her neck sunken in and withered with time.

"It should be how you are going to *survive* it."

She opened her mouth, and moths burst forth from the inner darkness, fluttering in the hundreds. I screamed, scrambling backward, swatting at the insects. With my back slammed against the wall, the insects kept coming, diving in a sweeping storm, blotting out the firelight. I shoved my head between my legs, thrusting the hood of my cloak over my face to shield from the onslaught as the woman's voice echoed in my ear.

The shrill question fluttered upon wings. Far away, the door creaked open, and the sound of footsteps inched closer to the swarm.

I hesitated to look at the owner of black studded boots covered in melting snow. Yet there was no denying who the owner of the voice was when she spoke.

"When you are done cowering, I have something to show you."

Ayla's empty gaze pierced the very wall I was attached to, her cheeks red from the cold. She carried a small bundle of flowers and a somber expression, lips pressed thin. As the wind, icy and unrelenting, she strode out of the dilapidated tavern without another word.

I stood, brushing off the dust. I covered my nose, suppressing the bile climbing my throat as the scent of death and decay flooded my senses. I took one last glance at the dark tavern falling apart at the seams different from the time I stepped into the place.

There was once a prince who wanted to die—the familiarity struck a chord for reasons I had yet to know.

Twenty-Two

yla studied me from under white eyelashes, and cold blue hardened like ice. "People are dying every day, from a mysterious cause that normal doctors or apothecaries could not identify, much less cure—they could only treat until the end came. Yet you still allow him to live."

Ayla strolled leisurely through the streets, leading me out of the small village and into the tangling mass of trees at the border. She led us both into the unknown with me as an unwilling follower.

Ayla stopped, tossing her head back, and looked over with a heinous grin. "Unless something happened?"

I resisted the urge to bring my hand to my bandaged neck. The memory of the night before blared like church bells. After Silas had drunk his fill, we lay there among overturned black satin sheets. His face nuzzled against my neck in the aftermath, and he had been careful to limit the spillage of my blood and not take more than what he needed.

Or, at least, what Silas had assured.

As the euphoria died, I brushed the rough scars on his bare chest. I let lingering fingers wander and touched his maskless face. Intimate and dangerous, it was a thrilling combination of dangerous consequences—one I had embraced in the dim chamber.

All of it was a dream as Ayla stood before me, repulsed at what I had become. Perhaps I was nothing more than a plaything to Silas. Maybe I was a puppet, a silly little puppet who just wanted to live.

Ayla's cruel gaze narrowed with suspicion, awaiting an answer—the right one—rather than the lie.

I slowly allowed the lie to form. "I am not sure Silas is entirely responsible. If anything, how he has treated me has—"

Ayla trotted down the snow-filled path, beckoning me to follow close without a word. Feet sunk into the white-laced bank, the walkway becoming buried underneath thick blankets of white. The village was a blot behind us, and the castle loomed ominously in the distance, hovering above the evergreen branches. Weathered and worn, the castle's roof littered with large holes opened to the wintery hell. Tall spires stretched toward the sky, the crumbling stones failing to make the climb under the late afternoon sun.

The castle stood still, an abandoned home to wayward spirits.

The bells tolled the hour, ringing out among the gravestones.

Passing the wrought-iron gates of New Day Cemetery, Ayla wrapped her arm around mine, pinning me in place, and hissed, "Watch and then tell me if you still believe him."

Ravens cawed, circling overhead, watching keenly as omens do. Six people walked out of the small church carrying a tiny wooden casket, a procession following. Silence nestled among sober faces, the pallbearers in step as soldiers to deliver the deceased into death's hand.

Ayla and I walked, heads bowed in respect. We took our places behind the procession, following the mourners to the freshly dug grave.

The men shouldered the casket onto a pulley system, securing the corners to the ropes. A priest hobbled to the front, holding a large leather-bound book. Clothed in holy robes, he blended in with the white grim surroundings, flipping yellow pages, and began to recite prayer.

The words were harsh and unfamiliar, a language unknown to me, but knew the rolls of vowels and the hushed sobs of what it truly meant.

A prayer to ferry the dead to the afterlife—the final passage.

From the crowd, I picked out the mother we had visited nearly a fortnight ago. Eyes were rimmed red, cheeks wet from tears. She looked more fragile than the desperate mother I met She watched as her little girl was lowered to the cold earth.

Ayla squeezed my arm, her frown twisting further. "It's the little girl from last week. Shortly after we left, her mother informed me that she passed away in her sleep. Want to know what I found when I examined her lifeless corpse? Bite marks."

The priest finished the prayer as mourners walked up and tossed dirt upon the casket. Many left with tears on reddened, chilled cheeks with others holding onto loved ones steeped in grief. Wails drowned the cemetery in a haunting chorus carried on by gentle falling snowflakes kissing tears away.

The mother stood alone at the grave, clutching tulips of winter white contrasting the rippling black of mourning clothes rustling in the soft quiet. Her somber gaze down cast to the casket below, she hardly noticed our approach.

Ayla spoke with honeyed words. "My condolences. I know it's been a difficult time for you."

From under the dark veil, the woman's lips parted as she shook her head. "It was to be her tenth birthday today. My little girl is ten today, and I had to bury her." She sniffled into hands.

Her shoulders shook with hard sobs escaped her throat.

Ayla threw a rose onto the casket. Its scarlet bloom stood out from the dustings of white. The gravediggers shoveled dirt onto the casket, burying flowers, snow, and the innocent little girl into the cold ground.

The mother was ushered off by someone, her sobs the only sound in the cemetery. Snow fell softly, covering the ground once more in innocent white.

We had buried Father in the fall of last year, months after that—I became sick. I kept it from the household for as long as I could until Miriam had suggested we visit Father's grave to pay our respects on such a winter's day as this. Among those stones, Miriam and I traveled just as the mother did—weaving ourselves around worn rock, the ground patched with dirt and snow with some plots newer than others. Huddled at the face, the secret burst from lips, blood bubbling onto the white and staining it crimson. I had watched as Miriam's expression fell into despair.

"You're not sick. You can't be," she had whispered among the graves with her sorrow-filled blue eyes coated with tears. "You can't be."

I nodded, the words lodged in my throat. It was funny to think about mortality in this way only a year later, the fear haunting me well before then. The oddity of the fear still haunting mortal dreams kissed softly as death.

A pang shot through my heart. I wondered what she would say about Silas, Ayla, the village, everything. Would she see them as pawns to use as she had me? Or would she see it as that night in the study, taking life for what it is?

Ayla scowled, "Are you happy now? She's dead. The monster is better off dead, yet you dally with the lives of the villagers."

My heart sank to the depths of my chest. Silas was not involved. He gave me his word. Despite this, there was hardly any other person or reason for the villagers' afflictions. I didn't meet her hard gaze, in disbelief at the truth I refused to accept as willing as others had.

"Look at me," Ayla shrilled. She grabbed my wrist, jostling me forward into the mud. I knelt at the foot of the girl's grave. "What more proof do you need? He's a killer, and if you don't kill him—he will kill you."

"I can't," I choked up as tears welled. Her grip on my neck tightened as the taste of dirt flooded my mouth. "I can't. He's not doing this—he gave me his word."

"You trust the word of a monster over the faithfulness of your friend? How absurd!" Ayla hissed, her fingers digging harder into my neck, grazing over the soft, tender flesh and the bandage. She yanked upwards, dragging me to my feet. "What do we have here?"

"No! Don't! Please!" I cried, struggling against her. I tried with all my might to pry her fingers off my neck.

The air snatched from my lungs, depleted in one swift movement that blurred altogether.

Ayla ripped the bandage off, revealing the two neat pricks upon pale flesh, rubbed red from the cotton.

"What have you done?" She gasped, releasing me to the ground. "You let him drink from you? You were supposed to kill him, not become his lackey!"

My hand flew to my neck, covering the awful truth. "He would never hurt me. He isn't the one doing this—please believe me! There—there is someone else involved."

"You can't trust what that beast says. You are brainwashed—*brainwashed*. Probably will kill us all if given the chance." Ayla's lips curled into a heinous smile. "You'd kill us all."

The shadows fell across the stones, and the bell's thunderous baritone struck free, shattering the eerie gloom and replacing it with such darkness. They curled around Ayla's feet, gliding with her as she strode toward the gate.

She tossed her head back, blonde spooling out from her cloak. "Defend him while you can. It won't last." She walked off, the snow falling harder until she was nothing more than a speck of blue among the landscape.

Darkness followed after her as I stood at the gate, condemning us to a path where neither of us will ever cross again.

That was the last time I saw Ayla Wallace.

Twenty-Three

A harrowing darkness, unlike anything else I have encountered, curled my toes in icy heat. At the edge of the bed they festered, flinging itself to the high top of the canopy and entrapping its prey with deadly force.

I did not dare to open my eyes to the dark gnashing its teeth, whispering in my ear, daring me to look.

I curled at the head of the bed, shielding my feet from the intruder's coldness, patting down the duvet to form it as armor.

It had to be a dream—it was a dream.

Any moment, Silas would whisper sweet words or chastise me for such absurdity in having a fear of the dark. The shadowy darkness did not speak, nor did it avert its gaze from where I slept. I didn't need to crack an eyelid to know they were there.

Tall, lanky wisps licked at my ankles, scraping talons onto the duvet. *"Valeria . . . Valeria,"* it hissed. *"Come play, sweet Valeria. Let me carve out your insides . . . she'll be happy. Oh so happy."*

I sprang from the bed, ducking into the corner of the nearby wall, toppling over the nightstand. Compared to the shadows from the forest, the figure was not fully formed. It was feathery and similar to the ghosts. It shifted its form from a wolf to a tall lanky man, garish and enigmatic, it reminded me of what I had envisioned Death to be like. Nothing more than a shapeless being with a hunger for life stuck in the precipice of the world.

The shadow circled me closely, corralling deeper into the corner, snapping its jaw and hissing my name.

"Just a bite, Valeria. Ah, Valeria."

The balcony drapes flapped soundlessly, the cold wind blowing sparkling flakes under a budding moon. The room was washed in silver, drowning out the solid hold the shadow had on the ethereal plane.

I grabbed for the knife, scattered upon the floor beside the discarded ashes and the vial. Hands shaking, I pointed the blade at the shadow, prepared to fight.

Prepared to die.

The shadow was fading back to wherever or whoever had sent it.

I stepped forward, and my body screamed to run from the danger, but I couldn't run. Not when there was a storm on the horizon.

The shadow did not lunge nor react. It remained out of reach, hungrily circling for an opening to take a bite where it can. The mass grew eyes, dotting its body in grotesque hideousness, all flickered between the knife and the ring—Silas's ring.

I touched the ring. A soft sense of his protection warmed my conviction as the scarlet jewels twinkled under the light. "I am not afraid. Tell your master I am alive, and I will fight to save Silas even if it costs me my life."

The words were heavy, aloft even, but with the ring upon my finger and the budding in my chest—it was becoming difficult to ignore what I had to face.

I was linked to Silas, and he was linked to me. The danger would only keep coming if I remained ignorant to this fact.

It reared on its hind legs, standing taller than a black bear. From its grotesque jaws, it howled a blood-curdling scream into the night. Inky blobs flew from its body, circling the ceiling and joining the blackness.

The shadow was gone, and I was alone to the soft darkness enchanted by the waxing moon.

The knife clattered to the floor.

Smoke rose from my lips, rubbing at my arms as I stalked to the balcony window. The faint breeze rustled the curtains, showing a most beautiful sight of the garden and of the man sitting among the frost-covered roses.

Silas sat on the stone bench, head bent upwards to the moon in stilled silence, watching the night past him by. Loneliness and solitude rested upon his shoulders, trapped in a conversation between the ghosts he harbors and the night that sees all his sins. The pale moon kept a tormented man company in solace.

Without another thought, I grabbed a robe, threw it over my shoulders, and joined Silas.

The December air chilled me to the bones, and I shivered as the night winds danced among petals in the sacred place. Down the path of stones in the back of the castle and past hedges of wilting roses, Silas dared not glance as I settled beside him. Bitter cold pressed in from the bench, but I do not let that show.

"Tell me, what are you doing out here?"

Silas's eyebrow quirked, and a dry laugh escaped from pale rose lips. "And why are you awake?"

I smoothed out the robe, the satin gliding across skin smooth as butter, doing little to stave off the cold biting at exposed flesh. I leaned forward, meeting his gaze. "You are deflecting my original question."

Silas shook his head. "I can see that I am not getting rid of you anytime soon." He closed his eyes, perhaps picturing intrigue playing across his lids as a silver screen does. His mouth twitched, parting softly as waves crashing the shore, only to remain quiet.

Silas clasped his hands together, the silver moonlight kissing the crown of his head with loose strands aglow in heavenly darkness. Gold cast to the crimson roses, jaw hardening, before turning back to me.

I sighed, "Do you at least want to know why I am out here in the bitterly cold?"

No response.

I drummed my fingers against the stone bench. "A shadow snuck into my room and attacked me, the frightful thing that it was. It was weak, fading into nothing before hurling itself out the window." I continued on with a smirk.

Silas's eyes widened. "It was here! Are you sure?"

I nodded. "Yes, and I am quite positive."

Silas ran a hand through his hair, snagging his fingers among pale moonlight. "Then, it has already begun."

I cocked my head. "Silas, what are you not telling me?"

I truly took him in and noticed faint scratches, red and swollen on his neck and arms. As if something with long claws raked against him. He was not wearing his white mask, his silvery hair instead covered enough of the scars to hide them from view.

"Do you see the roses?" His body shifted toward me. His hands grabbed mine with such tenderness I shivered, not from the cold but from each stroke of his thumb upon my palms. Silas gave a breathless sigh. "They have been wilting, decaying, and soon, they will die."

"As flowers do."

"Not these ones. Never these." Silas squeezed my hand, brows furrowing. "The castle, the roses, even the mists that prevent you from leaving this seclusion are all tied to me, and I am running out of time."

The fog crept up to the gates, letting us know that there was nowhere out of its wispy grasp. "Silas, if this is about the other night, I—"

"No, no. I wished—I wished that I was explaining myself better." Silas stood, his hands still folded with mine. "Perhaps if I showed you, it would all make sense."

I rose to my feet. "Then, show me."

Silas guided me through the warping maze, the sweet heady scent of the roses becoming stronger the further we went. Petals scattered the snow-covered path, a small trail for us to follow with only the moon to provide us with light from the encroaching darkness.

We entered out from the winding hedges to an open area. My eyes took a moment to adjust to the expanse of the space as Silas slipped from my grasp. He kneeled at a stone marker, saying words in ancient tongue before placing two fingers to his lips, kissing softly and setting it onto the gray stone.

Red roses shifted to white silver, flowers suckling in the budding moonlight. The grounds were cast in a sickly glow with the buds illuminating the enclosed alcove. Long strings of vines wrapped around stone, seizing all it can from the lone bench sitting among painted glass to the statue that loomed.

The statue was of a woman, her face round and poignant, smiling down at anyone who sat below her for a blessing. The statue, draped in Greco-Roman finery, was sculpted with sensual care. A single breast poked out from underneath carved flowing fabric, her long white hair cascading over the growth. Nestled in it was a crescent crown glittering against glass. Her head was bowed in reverence to the lovers.

"They called this a moon garden, perhaps in honor of the moon goddess." Silas stepped toward the bench, fingers tracing long-forgotten grooves. "This is the place in which I had been happy and it is the same place that has caused me such despair."

I gasped as both Silas and the black-haired boy approached me, a crown of silver upon dark curls. His blue eyes gleamed brightly, whispering sweet nothings to ears that will no longer hear his voice after that night.

"Your curse," I started, gaze fixed to the lone tombstone. I bent down to touch the fine carved words, *Vi et animo*. "Tell me, the vision with the woman and the men, the night I found you trying to kill yourself—it's all connected to your curse."

The gorgeous scene had been looked after. Not a vine touched the white marker, nor was there a speck of dirt.

"It began with her death, and it ended with my torment. I try not to remember, but my name binds the curse, or so I was told." Silas slumped onto the bench, the painted glass from windows reflecting onto him in a beautiful array of colors.

It was just as it had been many moons ago.

"The woman you say you saw, she had been my betrothed when I had been a prince. Our countries had been at odds for many years, and both our parents agreed a political marriage was necessary to ease rising tensions. I had been a fool then. I wished for nothing more than the endless hunts and to be locked up in my study, learning about the world that I was not able to freely see. I often hide in the garden to get away from most of the courts and my parents' attempt to secure a match for me." His lips tugged into a tight smile, gaze lifted. "It was here I found her, sitting here staring at the roses. I came to find out that a rival for the throne had played a nasty prank on her, so she had come for a little solace. She was the beginning to my end."

The cold numbed my skin, snow crunching underfoot as I took up a seat next to Silas. He shrugged off his coat, draping it over my shoulders, and tucked me in close. Heat bloomed across my reddened cheeks at the intimate act, heart drumming wildly in my chest.

I wrapped the coat tighter, not letting his presence distract me.

"Not long after she died, I was approached by a woman who promised to ease my suffering. I thought that she had meant she rid me of the memory of her or perhaps the ache of longing. I paid more than what I was promised. I condemn both her soul and mine to this hell. She, already dead, cannot move on fully, and I can never die. I can never join her in the hereafter to hold her, to touch her, to even talk to her."

"Why can she not talk to you?" I rubbed my thumb as he talked, wishing I did not let the past affect me so.

The fire burned in my chest as the innate sadness joined it.

Silas nuzzled my ear, breath hot against my neck. "Her soul is split in two. When I made my deal, she had been long gone, so what was brought back was her but a mere fraction of what once was. She can no longer perceive me nor any of the other residents in the castle. She instead haunts me in the west wing as a hollow companion to me."

"Just like her, we were all frozen in time and removed from the world. The fog created a barrier to keep us in and to keep those who wish us harm out. The only reprieve I've had is glimpses from your world," he said, taking my hand and intertwining our fingers, his thumb brushing the ring binding me to him.

The ache in my chest grew. How long had I been denying myself or even Silas? Every moment I had spent left me with a dizzying spell of what I should or shouldn't be. Mama and Miriam wanted me to be the elder daughter that sacrificed herself for her family. Ayla wanted me to the sacrificial goat to the slaughter and kill the man who had only shown me kindness, and Silas—Silas had let me be what I wanted to be outside of what I had been told I was.

What I had to be?

"That night, the engagement party," I closed my eyes, seeing it play out once more and letting myself relive it even if for a bit. "You found me at a time when the world was falling in around me. I had thought you were an angel ready to sweep me away from the darkness that harbors in my soul."

"I am no angel," Silas attested. "I am a thing of damnation, a demon, a bastard of the gods. I condemned her, and I'll condemn you if you let me."

"And if I let you"—I swallowed—"condemn me to the hell that you have walked alone for so long."

Silas stared out at the roses, throat bobbing as he struggled against the tide to speak the words he was so desperate to say. Silas had been alone, drifting as I had been with the tides of the world, watching it slowly change without him.

Does he ache for the world badly, or does he ache for death more?

A petal fell, caressed by the glistening snow. "In a few weeks' time—if that—I'll be nothing more. Anyone tied to Castle Briar will disappear alongside me. The fog will lift, and perhaps the villagers will be able to leave this trapped space. I cannot be certain of their fate, but I can be certain of mine." Silas grasped my cheek, and I leaned into his touch. "I can't let you share my fate."

Just like many times before, I stood there on the precipice. If I turned back, just who would I be? If I turned back, would I still be nothing more than a puppet to the people around me pulling the strings to enact their own wishes? If I turned back, would I still be the girl who'd follow them with a sad smile? Would I still wish for more and never get the chance to do so?

But if I let myself have this one thing—to love and be loved by a man who had forsaken life, what would that mean for my future? Would the ache in my chest ease? If I chose to tie myself to a damned man, would I still live in ways that I had thought was never mine to choose?

I whispered, slow to announce every syllable that passed from my lips, "I love you." The aching in my chest pressed into me as if there was nowhere else to go. I held myself there—among the bitter cold and the truth I had been running from since the beginning. "And it terrifies me endlessly. But when you say such words, I am frightened not for me but for you. When I first laid eyes on you, I knew that you'd consume and ruin me."

Silas brushed a strand away from my face, and I shivered against him. His lips hovered over mine, heat blooming on chilled skin. "Have I, Little Dove?"

My breath hitched, and for the second time, I didn't think.

I kissed him, soft and inviting lips greeting mine, hands woven through dark locks. Fire coursed through my chilled bones, building with each stray touch. Silas tossed me over his lap, and I straddled him, cupping his face while his hands traced up my back. I softly moaned against him, wanting to get lost in the fire and electricity.

I was selfish, a very selfish woman.

Silas broke the kiss, cupping my face as his eyes searched mine. "You make me feel alive, Valeria.

Something I have not been—have not felt in such lost years. I am yours."

"And you are mine." I let my forehead rest against his, sharing in the softness among the dying roses as if it was to be our graves.

They could have very well become it.

Cool stone braced my back, strewed on the bench below the smiling face of a goddess, watching as Silas feverishly worships under her watchful, loving gaze. His lips caress my neck, heart beating in tandem to his touch. Beneath the thrones of the gods under the moonlit night, I was sinning for this man to take me wholly unto his own.

Silas stroked my leg, pushing the robe and the chemise high upon my chilled skin. Mouth working down my neck and kissing my breast gently, he flickered his smoldering stare as his hand shifted lower to my inner thigh.

A gasp escaped from my lips, and I held his gaze, brimming with desire. Hunger as delicious as the smirk slid across his face smooth as the stone beneath. I struggled to keep my thoughts in order as his fingers slipped underneath the fabric and climbed to the apex of my thigh.

Silas teased, his fingers never straying too close to my center as I writhed under him, begging. He hovered over me, lips upon my neck as his fingers splay me open, diving into the ocean tides. I moaned as he stroked softly and nestled my hands into silver strands, pulling him closer to me. Our mouths collided, intense desire pulsating through my body—the fire spreading, licking at the frozen air.

I needed him as a dying man needed the gods, whole and absolute. Between us, rawness to lust became animalistic, threatening to claim us both. To consume our souls the higher we ascended to the blissful heavens.

Silas pulled away, and I didn't hesitate to bare the soft flesh of my neck. He kissed the skin softly, careful to tug at the bandage. He skimmed tender flesh, and I awaited for the singular moment of bliss, where my body fell away to fly under the moonlight. I tipped my head back, moaning out his name.

He groaned, fingers sliding into me, moving agonizingly slow. I throbbed under him, limbs alive with electricity I was sure to combust. I arched my back, Silas swinging his legs over me, setting a knee between my thighs.

"Silas."

I whispered his name as a prayer to a god. A God wholly worshipped my mortal, fragile body until I begged for more. Until I no longer knew my own name or where I was. The only name to tether me to this plane was his and only his as I was pulled over the crest, shattering under him bit by bit.

I was his, and he was mine.

I cried out, holding him against me, cloves and spice anchoring me to the realm of the living for a moment.

Silas's teeth sank into my neck, drinking deeply as another wave of ecstasy pulsed, and I faded again.

Drifting to the vastness of pleasure, soaked into my body until Silas faded away and so did the troubles that the statue overhead reminds us of.

Silas released his hold, panting as bright crimson drips from his mouth. What I once had thought to be garish and barbaric I gladly held in the palm of my hand.

"I love you."

Silas nuzzled my hand. "Say it again, Little Dove."

I kissed him, breathing against him. "I love you."

"I love you, too," he said against my lips, holding me tight. He lifted me up into his arms, his body warm against the blistering cold. "Come, Little Dove, let's get you warmed up."

Twenty-Four

J curled my fingers around the bound leather of the book, the smooth crisp pages worn from time. I searched the library for the country of Amaris to find a clue to Silas's name. My search yielded nothing besides this journal. Nearly identical to the one back in my room—except there were less letters and correspondence, appearing to be written by one person.

From one, there is none but from more there is the beauty that even the gods have never told before. This is what Cecilia had told me this morning. It was a saying that her mother used to say. Her mother died due to the war that rages on near our borders. I must put a stop to the war before more unnecessary bloodshed and deaths

mount. I can already feel their deaths on my hands since Father died.
I am unworthy of the crown.

The last line looped in my head. I pictured a lost man trying to figure out how to run a kingdom in the midst of turmoil. The death of his father, his lover, and the mounting pressure from the council was too much to bear. This Narcisa character seemed to have ulterior motives despite stating what was "best" for the people.

I slammed the journal shut, squeezing the bridge of my nose. I had hoped for clues, for places that even Silas had not checked in the hundreds of years he had been held up in the dusty castle.

"What about this book?" Ebony spouted from the top shelf, her translucent body slithering down with a book. "This one seems to tell a similar tale to the one that you are looking for."

I flipped through pages, finding that it was nothing more than a secondary source to what I was after. "Unfortunately, no." I slammed the book shut and squeezed the bridge of my nose.

I had hoped there was something Silas had missed. Something to point to try and solve the begotten mystery, but there was nothing. There was absolutely nothing. Any mention of Silas before the curse had either been blotted out by black stains of fragile documents or were missing.

Ebony's ghostly fingers picked the book up and placed it up on the table. "Cheer up, Valeria. We'll find it soon enough."

I turned to her. "Aren't you scared? What if I don't do something and you disappear?"

This had been my second look into the stacks. We had started that morning in the study to find Silas's personal collection lacking any historical context of what happened to predate his curse. Even with the historical collection, it seemed more like an impossible task.

Ebony floated down next to me, appearing to sit upon the soft cushion. Cold wafted from her iridescent form, biting into my long-sleeve dress. Books scattered across the floor, bits of papers rustling against my feet as I strode to the staircase to pull out another book from the spiral tower leading to the locked door.

Ebony wiped her hands onto her apron, forever stained with blood. "Of course I'm scared. Most are. We are scared of the unknown and where we all go after we die. We have existed for centuries in this castle, and we don't know life without it."

Which meant there was no way of telling what would happen if Silas disappeared and the castle was destroyed.

The morning sun passed through her form making it, so she was nearly transparent. The sunlight bounced from painted glass, shedding a spotlight onto the lone piano keys. If I did not find the way to break Silas's curse, there would be no more leisurely playing if the castle collapsed and, with it, only sorrowful tunes would haunt us underneath the rubble.

I strode to the bookcase, fingering spines of worn titles where the faded print no longer told the titles of the books themselves. I walked along the case, climbing the wrought-iron stairs. Thousands of books lined the shelves, covering an array of subjects with historical references appearing older than the heavy gray lines. A book at the top of the tower was untouched by the dust.

I touched the spine. The rough, broken cover crumbled underneath my finger. I carefully extracted the book from the shelf, the jacket disintegrating. The raised lettering was etched out of existence, but in my hands, it didn't matter.

"Valeria." Ebony floated up. Her chilled presence added to the goose bumps along my skin. Dark orbs gazed down at the open page where a silver key was tucked between its decaying pages. "Where do you think that goes?"

I tucked the book back into its hole, grasping the key in hand, and flew up the stairs to the lone door at the end of the long climb. The door at the top called to me, my skin itching with the memory of their invasion.

I placed the key into the lock, turning it until a hard click set into place, the cold biting into my palm. "Ebony, whatever is behind this door was hidden for a reason. Whatever happens, I need you to pull me out at the very last possible second."

Ebony's form flickered, black orbs scrunched together in worry. "Whatever is in there is best to be forgotten. Why don't we wait for Silas? I am sure that he can—"

I shook my head. "No, this cannot wait, and I don't certainly want him to know, not yet anyway."

Ebony disappeared down the banister before reappearing with a candelabra in hand, candles aglow. "At least take this for protection. They will get close enough but not enough to harm you while holding a light."

"I suspect you know what is behind this door, then," I said and grasped the black stand, the soft heat burgeoning out of the cold.

She gave a half-hearted nod, wringing her hands in her apron. "It's what all ghosts see when we die, and it's the one thing we fear in the hereafter."

The fact there were two doors harboring them gave me some pause as to why. What was so different from the other door I had encountered on my first journey to the west wing? Palm laid on the knob. There was only one thought—the hope in the darkness lay the key to the puzzle or a clue we had missed.

I strengthened my conviction, turning the knob and tightening my fingers around the stand. I opened the door, and the hinges creaked as if it was sighing for the first time in centuries. A fathomless darkness greeted me as did the hungry whispers bubbling coldly from inside.

Have you come to free us, child of man?

Oh, how delicious. She has met the others . . .

And live to tell, no doubt. Interesting indeed . . .

I crossed the threshold into their domain, praying Ebony would do what I needed her to do. I held the candlelight overhead to the writhing black mass swirling above me. Thousands of eyes narrowed on me, their eerily human-like irises shining with amusement. Their cold presence crept up my spine, grasping my neck with their long tendrils.

Heart drumming loudly, I was sure Silas would know I had opened this very door, but I couldn't turn back. Not when their riddle had haunted my waking nightmares, and the faint whispering of words was still etched into my skin.

"Tell me, how can I restore Silas's name?" I asked, my voice carrying in all manner of directions.

Too easy, girl. He is trapped here as much as we are, so why would we want to free our captor—our brethren? We are all communally damned, never to see peace, writhing in madness. The question you should be asking is if the others damned beside ussss.

The black mass darted to the open door, only to shrink back at the budding beams cast by the afternoon light. It hissed and slinked to the dark corners.

My fingers shook, the flames wobbling. "Are you speaking of the person responsible for the deaths in the village? Tell me something, children of darkness."

The black mass hissed, *Ignorant child, we are not them. Mindless, mischievous creatures, they are. We are far older, seen the darkest pits and fed on the sweetest of despair. We are all, and we are one.*

"Tell me what you know. They have shown me the past. Can you show me what the future holds, perhaps?" I pressed, and blood roared in my ears as a searing icy cold ripped through the warmth of the air.

I swallowed down the blaring warnings. "In exchange, I'll give you what you want."

The mass of eyes lowered to meet me at face level, flickering to a collection of color. A tendril caressed my cheeks, retracting it quickly as the light burned the darkness away.

Solve our little riddle, and perhaps we can find common ground.

Yesss—solve our little riddle, and we'll tell you all you need to know.

The mass darted once more across the room, blending in with the shadowy corners.

I stepped carefully around the mass, candelabra held high to find three candles remained lit. Panic set in as I watched another candle extinguished to the harsh laughter of the shadows. "You tell me how to free Silas, the ghost, and everyone from this curse, not some stupid riddle. I don't have time for that!"

Careful now, you only have so much light left. It smirked as thousands of its eyes scrunching together. *But there is something we desssssire, more so than sweet despair, and it'd behoove you to take what we are offering, child.*

"Then, get to the point," I growled, patience running thin.

Candles flickered, and my palms were clammy as I shot a glance back to the door behind me to Ebony, so out of reach.

I began small, hungry to grow. We consume all, devouring everything in turning tides. I dance and make merry before I destroy all in my path—what am I?

"Too easy." I smirked. It did not take me long to guess as I held the key. "I am a flame."

Its eyes smiled. *Excellent. What you desire is found in a labyrinth, hidden by passages of time. Blood spilled upon a name for the burden to be shared by a lover's kiss.*

Another candle extinguished, smoke rising as a warning. "You told me that you would tell me all I needed to know!"

And we have, it hissed once more, voices reverberating from its inky mass. *You never asked us how. In exchange, we want a promise from you, child of man.*

The last flame flickered, and I edged for the door. "Why should I promise you anything? You have not said a single thing that was useful."

There will come a time where you need us. When the time comes and all you have learned becomes pain shall be the time you release us. A time when the agony of my brethren wreaks upon this plane—then you shall free us. Free us as repayment for your troubles.

The mass stalked toward me and kissed my ear with its icy breath. Cold tendrils wrapped around exposed flesh as my chilled hand closed around the wrought-iron banister. It slicked back, the dark trapped behind the threshold, unable to cross over the light.

"Shut it!" I screamed at Ebony.

Her ghostly hands slammed the door shut in the mass's face.

The door bucked a few times, its hinges shaking, tossing the key aside as the shadows hissed in delight.

I scrambled for the key and slammed it into the lock, forcing the darkness out. Ebony's form shivered

as we stepped back from the door, watching—waiting
for the screams to begin, but they never came.
    Then, just as before, it all went quiet.

Twenty-Five

"**Y**ou're looking a little stressed. It's far too early for that, Little Dove." Silas stood in the doorway, his lean body pressing against the mahogany frame.

He was dressed in dark trousers and a red silk blouse eerily the color of blood with his black mask affixed to his face in accents of gold.

Silas's lips quirked up into a smile before he shifted off the frame and sauntered forward. "I assumed you'd be in town and not here, of all places."

"You did say I could come here whenever I wanted," I said.

My fingers felt worn from shifting through stacks of books. They itched to play the piano and get lost in the music—to forget the impending doom on the horizon and the accursed riddle.

After we were sure the mass behind the door was no longer a threat, Ebony and I had begun shifting through the stacks for a clue to the riddle the damn thing spouted. All we managed to find was nothing, and the book that once held the key was nothing more than a simple nursery tale about a princess trapped in a tower.

Silas picked up the book I had set aside. "Where did you find this?" He placed a hand over the rough cover, his face unreadable between the mix of emotions rolling deep under his skin. The world halted at that moment. The planets ceased spinning as Silas uttered out, "Valeria, where did you find this?"

I dropped my hand from the shelf. Ebony and I shared a glance. "I'm not sure, but I guess it would have been somewhere about the tower."

Silas stared at the ascending tower of books with a look of a man who wished to not remember the darkest part of their souls. Ones in which they drowned to forget.

Silas sauntered languidly as if in a trance and placed the journal onto the shelf nestled between history and dust. Silas took my hand, lightning caressing skin, a lifetime shared between us as lovers born of different centuries never to taste the other. The same visions crammed themselves into my skull, yet his touch ground me into the present.

Silas ran a thumb over the ring, squeezing my hand tightly in his. In moments like these, I am struck by the strong deep feeling in my bones, the aggressive electric sting leaving me breathless.

I craved him as I do air as if my own existence depended on it, a fact I tried to deny for so long.

"Valeria." Silas's husky voice tickled my ear, pulling me in tight until I could taste those lips. "Promise me to never go in there again. Whatever they promised you, it's not worth freeing them or your life. I cannot lose you, not for my sake, not again." He kissed my hand softly, gaze lifting, and his mask shifted with mournful shadows, courtesy of candlelight and the dying day.

There was a newness, one I had not seen since coming to know the man, a fathomless depth of golden hues straining against the darkest parts. Struggling between the past, the gold locket tucked into his pants pocket, out of sight to the world kept close like a boundless chain, and the future, hand enraptured in mine. There was a long-begotten crossroad he must travel, waiting as one of his ghosts haunting him just as Cecilia had.

I squeezed his hand. "There is nothing you have to worry about. They offered me nothing of value. For now, let's focus on finding your true name." His palm caressed my cheeks, and I leaned into his touch.

Silas tipped my chin back. "I'd give you the stars and the moon. I'd give you my life, just, please, never go near that door."

My mind raced at his warning, but before I could refute, soft lips brushed against mine, tentative at first.

I fluttered my lids closed as fingers stroked my buttoned, lace back. Desire pulsed through my body, fluttering in fiery heat. I wove my palms through his hair as he pushed me up against the shelf. Books fell from their hold and scattered below us as we breathed life into dusty books. I wrapped my legs around his waist, and hands cupped me as he whisked us onto the sprawling cushions of the recamier. Silas broke the kiss, eyes wild with untamed need reaching a hand to stroke my cheek, twirling a black strand.

Fangs protruded from his lips as his fingers swept across mine. Silas descended once more, pressing kiss after kiss lower down my body where flesh gave way to fabric. I strained against the restrictiveness of the dress. The lace stretching with every shuddering breath. The long-sleeve and sweeping neckline meant to keep me warm seared my flesh with each press of his kiss.

Silas untangled himself, breathless and hungry. "Turn around."

I stood, brushing my long hair out of the way of his working, agonizingly slow fingers unbuttoning. Each slip, he pressed a kiss to the bare skin underneath. Goose bumps raised as burning fury pumped through my veins.

I dropped my head back, a soft moan escaping, palms pressed to the falling dress as the final button released from its prison. Silas spun me around, his lips crashed onto mine, and I forgot all about the garment pooling at my feet, leaving me in undergarments and at the mercy of Silas's relentless attack. Hands gripped my thighs, and our kiss turned into teeth and tongue colliding with one another.

Silas's mouth caressed against my neck, kissing gently, his hand exploring the rest of my body. I arched into him, delicate strands of moonlight spooled between fingertips. The study fell away as the heat mounted in my belly. Hands brushed my chemise aside, fingers grazing bare flesh. Fire thrummed through my veins, scorching my flesh in the wake of Silas.

I gasped.

Silas dragged his fangs against my skin, hot and heavy breaths kissing my neck. I closed my eyes, anticipation drumming so loud I swore the gods heard the beating of my heart and how fast my blood chased at it. The pressure built upon my neck until his fangs sank deeply. My breath hitched, blood shrilling in my ear.

Pain bloomed into blissful pleasure, enveloping and complete. My own body separated from me, weightless against him, and I fell into an endless escape cast me into the great beyond and into the veil.

Don't you wish that we could be different?

The boy from my vision floated beyond reach, an infectious grin on his lips as the sunshine kissed his skin. Summer grass lazily danced between us, tickling my nose as we lay among the soft green fields. A hand stretched between us, and sparks flew across as the boy's own mouth moved, saying words that fell upon deaf ears. The warmth of the sight started dying as blood drummed, beating in its own accordance, staining crimson in its wake.

I opened my mouth, words spilling out as the scene shifted and formed, colliding in vivid colors. Words, unfamiliar, raked claws against my brain, begging for me to hear them, to carry them back with me.

The separation between the vision and my own body was thin. I was here and not. Forever in the golden sunlight of the field mingling with the dreary darkness of the castle's library. It called to me—dreams dancing sweetly on waves of euphoria.

"Valeria."

Silas's voice snapped me out of the vision. Worried eyes tethered me into my body once more, head pounding as the room tilted and shifted.

I focused in on his face, blood smeared across his lips, coating his tongue as he murmured softly to himself, "I went too deep. I should have stopped. Your heart slowed, so slow, and you were speaking softly. Whispering to me, unscrupulously in a language I hadn't heard in over five hundred years. I'm sorry, the hunger . . . it's getting worse."

He placed his head in his palms, turning away. Blood coated my tongue, and I realized all too late the consequences of the taste of metal and golden summer fields.

I shifted, the world tilting along with me and took his cheek. My mind struggled to form the words I desperately wished to say, as his blood circulated slowly within mine. The haze clouded my head as I scrunched my brows in effort.

"I'm—I'm alright."

The room ceased spinning, then sharpened into focus so violently I had thought I'd become sick. Silas cradled me in his lap, a halo of silver draping over us and heavy arms wrapped tight against me. Blood dripped from his lips, staining the white blouse. I dared not look at my own state of dress.

"I saw him again. In another vision."

The room fell away as green grass swayed in front of the black hair boy, lips moved with words so far out of touch—so out of reach that they were lost on me. Important words they were yet it pained me to not know what they were. There was a connection I felt in my bones as Silas reached for me, as a phantom weariness took hold. Those simple words were out in the ether, awaiting to be heard. Their very memories seared themselves into my brain.

"What did you see, Little Dove?"

"A dream," I replied, my own voice sounding strange and distant. "A beautiful dream."

There comes a time to wake up from the dream and endure the nightmare to follow. We were living on borrowed time, where days ticked away by mere minutes. Tucked under Silas's arms, the shadows lurked beyond the reaches of their cavernous corners. Watching. Waiting to devour the little happiness dared to exist in the dark.

I wondered if the dark-haired boy was swallowed up by the darkness. Cast in shadows far from the sun lit summer fields of happiness.

I nudged Silas, sinking deeper into cloves and spice and drifting into the golden light of the warm summer sun to the smiling boy under the willow tree.

Don't you wish we could be different?

Twenty-Six

"**I** want to visit my sister for the Winter Solstice."

The glass dropped to the floor, and shards of brilliant purple and blue shattered as blood pooled between us. Resignation reigned on Silas's gaze as if he had come to expect the question from my lips for quite some time now.

"I am not sure if I can grant such a request, Valeria. Not that I do not wish for you to see your family, but I am unsure if I can even make that possible."

His voice wavered, snapping at the ghosts who swept the glass away.

Dinner was a feast of roasted turkey covered in cranberry sauce, delicious but brought forth an ache. Seeing the food reminded me of the season that was upon us, a turning of the tides. Days had turned into months, and the guilt I carried expanded as I imagined Miriam grieving my death.

Dressed in mourning black, she'd travel to the family grave site placing wreaths at the headstone marker of Father and my own. A stone without a body under the ice-cold earth, mumbling the prayers with Mama standing there with all the stoicism she had, watching as Miriam cried and never shedding a tear.

"You passed through the mist when you met me. Surely, there is a way through," I argued, my own voice betraying me. "Please, I just want to see them for the Winter Solstice holiday. To let them know I am still alive, and they do not have to worry for me." I took his hand, warm and soft within mine, squeezing reassuringly.

The regrets trembled on lips pressed softly by the one I had thought of as a villain. Much had changed, and there with it, a regret I needed to right before I could allow the final piece to fall for me. The vitriol I undeservedly said to Miriam, her face sunken at the idea I was lost—handed a death sentence at the time only to be revived. I had to let her know I was alive—I was no longer on death's doorstep but instead was courted by him.

Cherished by him.

Loved by him.

My darkness would never touch the light of her purity, would never harbor the guilt of being the loved child. Would never shadow it again. I did not want her to move through her life with regrets or the singular thought that she was a terrible sister when it was, in fact, me. I needed to see her to make amends as if for the last time.

Silas's gaze shadowed the softness of the evening light, conflict and desire dancing across his face, a battle in which there was not an end. He scooted his chair back, coming to rest at my side, his thumb tracing the inner parts of my hand. Silas's throat bobbed as if he were descending to the sinking depths of fear. I'd imagine it building, pressing against him at the weight of this request, the centuries stretching beyond him, alone and frightened as each day passed and more of him wore away.

Like a rock beaten against the raging storms.

His hand felt firm against my back, bringing me into a shared embrace, bodies melded in perfect unison as if to share a secret or a last rite. Releasing me, he took the ring from his finger. It was a band of dark tungsten set with bloodred rubies, pairing with my ring. It vibrated with power.

Silas pressed a kiss to my hand before sliding on the heavy ring opposite to his on my left.

I watched as the ring slid itself down onto my finger, the once thick band having turned thin, matching my own ring.

"This ring will assure you safe passage through the mist under the care of the full moon for the next three days. You will act in my stead on this solstice night as you pass over to Endovier and roam among them." He kissed the ring and gazed up at me, gold irises flickering. Touching my cheek, he caressed it as if for the last time. "Try not to dally too long, Little Dove."

Silas kissed me, tender passion igniting, carving us both until we were hollow.

I cradled his face in my hands, fingers tracing the lines of his scars.

Sorrow sat upon his gaze as it danced between fear and hope.

The weight of his ring heavy upon my finger. I needed to leave before I would decide against it. Before I let this man consume me, once and for all. Before I let him take my life in his. Life was short and death so permanent. Death does not discriminate among the rich or the poor, nor does it care about the prayer we heed. No amount of prayer can erase our transgression in the end.

With lips trembling, I lifted my head high, getting to my feet. "I should be back in time for supper tomorrow night."

Silas grinned, sorrow lifting slightly. "I'll let Ebony know to expect you."

I strode to the door, heart accelerating with anticipation.

Silas followed, as did a small audience of resident ghosts, straining to get a look in front of the pale crowd. "The mist will take you to the outskirts and into a back alley of Endovier. Valeria, promise me— promise you will be safe."

I nodded, not turning back.

I could not bear to see the worry knitting his brow. To see the crude thought play out on his lips as it trembled.

"Silas," I said, opening the huge doors revealing the cloud filled night, the solstice moon greeting me. "I made a promise to help you find your name. I do not intend to break that promise. I will be back. Do not fret."

I stepped into the night and down the road, drifting into the mist.

The streets bustled with activities, newsies slinging the current events into the faces of people trying to go about their business. Men in their best suits strutted the street, tipping their hats in greeting to young women. The ladies fluttered, absorbed in their conversation, bumping everyone within their path, berated harshly by the group.

I gripped the umbrella, knuckles straining as I wove in and out of the foot traffic. Snatching it from an unsuspecting shop had not been the brightest of ideas but as the rain poured, it soaked anything caught in it to the bone.

I made my first stop at the church. Its pristine stained glass work and towering spires were not at all different from Silas's castle. Taking one granite step at a time, I entered the sanctuary in a flush of dead silence. Not a soul dared to utter a word, heads bowed in prayer in pews of oak.

In the corner of the sanctuary, a table of towering tea light candles offered solace to those who lit one for the dead. I sat next to a woman in prayer. She was past her prime, gray hair giving way to white underneath, with wrinkles sunken into sharp cheeks. Shaky hands held a pewter stick of flame to the candles, lighting several one by one.

I took a stick, lighting it under a small taper candle and lit three. One for Cecilia, one for Silas, and one for me. I cited the old prayers, the ones I remembered the most and hope it'd bring solace to myself and to Cecilia and Silas stuck in a never-ending web of suffering.

"Valeria?" The gray woman lifted her gaze. It was Mama taking her place. The rueful scorn deepened her wrinkles, aging her ghastly. *"How?"*

I sighed. "Hello, Mama." I placed the pewter stick back into the basket and rose to my feet. When I smoothed out the fabric of my dress, the crimson hue danced with the flames catching the small droplets of chains from the waist chain around the corset.

"You look well. I'm surprised nevertheless. Have you come back to save your family—the ones that you abandoned in their time of need?" Mama twisted her lips, the light in gray-blue eyes ignited furiously. "Miriam is beside herself and too delicate to understand what it means for our family. The kind of vultures that'd eat us up if word was to spill. I was lucky enough to be able to sell the last of the household goods that had any value. With you here, we can resume things as normal, and we can—"

"No."

Mama pursed her lips together.

I fiddled with my ring—the one Silas presented me many moons ago in the same sanctuary I now stood in.

The church was the same, the red carpet pleated by sunlight streaming through colored glass. At the altar was the podium carved into the base of the stand. The depiction of the gods I so long ago had felt were lost.

"What do you mean, 'No?'" Mama sneered.

I squared my shoulders. "I mean no. I came back, not for you. I came back for Miriam. I came back to say goodbye."

"Do you not realize what Miriam had to suffer through while you were gone! I had to offer her hand to William lest he spilled what had happened in the church the night the beast took you away from us." She pulled me in tight, bony fingers digging into the soft felt of my cloak. "Are you so heartless to condemn your own flesh and blood?"

I gripped her hands, biting my tongue at the worst of the curses I wish I'd uttered every day of my life. Since Father, it had been nothing more than how to save the family from ruin. I had been used as a pawn designed by Mama to escape the fate that was helplessly bestowed onto us from a dead man. There had been other ways, I am sure. Ways that would have not guaranteed us to stay in the limelight of society but ways nevertheless ensured that Mama's own daughters still had choices they could make.

Instead, she had led one daughter to the wolves to be swallowed whole without a second thought all for a name that would never deign the legacy she so claimed it ought to.

Mama's wrinkled face showed much in the months I have been gone, worried over such trivial matters of a broken name, withering away as I had made me second-guess if she had succumbed to my illness. With Silas's blessing, I offered one kindness left to the woman who was no longer my mother, not in the ways that truly mattered.

"If you thought I was here for you or the family, you are sorely mistaken. Meet me at the Tearoom at sunset. Tell Miriam as well. You will do this for me, or so help me God, Mama, I will tear you down with me," I growled. Before she could utter a word, I spun on my heels and left the church.

Twenty-Seven

Outside of the Tearoom, trepidation thundered in my chest as my fist clenched at my side. I fiddled with Silas's heavy ring, the metal cutting into my finger. I drew the umbrella down, the sun kissing my brow, took a breath in, and opened the door to the shop.

It was as I remembered, tables clustered in the shop with ladies engaged in chatting, enveloping the space in cacophony. Steam rose from hot cups of tea nestled in fine china. Waves of lavender, rose hips, hibiscus, and earthly roots crashed into one another, turning about the establishment as spirits. There were earnest looks as I entered from the women sitting at the packed tables. It was not that long ago I was one of them, listening to gossip and converging with the masses for the simple hope of what every young lady in high society wanted, a love match. That had been off the table for quite some time during these meetings.

I glided to an open table, and a cup was turned over.

A lady rushed over, her service uniform a mess of wet stains all in variance of hues. "Apologies, ma'am. Hope I was not keeping you long. What can I get you?" She clasped her hands in front of her, wryly wringing them.

Her shoulders were pensive as she bit her lips, waiting for a lurid of harsh words to be hurled at her again.

I inclined my head toward the tea bar as glittering bottles and jars beckoned from their glass case. When I spied a bottle of green, a smile crept upon my lips. "Tell your barman that I'd like la fée verte."

The server's eyes widened. "Oh, no, ma'am, we do not serve that sort of drink here. I do not know where you are from, but liquor, especially la fée verte, has been banned for quite some time."

I leaned closely, dropping my voice. "I think you'd make an exception for me. After all, to any untrained eye, they might be a well-disguised jar but dangerous to one that knows." I pulled a coin from the pouch, sweet elation pulsing. "Here is something to sweeten the deal. Tell your man there is one with his name if he were to look the other way." The server frowned to where I pulled another coin from my satchel. "Some advice is to make the bottles indiscreet by putting them in brown bottles and out of the limelight. Would be ashamed if this place were to close due to a little issue such as that."

The server took the coin and flipped it over to examine its validity, then deposited it into her pocket before striding to the bar with her mission.

I leaned back and watched the exchange between her and the bartender. The man's gaze flickered toward me, brow raised as he argued with the woman. He did not appear to believe her until she pulled out the lone coin. He glanced back, and this time, I smiled and waved. The man quickly worked, pouring the green drink into a glass. Setting a sugar cube upon a silver spoon, he dripped water onto it and into the aphrodisiac, spiriting the glass body until I was face to face with its shape.

I placed the other silver coin into the palm of the server. She only nodded before slipping back to the bar.

I sipped the absinthe, the taste of black licorice and anise dancing upon my lips. I tried to push the thought of the possibility of Silas being here, sipping the delightfully banned drink alongside me. The ache clung to my heart and my empty left hand.

I swirled the green around the glass, watching the door for Miriam. I had not the slightest clue what I was to say, and in the months I had been away, there had been many things to say. She did not have to worry about my health or my safety, the books I had read, the lessons I had learned under Ayla and Silas's instructions had filled my days in ways that mattered.

Delightful ways I had often yearned for more so than for any man. I was a corpse when I left, and upon returning, I was alive again.

For so long, I had been made to be someone I was not. That I had to be for the sake of Miriam and the fate of our family in the wake of Father's death. I had to take the role of the older sister and take the brunt. Feed the ostentatious lies Mama had hoped would save our family.

Now, the person that sat in the tea shop sipping absinthe was no longer the same quiet girl.

This woman had venom.

"I would have thought you a stranger if it wasn't for the fact that you seemed so familiar." Miriam clutched a small bag, jaw clenched as she took in the scene of the shop. Golden curls spilled from her neat bun, tickling the nape of her alabaster skin, likened to that of a porcelain doll. Her cerulean gaze trained on the glass in front of me. "Didn't take you to partake in forbidden activities. My—how the tables have turned."

I smiled, gesturing to the empty seat in front of me. "Please."

She sat, prim and proper as a lady does—beckoning a server who never asked for her order but deposited the teapot without another word and went about his business.

"We thought you were dead after not hearing from you in so long after that brute of a man whisked you away from us."

I sipped idly. "He is not much of a brute as he is out of practice. I'd written sooner, but there is not much of a mail system in which he lives."

"And now, what's changed?" Miriam's lips thinned. "As I have said we do not hear from you—Mama was beside herself."

I chuckled, imagining Mama's cunning plan fall apart as Silas had uttered those words in the place of worship.

Miriam brought her cup to her lips with a pout. "I do not know what you had to do—are you back for good? Are you marrying William?"

I nearly gagged. "William—what makes you think that I am back to marry him?"

She lowered her head, a grim look casting upon her frightening in the twenty years we had shared the same spaces was one that's beyond terrifying.

"Please, you need to help me. I can't—I can't—I'm not like you." Miriam reached across the table, grasping my hand with such urgency. A familiar gaudy ring adorned her finger. "Mama arranged it shortly after you left. We are to be married in a few weeks, and I-I . . ."

Her hand shook, releasing my arms and lifting the scalding liquid to her lips, sloshing out of the cup and onto the white tablecloth.

The door jingled opened, the sound of familiar footsteps clamoring our way, then stopping at the head of the table. The absinthe was working its magic, and the overwhelming thoughts of the last six months disappeared in a single moment. I was back to the wall erected between the horror of society and Miriam, the little angel. Envious little angel incapable of stains upon her delicate feature.

Mama stern eyes stooped to the green of my glass before setting upon my face. William's devilish smirk was that of a sword speared through me. William placed a hand on my shoulder, squeezing tightly.

Miriam's eyes pleaded, sorry that they were here. That she was going to drag me back to a life I never wanted. But it was her deal, after all, my life for hers.

It was not fair I was living carefree, when she had to take my place.

Why did she have to marry the brute she once had called handsome and admirable?

I bit my lip. "I'd say congrats are in order, but I am guessing it isn't what you had thought it would be." I gripped William's hand, sliding it off, not daring to glance up in his direction.

"I see that you are well, Valeria. It appears your color has returned. I am sure that everyone is happy that you are home," Mama huffed, having felt indignant for the last six months.

It was as if I had never left—that Silas had never existed.

I swirled the glass, the contents a reflection of my own head. There was not much I could do to help her, not without outright killing the man. The fact I did want this man dead shivered through my warmed body. Not that Silas would oppose murder. But I refuse to commit to bloodshed. Miriam glanced expectantly at Mama and at me, lips pursed as frustration knitted her brow. William enjoyed the show he was promised to, and judging by his presence, he wanted to ensure we were not getting out unscathed.

I lifted my narrow gaze upon Mama. "What is it that you want, Mama?"

"You, to come back. What else is there, child?" she mused, shooing away the waiter and anyone else in the vicinity.

"I am not coming back, Mama."

"Oh, I think you are. After all, you did run out on William. You were the talk of the town for quite some time. Not only did you embarrass yourself but him and the rest of this family as well. Think of your sister, Valeria." She cocked her head, graying strands spilling over her shoulder in simple elegance.

Mama was putting forth her best class act. Our conversation in the church spooked her—this, I was sure of. Since then, she was creating a farce in the public to gain sympathy, a game she was often used to and on that may have worked months ago.

I growled, "You know damn well that is not what happened. If anyone ran, it was this fool." I nodded toward William, his smirk transforming into a harsh scowl.

"Mrs. McCallister, I was promised to wed one of your daughters in exchange for my assistance. I hope you do not intend to break that agreement." With a click of his tongue and a tug of his lips, he added, "A woman such as Valeria is one that has had challenges especially with living with a beast for so long. I doubt she would have a proper prospect if anyone were to find out the circumstances of her disappearance and possible defilement of another man."

"I am sure some arrangements can be made. After all, we had agreed upon our terms, and I see no reason to change since Valeria has returned." Mama fanned herself, watching the heads of ladies giving her nods of approval.

As if the matriarch of the illustrious McCallister family had any worth left and was not the fraud she truly was.

"Yes, and I do not like to let go of my toys." William cocked his head with an awful sneer.

Blood shrilled in my ears, my stomach bottoming out. Under the table, I shifted Silas's ring on my finger, not even registering the words until they hung heavy on their grim faces.

"I am sure that will be no problem." I whipped my hand from under the table, showing them the band. "I am sure I can ask my *husband* to ensure the welfare of my family and not depend on a man who would rather be in the company of prostitutes than of a proper lady."

William sent the chair flying back, shaking. Fury raged in his gaze, a vein popping out of his forehead becoming clear as he lowered himself to me, finger pointed high.

"You say another word, and I will not hesitate to kill you," he whispered. "You may have gotten away from me once, but I will not let that happen again or your sister, such a submissive woman—you should take after her lead."

I pondered, knowing everyone within the business is watching with eager eyes, frothing at the mouth for the drama. I let the burn of the absinthe coat my throat, pulling myself to my feet, for all I had endured the last six months—this small man meant nothing to me now.

I raised my head, lips curled. "You are mistaken, William. You ever touch me or my sister again, you will die. That, I am sure of." I dug through my coat, brandishing a pouch of gold and silver with more than enough to live a comfortable lifestyle. I tossed it toward Miriam. "Take it and find yourself someone who is worthy of you."

Miriam swiped the pouch from off the table, quick enough before Mama or William had a chance to take it from her. She opened it and gasped. "Valeria . . ."

I glared at Mama, letting the next words ring out into the space. "If you sell Miriam to this abusive man, Mama, you will have sealed not only William's but your own deaths. I nor Miriam are to be pawns. Is that clear?"

Mama scowled.

Miriam's eyes widened, nodding in appreciation. She would have never fought Mama in the matter. Never saying a single word about objecting to the notion of saving our reputation—our money for the sake of this man. No, she would have gone on to marry William, enduring the daily abuse only to become burdened with a child, unable to leave or worse.

Dead.

This was the one thing I could do for her, this one small mercy. She'd find someone, maybe not from Endovier or someone rich, but one who'd keep her happy for the rest of her days. That is the best gift I can give her before walking out of her life for the last time.

For the last time, I took in Miriam's soft features—always the opposite of me. The light to my dark, the soft to my harshness—innocent and pure more than I ever can hope to be. The last tie I had to this side of the mortal coil. I strode to the door of the teahouse, aware of the eyes upon me, but I dared not to look.

I twisted the ring, heat singing under the band. Silas was waiting. One foot after another, the path opened for me, becoming clear and unhindered. Whispers of both the past and future collided with one until they were one voice, urging forward through space and time.

I would not dally any longer. I had a promise to keep.

Mama cleared her throat, catching me off guard as my hand rested on the knob of the door, the mist closing in on the city streets. The simple sentence laced was with venom.

"Happy birthday, Valeria. May you live long and happy."

I stumbled back through the mist and onto a familiar dirt road. The castle greeted me as the ring upon my finger seared onto my hand with the pain barely registering. I walked the long path up to the grand wood door.

Ebony greeted me with open arms, but I just opted to travel up the long staircase up to my room—to the darkness that was eager to either greet me or to feed off on.

I shouldn't have been rattled.

Miriam was saved from a life of torture and pain. I should've been happy about that. I tossed myself onto the soft cushion of the bed, the scent of Silas having faded on the silk sheets. I yearned for the simpler times when I had thought I knew what was right and what was wrong.

It was my birthday, a day of supposed blissful happiness to celebrate the turning of another year. I survived to see another year turn and no longer thought to be at death's door. So why did I already feel as if I were dead?

The evening sun set in the west and the darkness greeted me eagerly as it always has.

Twenty-Eight

That night, at dinner, a huge box wrapped with suspicion and intrigue sat on the table in my seat. Silas grinned ear to ear, lounging in his chair, watching me intently, dressed handsomely—devilish even wearing a suit cut from the darkness itself. A vision of shadows shimmered under the bright candlelight. Flecks of red and gold accented his collar draped in fine gold and rubies. The only piece missing was a heavy crown of silver on top of his—

I snapped back to Silas, piercing gold eyes watching me closely.

"Everything alright, Little Dove?"

Silas indeed wore a suit, but it was not the luxurious one I had seen moments ago. It was simple, as fine silk glimmered softly.

I gripped the back of the chair, returning my perplexity to the enormity sitting among delicacies, the red bow draped the white of the wrapping paper with eagerness and haste.

Ebony appeared to be in good spirits, smiling wide enough to reach the empty black sockets as her form flickered from translucent to opaque. Unease rocked my belly, an itch crawled up my skin, staring at the large package.

"What's with the box?" I asked.

Ebony fluttered down from the chandelier, and goose bumps raised across my skin as she came to rest by my side. Ebony held my hands, her form more solid, as if she was truly here. "Open it! Oh, it is simply lovely! I promise you won't be disappointed!"

The candle's flames brightened as her smile threatened to burst the entire room in light. Silas attempted to hide his smirk by scratching at his chin, only to nod my way.

I tugged at the bow, coming undone in a few simple strokes. I carefully ripped through the paper to a black box underneath. Ebony nodded profusely, one second away from jumping in herself to open the box as her phantom hands inched closer.

I opened it and nearly dropped to my knees. "Silas, I . . ." My voice drifted to Silas's warm and adorning gaze, unfazed while perched over his glass of wine. "I can't . . . This is . . . Gods . . ."

"You came home distressed after your visit. I gathered it did not go well, and I had Ebony look into a few things for me and came to find that it had been your birthday."

Ebony touched my shoulder, finger firm and cool. "I told this lug that we simply could not possibly pass this important day up. So, while you were moping about—I procured a list for this brood to go get for tonight." She stuck her tongue out at Silas, an amusing gesture.

I laughed, and it sounded odd passing from my lips. I let my hand pass over the ornate fabric, satin and beading raised against my palm.

The dress was gorgeous, wrapped pretty in the shimmery gold and gossamer. An over-the-shoulder gown with black and crimson trimmings laid together with exquisiteness made for a queen. Silk gloves sat on top, along with a necklace statement piece, a single tear-shaped ruby and a black velvet strap.

I blinked in disbelief as reality set back in. One does not wear such a gown for a man and ghosts but for a grand ball. To be admired by some and envied by others—all eyes trailing after desire incarnate.

Mama would have considered the gown to be ludicrous and sinful, especially a gift from a man, a scandal waiting to happen. Miriam would have thought it bold and a gorgeous sentiment from a lover's eye.

I set the dress back into the box, the ache heavy in my chest. "This is gorgeous, but I'd have nowhere to wear such a gown."

As if on cue, Silas flashed from his seat and cupped my chin. "I thought you may say that, so I had arranged a ball here. The residents are preparing themselves as we speak. It has been so long for them, too, that I hope you would give them the honor of wearing this." He kissed my hand.

"Silas, what are you saying?" I said, mind envisioning the grand occasion.

The difference between the engagement ball and this one swirled in my head.

Silas's devilish grin widened, and I fought the urge to shamelessly kiss it off him. "Valeria McCallister, would you do me the honor of accompanying me to tonight's ball?"

His hands wandered down, tracing the edge of my hips and up the length of my spine.

I leaned into his scent of cloves and spice and wordlessly kissed those fine lips of his. "You are simply too much."

Silas pressed a kiss to my forehead. "I'd do anything for you. That is a promise."

Ebony twisted my dark hair into braids that tickled my bare back, folding the plait in on itself and pinning it high. "Alright, open your eyes!"

In the mirror, an endless, bewildering forest-green stare greeted me. The woman reflected back was regal, only to miss a crown to adorn the infinity blackness of her dark hair. My own body was foreign to me, fuller with curves prominent accentuated the dark trimmings of the dress. The fabric was smooth against my hand, the beading glimmering in the moonlight.

I was crimson and nightshade, akin to Silas and his dark beauty.

The full moon gleamed brightly into the room from the balcony as I took to the evening air, the harsh cold filled my lungs. Moonlight gave off a distinct red glow, casting an eerie scarlet color reflecting off the roses. The greenery of the rose bushes took on a whole other color, darkening to a nearly black hue. The frigid air bit into bare skin, my own breath whispered past my lips into the glittering of stars off in the distant winter's night. I draped my arms over the stone ledge and stared up to the jeweled thrones smiling down on mortal flesh.

At the edge of the garden, I spotted a tall, lanky shadow lurking among the roses, hunched over. It crept out of sight, disappearing behind the thicket of the maze.

I leaned over the ledge, searching the lower grounds for the figure.

"You look stunning." Silas leaned against the doorway with a half-cocked smile gracing his beautiful lips. "Everything okay, Little Dove?"

I strode to him and set a cold hand in his. I shook the thought out of my head. I was not going to let anything ruin such a moment for me. I may not have many more moments like this after tonight.

"Yes," I said, placing a kiss upon his lips. I looped my arm in his and allowed him to escort us down to the booming voices and swell of music.

I drank in Silas as I did the music, as if it was my very last.

Twenty-Nine

hosts danced in mid-air with masks adorning their faces, lost to the shrill of the music sweeping them higher into the air of the grand ballroom. We came to a stop at the head of the staircase. The music died, and the ghosts turned their attention to us.

"Ladies and gentlemen, your host, Silas," Ebony shrilled from above, floating between us and the residents, then straightened her hand, "and his lovely guest of honor, Valeria McCallister!"

She wore a capped-sleeve dress reminiscent of a cloud dancing among the blue sky. She, too, wore a mask of glittering silver, and her hair swirled around her as if she was submerged in a grand river.

The room erupted with a roar of applause as ghosts hollered in delight from all directions, and the music began again.

Silas squeezed my hand, guiding us down the steps and onto the ballroom floor.

"Ready?" Silas said, voice low and seductive against my ear. With a hand, he braced my back, and heat swelled like wildfire ready to consume me on the spot.

Bewildered, I said, "For what?"

Silas swept us into the waltz, our bodies moving together in synchroneity. The intoxication of the music spun us around, blurring the crowd of faceless ghosts behind us as our steps quickened. The melody roared loudly with delight, shrilling of violins danced with us, constant bursts of energy as we twirled higher and higher. Our feet hardly touched the ground, meeting the ghosts high above the air with such ease as Silas held me with such care.

It was one, then two—and three waltz Silas guided me into, never straying for a single stolen touch. Each spin fanned the fire budding in my chest outward. The desire for more grew with burning intensity.

I squealed with delight as Silas tossed me up into the air, my skirt blooming as a rosebud, catching me with grace and ease. Breathless and hungry, I threw my head back and laughed as the music crescendo into a soft piano forte.

When the dance came to an end, Silas's eyes twinkled, kissing my hand softly before escorting us off the dancefloor and out onto the terrace overlooking the garden.

The bloodred moon kissed the grounds of the castle, illuminating the mist in crimson floating about in licking whips. The snow-covered bushes in thick clumps. The snow dusted the petals and fell from the shrubbery, weightless as if it was raining roses upon the snow-covered path into the gardens.

Silas ran his thumb over in my hand, wearing a tense expression overlooking the scene.

I cupped his face in my palms and kissed him softly. "You're tense."

"I am not." He pressed back against my lips. Silas wrapped his arms around me and held me tightly. The music began to play a soft serenade, mournful in its melody as the bows of cellos lengthen their notes to curl in the midnight air. "If this were to be my last night on Earth, then I hope it is this one."

I stroked his face, trembling as I pictured what life would have been had I met him sooner. What future would there be for us in the end, trapped behind decaying walls and a curse at its end?

"Don't," I began, "say things like that. I haven't given up. The answers are here, that I am sure of. We still have time to . . ."

Silas's lips captured mine, cherishing tenderly each gentle gasp. His hand on my neck wandered down the length of my body resting upon my hips, pulling me in tight against the furnace consuming us whole.

I wrapped my fingers into his suit coat, draping over his shoulder nail and raking his back. Breathless and enraptured, the Earth began to shudder to life as the music came to a stop. Chunks of the roof collapsed into the garden, rose petals scattering into the winter night.

Ebony flew in and whispered in Silas's ear.

Silas turned from tense to pensive, worry laced thick upon his brow as Ebony departed. He gave my hand a reassuring squeeze. "It appears we might be. But let us not dwell on that. Tonight is about you, Little Dove."

The structure resettled, and the music continued on unhindered from the small shake that rocked it. The castle was slow to succumb to its illness as much as I had been at the start. It was slowly dying, which meant Silas and the other residents had a shorter time than what we thought.

There was no more time for dancing and sweet kisses.

I needed to find his name before the stones collapsed down on us and buried the truth with it.

I relinquished my hand from his as if for the last time. "Silas, this is not the time. Where else haven't we . . ."

Out in the distance, fire light burned beyond the gates. Shouts and hollering traveled up from the gravel road. The wrought-iron gates clanked against the night air in earnest as the shouts grew closer. The torches flared in the night, beckoning the mob.

"Silas," I wavered from the balcony, "the villagers—they're armed."

"Quickly." Silas shuffled us inside as the first gunshot rang out. We ran for the back entrance of the castle. I tripped over broken stones, knees scraped from the impact. "Valeria!" Silas gathered my skirt, lifting me to my feet in a single motion.

"I'm fine. We need to get—"

Banging reverberated on the doors against the hushed moans of the spirits above us. The door splintered upon impact, the victorious cheers resounding from outside.

"Kill the beast!" they screamed in chilling unison.

They were almost through the door, the splitters widening with every swing bashed at the wood.

I grabbed Silas, searching for any way to go.

The grounds would be flooded with villagers out for blood. The ghosts erratically screamed, shifting from this realm to the next. Some of the ghost forms barely held on before disappearing into the crumbling walls altogether. If the villagers would have made their way inside, what was stopping them from making their way to the west wing, to the shadows and to the ghost of Cecilia, who'd possibly rip them in two?

I spun around only to be caged by Silas's protective arms, creating a barrier between me and the shadow at the garden entrance door. Mud-coated black trousers and his long coat shielded him from the worst of the winter cold. Hair skewed from the blast of wind as the snow picked up with wild eyes staring from behind the rear sight post of a rifle.

William cocked the gun back, the barrel aimed at Silas's chest. "Get your hands off her, demon!"

Thirty

"Stay behind me," Silas whispered to me.

The beating of the door drummed louder, threatening to burst from the hinges. We were trapped between William's gun and the mob, with our only exit being the balcony.

Silas's body towered over mine, a shield from William's cold, hard gaze.

"Don't make me say it again, beast," William growled.

"When I say run, run to the balcony," Silas commanded. "I'll be right behind you."

I nodded, aware of the cries for blood. Aware of too many things as the world threatened to plunge further.

"Run!"

Gunfire rang out, and I scurried to the ledge of the balcony. Footsteps quickly shuffled behind me before sweeping arms took hold of my waist and dropped us ten feet down into the snow-laden earth. I tumbled out of reach, groaning as pain fired up my limbs from the impact. To my right, Silas laid still, bleeding profusely from his chest.

I scurried to his side. "Oh my gods, Silas!" I shook him, trying to stop the bleeding—anything.

Silas moaned, taking his hand into the hole and extracting the bullet. His chest heaved as the wound slowly tried to heal. "I'm fine. We must move."

Another shot rang out into the night.

Silas jumped and covered me with his body as it made an impact. "Argh!"

William stood atop of the balcony, the rifle barrel pointed at us dead center.

"Can you walk?" I asked, draping him over my shoulders and mustering up the strength to make it through the night.

Silas nodded, wrapping his arms around me. "Hold on!" As another shot rang out, we disappeared into the garden.

Part of the way into the maze, Silas came to an abrupt stop, coughing up black blood and crashing into the statue. He collapsed, chest heaving as the wounds showed no signs of healing.

"What the hell were in those bullets?" he croaked out.

I took a hold of his hand, watching as his breathing became more erratic. "Silas, you need blood." I shoved my hair aside and ripped off the bandages to days' old wounds.

"I can't, Valeria. It would be more dangerous now than ever. They will kill both of us, and they are armed to the teeth," Silas grunted as he shoved his finger into his abdomen and extracted another bullet.

The silver bullet was intricately engraved, coated in white ash within the grooves, similar to the ash that had been given to me sometime ago.

Silas tossed it aside and sat up against the overturned bench. "It won't be long before they find us."

The lone gravestone stood, watching this play out all yet again with its carving of *Vi et animo* etched into its surface, mocking us.

I once again urged Silas. "Drink. You are right. We don't have much time. But what I do know is that they are out to kill you—not me. Drink and hide until this can pass."

The sound of footsteps entered the maze, a stampede on the hunt. They shouted, winding themselves around.

Silas held me tight against him, doing what he had done thousands of times before, it seemed. He kissed my neck before piercing my flesh. The burning made way for the ebbing ecstasy flooding my veins. Silas pulled away, gasping, as blood trickled down his mouth and his wounds stitched themselves back together.

Silas kissed me, blood coating my tongue entwined with cloves and spice. The footsteps pounded closer nearly upon us. The taste of salt mixed in with blood as tears welled.

Silas cupped my face. "I promise I won't be long."

Within moments, the crowd descended upon us, and Silas was nowhere to be found.

I leaned against the stone, blood coating my lips, as the crowd trampled through.

William spotted me, and his lips curled into a wry grin. "It appeared that the beast had left his lover off in a hurry. Care to tell us where he went?"

My legs wobbled as I stood to confront William. The crowd behind him simply whispered, unsure of the sight that was before them.

"Are we sure that this is the person? She seemed awfully familiar?"

"Wasn't she the girl always seen with Ayla?"

"Why is she protecting the demon? Do you think he has her in his thrall?" William tossed his gun to a man, grabbing me by the scruff of my dress.

"Where is he?"

Alcohol laced his breath, as did furious rage.

"I won't tell you." I spat in his face.

William dropped me to the cold, hard earth.

I flinched as his foot came within an inch of my face.

A man grabbed his shoulder, yanking William back. "Sir, it is highly inappropriate to strike a woman. We are here for the demon, not the girl."

William shook the man off. "I will do whatever I please even if that means that she comes with me."

I gathered myself to my feet, squaring up William in the presence of those who I consider an enemy. "You would have to kill me before I ever go with you willingly."

William contemplated a moment, a heinous grin sliding across his face as his eyes flickered to the space behind me. "I'm sure that won't be an issue."

"What—" I began, blinding pain erupting against my skull and my legs crumbled from underneath me.

William and the mob blurred together with the faint torch light and the blackness swimming in my vision.

He dropped to his knees, and the last image I saw was the heinous smile. "Should have listened to me."

Thirty-One

Drifting.

Falling.

Dreaming.

I awoke to the soft grass upon my feet, the giant willow standing firm in front. The summer breeze rustled through dark curtains as the warmth of the late afternoon sun sank into chilled skin. I searched for the boy often here among the grass, lips tugged high into a lazy grin. But he was not there upon the red flowers resembling blood. The dread swelled during the ball and exploded into a million pieces as my gaze landed on a single skull sitting on top of a freshly marked grave.

"I don't have much time, Valeria."

Standing out in the field was a woman with hair that of fire and deep emerald eyes with lips drawn thin into a sly smile. Her pallor was a sickly alabaster, so pale that blue marred her skin in spider web veins and eyes, a ghost shade of white.

She regarded the skull for a moment or two, picking it up and cradling it in her hands.

"Cecilia," I said.

Those eyes settled on me, staring right through mortal flesh.

"Cecilia." I took a step, heels sinking into the grass and the mud. I tugged at my foot to free it and found that I couldn't.

Dark clouds moved in, gusts of wind kicking up flowers and dust high into the air. Thunder rumbled, and lighting crackled across the blooming sky.

Cecilia's hair whipped wildly around her, unbothered by the shifting storm. "Save him."

Lightning struck the tree, engulfing the scene in bright white light. Her scream cut through the howling wind, shrieking with urgency.

I flung to life, crashing into my body with warm arms wrapped tight against my chest pinning me in place. Soft cushions braced my back and fingers, and a blanket laid curled at my feet. I glanced about the room to stone walls and familiarity.

I was in my room. I was still on the castle grounds.

My attention was drawn to the hands wrapped around me, clearly not the ones I had gotten accustomed to in the many months at Castle Briar, with their scars and calluses. These were ones that had seen horrendous violence, white scars and fresh cuts across knuckles. Revulsion curled in my stomach, bile stung my throat.

"I wondered how long you'd be out for." William snickered, slicing into my skin more so than his hand on my wrist.

Thousands of questions flitted through with only one that truly mattered. "Where's Silas?"

"She was right. You truly are brainwashed," William sneered. His mouth dropped to my ear. "Now, why would you want to know where the monster is? Is it because you fancy the abomination more than your own?"

I shoved my elbow deep into his side, lessening his grip, and stumbled out of the bed.

Fingers grazed the door when it opened of its own accord.

Ayla stepped through the doorway with a sword pressed firmly to my chest. "What did I say in making sure she stays put until the trap is set?"

"Not my fault the bitch decided to make a break for it," William scoffed.

Ayla's cold gaze lashed onto me. "I do not care for the drama this has caused, but what I do care for is killing that vampire."

Biting back tears, my cheeks burning as rage and disgust brewed within my veins. Ayla was in on his plan. The person I thought of as a friend was now using me as bait to kill the man I love.

I braced myself against the bedpost, far away from Ayla's sword and from William. The cold air did little to the torn dress, the bodice hung by mere threads and the train ripped to shreds. Holding the bone plate close, fury guiding upwards meeting the revulsion pulsating its way through my body.

"Whatever it is you intend, I will not help you," I gritted out between bared teeth.

William jumped off the bed, corralling me toward the wall. I was met by cool stone and William's wicked sneer was as close as I had ever wanted to be. He was a hair's breadth away, dropping his lips to my ear.

"Protecting it, are we? I wonder how we can remedy this." He snaked his palm up my thigh, teasing menacing across my naked skin.

I froze, breaths coming in heaving heavy gasps. Instinct took over, palm stinging as it flew across his face. William stumbled a few paces and clutched his cheek, his cheeks redder by the second, murder blazing high in his eyes.

"You little bitch." William lunged for me, pinning me against the wall by the neck.

I clawed, nails biting into flesh, drawing blood.

The harder I fought, the tighter his hold became as dark spots danced high in my vision.

"That's enough. Any further, and we give him a reason to kill the both of us."

Ayla's cool voice echoed with the grip around my throat loosening.

I dropped to the floor, coughing for air as I doubled over onto the cool stone. Pain laced my scalp, lifting me to my feet. "Why don't we cut the crap and you tell us where Silas ran off to?"

I screamed, pain lacing itself through my flesh. Struggling to gain my bearing, I scraped William's hand, crying out, "I won't. I won't. I won't!"

Tears welled in my eyes with each parting syllable.

William threw me across the room, sending me into the nightstand, shoulder hitting against the hardwood, which fell over on impact. Hot blood trickled from the head wound and from various scrapes.

Contents from the drawer scattered across the floor. The vial of Silas's long-forgotten blood, the journal, and the dried rose from nights ago splayed out.

William wrapped his hands around the fabric of the falling dress and hauled me up. Terror seized me, and I squeezed my eyes, bracing for the next blow as his hands tightened around me.

William laughed. "I wondered if the beast has had his fun with you yet." He tossed me onto the bed and unbuckled his pants.

I scurried to the opposite side of the bed, mind racing.

The balcony doors were nearby. If I could pry one open quick enough to drop down, escaping into the garden's maze should not be an issue. The drop was only ten feet from the ground at best. I'd simply be bruised. At worst, I break something in the fall.

I inched closer to the door.

William's hungry eyes grew ever closer until he was climbing across the bed, licking his lips.

Ayla coughed into her hand, drawing William's attention away. "I have a better plan. Silas is still somewhere on these grounds and could not have gotten far with that gunshot wound. We need to lure him out, and she"—she swept across the room, pulling William to his feet, who was completely enthralled—"is the ticket. Don't you think it would be fitting to repay the debt?" Cold blue eyes swept to me. "A perfect catalyst to end all of this for once and for all."

William's cruel smile widened as he hopped off the bed and buckled his pants. He called to a few people, their bodies shadowing the door to where I did not make out clearly who they were other than to guess that they were a part of the village. He whispered to them in soft hush voices that I only made out a few words.

"Lure" and "ready." Without much context, my heart sank. I was either going to draw out Silas, or I was going to marry William.

William turned back to us. "I'll prepare the arrangements for the ceremony, and we shall have our beast before the blood moon is over."

William disappeared down the hall, shouting orders at those wandering. I did not stop to think how they got past the ghost but knew that they somehow did. I dare not to picture Ebony alone and terrified, trapped in an endless abyss and watch as her castle and master were taken all in the same night.

Ayla followed, and just like the many times before in this castle, the person standing in Ayla's place was not her but a long-forgotten form. In some manners, it made sense as the truth fumbled its way out.

"What is it that you are after?"

She stopped dead cold, body rigid as she flexed her fingers. Ayla shifted, tossing her head back in response. "Vengeance of what I am owed and my right." Turning swiftly, she left the room, her heels clicked down the corridor.

Thirty-Two

Igroaned, scooting along the floor to rest my back against the bed. Muscles strained as I propped myself up to sit up properly. My foot nudged the diamond shape vial inches away, the glass chiming dully across the floorboards. It landed near the spine of the journal curled at the base of my thigh. I picked the vial up, the taste of blood from the garden danced faintly upon my lips.

Without a single thought, I drank it. Icy cold raced through my veins, skin stitching itself back together and the pain eased into a phantom ache. I sighed, settling into a fraying body.

I had to solve it—solve everything. That very night.

I leafed through the journal once more, trying to find any clue that could solve the mystery and make sense of what was happening. Cecilia, the shadows, and even the weird visions of the past yielded nothing coherent in leading me to the heart of the mysteries. I had read through this multiple times to find Silas's true name to come up with no leads. Yet part of me knew the answer had to be there.

It was my only hope.

I held the journal tight, adjusting to the faint scrawling. The last entry was written in terrible haste with some of the words not entirely printed onto the page properly. Black ink smeared, as if the author's shaky hand was becoming more and more unstable as he sat to write. Occasionally, the stroke of the lettering changed with most of the cases happening in the middle of the word. Then there were the matters of the stray letters tucked away into the flaps and the oddity of letters at the bottom of the correspondences.

I set the book on the desk, digging into the drawers for pen and paper. I hastily circled the capitalized letters, stringing them into a coherent name, ringing alarm bells inside of my head.

In the garden.

In the garden glared up at me, the dawning realization of what it referred to thrummed through me. *Vi et animo.* With heart and soul. The shadow's riddles.

I worked quickly, unfolding the anagram before me until the conclusion reflected in the moonlit room on crumbling sheets. I sat in disbelief at the two little words, my own stomach dropping, connecting piece after piece of what I had to do—what needed to be done.

I shifted the empty vial in my hand, a plan forming as I stitched together the shadow's riddle. I needed more time—time I no longer had. Squeezing my eyes shut, a knot forming as I sent up a prayer to anyone that'll listen.

Please, let there be another ways this ends.

The door creaked open as two men staggered over each other to get through the doorway.

I shuffled the journal and the paper quickly into the drawer and spun around to greet the two men.

Both appeared brute and roguish. One of the burly men stood at the doorway, a shadow against the bright candlelight hallway, while the other one stepped into the room. The man had seen better days by the look of the eyepatch, scars, and open sores dotting his body.

He held out a box draped in a black ribbon. "Order from the master. He said to put this on for the ceremonies."

The stench of infection rolled off him, smothering the room in sickness.

I crossed my arms, crinkling my nose in defiance. "And if I refuse?"

The one from the door piped up, sneering in delight. "He also said that you might say that. If you don't want the dress, then he has given us the order to get you there any way possible, even if that means stripping you naked and having a little—fun."

I snarled, taking the box. "Thanks, but no thanks. If that is all, leave me to change."

The two looked on, the sickly one blushing as he averted his gaze whereas the one in the door was unfazed by my comment.

"Leave."

"Don't get any ideas."

Then there was silence, and I was left with the box.

I set it on the bed and carefully unwrapped it. In it lay a gown of silvery white and a white postcard with Miriam's writing scrawled across the pristine paper.

A small wedding gift. Sorry, Valeria, for not being the sister you deserved.

I took the gown out, unsure of what she meant by small. A knife clattered to the bottom of the box, simple and understated with the meaning of Miriam's final words clear as day. I clutched the blade to my chest. I did not know what this cost her to get this here, but this was a sound message. This was her own attempt at making things right and, with that, a means to fight.

I readied myself, slipping the knife into my bodice letting a faint smile creep upon my lips. When the men finally come to collect me, I was sitting on the bed calmly with the same grin.

"What is with the funny look?" one asked with a grimace. "Finally change your tune?"

The cool blade pressed softly against my breast, the images of William's death played through my head.

"You can say that."

The ballroom was staged for the biggest charade and class act I would ever put on. The musicians swayed solemnly, holding their instruments tight, beginning to slowly play the dread march. Although it appeared that the ballroom was not where the ceremony was to be held. No, William's henchmen continued to guide me until we were to the double doors overlooking the garden.

One of William's men's arms was looped around me tightly, pressing into my body, forcing us forward. The garden was draped in elegance, and beauty from the roses glinted as rubies at night. At the end of the aisle, a priest from the town stood in audacious robes of white gold, pure as the snow that covered the grounds.

William stood to the priest's left, smug and grinning villainously. I had thought the gods might have to smite him for the awful look crawling upon his face.

I shuddered against the wind. The snow had begun to coat the rose bushes in earnest, falling faster than the petals could bear, which fell weightlessly onto the cold ground, framing the aisle lit by the glow of the moon, staining everything in red.

I was unsure as to why William had opted for us to lure Silas outside rather than inside. The weather was less than ideal. Even the fog that kept to the roads crept its way into the garden and spooling smoky tendrils. It appeared the castle grounds, too, sensed the end nearing.

The men pushed us down the aisle, and I stumbled, only to be yanked back violently. The grip on my upper arm tightened, constricting painfully as each step brought me closer. I prayed that Silas stayed as far away from these people. I fear for not only my safety but for his.

Silas, if you can hear me, please know I-I love you.

The words echoed across my mind in the same way that all that time ago I had reached out beyond myself to see him again. I was armed with the will to fight and find his name to end whatever curse that held him captive.

I stood upon the altar, and William forcefully grabbed my hand, shoving a silver band onto my finger. The priest began mumbling the wedding prayer, his tongue stumbling on the words as William's impatience was running out.

"Say the blasted words, Priest."

The priest, taken aback, grumbled out, "Sir, there are procedures in the wedding rites."

"I do not care about procedures. What I care about is taking what is mine."

His fingers dug into my arm, and I let out a yelp as I struggled to remain upright, twisting my arm to try and get out of his wrists.

The knife sliced against my breast, twisting with me as I wrenched myself out of William's grasp. His finger wrapped around my wrist, securing themselves into place. The little few words that came from the priest's lips were ones I dreaded six months ago and even more so now.

"In the eyes of God, I pronounce you husband and—"

The wind grew stronger. Rose petals danced gracefully in a tornado of crimson, obscuring my vision of the garden, William, and the priest.

I was enveloped in a storm of red.

Gentle hands swept over William's death grip, and long pale fingers wrapped around my wrist and my waist. In a flash, warm arms yanked me back from the altar, and cloves and spice sweetly tickled my nose. A deluge of petals dissipated to the sound of my heart beating a beautiful melody.

The priest cowered behind a rose bush, the old man shaking beneath his ropes. William was beet red and attempted to pull the man up by the collar as he pointed a shaky finger toward us.

"You!" he growled out.

Down upon the hand was a signet ring on his left, the familiar silver tungsten band.

I softened against him. "You came."

Silas stroked the bruises on my wrist, a playful smile pressed against the back of my hand as he offered a kiss, responding, "You called."

Tears welled, and I trembled against his embrace, enraptured by piercing gold dancing between regret and elation, the slender shape of his lips quirked in a serene smile, the crinkle of his brow and just him.

It was him.

"Silas, this is a trap. You need to run—now!"

William charged toward us, brandishing a knife. "I won't let you."

"Care to dance." Silas swept me into his arm, spinning us to narrowly avoid the blade. William stumbled before charging forward again.

Silas's grip tightened, dancing around William's crazed slashing.

"I. Will. Not. Let. You. Have. Her." He grunted between missed slashes.

Silas continued to gliding gracefully.

William called to his henchmen, "Don't just stand there. Get him!"

The men joined in the dance. Silas's movements quickened, avoiding the men's careless attempts at grabbing me while William tried to get close.

I clung on to the collar of his button-down shirt before reaching down the front of my dress to the cool metal. "Silas," I said softly as William's cries of frustration echoed into the night. "I want you to let me down."

Silas's leg slammed down on one of the men's skulls and then kicked the poor man into the other onto the hard pavement.

They groaned softly, both alive enough to be rendered unconscious and out of the fight, enraging William further.

He charged again at Silas.

"Little Dove, I do not think that is a good idea."

I held the knife. The heavy weight of it in my palm gave me enough courage to see this through.

Silas's eyes widened, mouth twisted into a small grin. "Never ceases to amaze me, Little Dove."

Silas deflected a blow from William, sending us back toward the castle as he created the necessary distance between William and us. William hunched over against one of the statues, clouds of ice spilling from his lips. Disdain glinted high upon his brow. Silas set me down gently on the cobblestone at the very moment William caught his second wind.

"You whore, letting this monster taint you," William spat, sauntering closer with the slim blade's malicious glint bouncing off in silver light onto the statues. "I could have given you everything, had you been a good little girl. I would have been a man of respect and power with you by my side had you not run off with a beast."

I stood my ground, the knife flush against my thigh.

This man wanted my life in the worst way. To control me, to make me nothing more than a doll. I had been a doll for much of my life. To uphold the lie that began with my father, a lie that William had pursued to his own end goals.

William stood paces away from me, bloodlust suspended in the air.

I sensed Silas's own uneasiness behind me.

William adjusted the knife high. "I could have given you everything. You brought this on yourself."

William brought down his arm, arching it high above me.

He missed.

I plunged my own knife into his chest, stumbling into him.

"Same to you."

The knife clattered to the ground with his gaze drawn toward his chest and the instrument of death protruding out from it. Blood spurted slowly from the wound, crimson coating my hand.

William gasped, pushing me away, dooming himself.

Blood swelled from the wound, a river of crimson coating the gray suit jacket in slick black.

William dropped to his knees, arm outreached as the realization of what I had done played across his face. "You fucking stabbed me. The bitch stabbed me." He began to laugh, clutching at his chest, then slumped to his side, lifeless eyes casting their unfettered gaze to the ground.

The knife dropped from my hands, legs buckling underneath with the dawning realization of having just killed a man. Bile climbed my throat, staring at the lifeless body of William, the light draining from him.

Silas's lean body wrapped itself around my shaking form, a hand resting on my hip as he pulled me upward. "Are you alright, Little Dove?"

I nodded, my gaze fixed to the splayed corpse. "I did not think it would come to this."

"I know."

I touched Silas's cheek as my soft skin met with salty tears.

Silas's rueful expression mirrored my own, of love and affection. Lips crashed against mine, a sweet poison expunged of all unearthly sins.

I cupped his cheeks, breaking the kiss with a heartfelt ache. I ran my thumb across the softness of his lips. I wanted to memorize his face, the firm edges and soft lines of his scars against my fingertips. I leaned closer, letting my forehead touch his, praying he could not hear my thoughts expounding in sorrow.

I pulled away, grabbing William's knife. "Ask me your question."

Silas smiled gently, oblivious to what I'd found. "Valeria, do you want to guess my name?"

"I do."

"Alright, Little Dove. Do not keep me in suspense."

The pain written in those pages, the pain of the prince who had gone through hell after losing his beloved, the tragedy consuming his life and the life of his people. Until he was nothing more than a stranger to himself in a castle full of ghosts. All trapped by a curse woven by blood only to be unbroken by blood.

"Valeria."

Silas's worried voice snapped my attention back.

I gripped the knife, "Silas, I—"

I spat up blood, stumbling back. I drifted downwards to the crimson blooming across silver down at my abdomen. Rich scarlet soaked through the silvery gown with the steady stream dripping onto the courtyard, staining the snow.

Drip. Drip. Drip.

Silas's horrid expression shook with gold flares drifting far beyond the hole.

"No . . . Valeria!"

I dropped to my knees, Silas catching in his arms. He held his hands over the wound, attempting to staunch the bleeding the best he could.

I removed his hand, the fire burning across my flesh, racing against the clock. "Don't . . ."

Laughter pulled me to where William's body lay, traveling to a familiar face holding the knife stained in blood.

"Miss me?"

Silas's expression darkened.

"Narcisa."

Ayla's lips curled. "Glad you remembered me after all these years."

Thirty-Three

Narcisa gracefully toyed with the knife, crimson dripping down cold steel. Silas attempted to stop the bleeding, going as far as to rip his own wrist open to force his blood into my lips. I only sputtered out more, the metallic taste coating my tongue. I pressed on the wound, the surrounding area burning and intensifying.

This time, no amount of Silas's blood could fix me.

Silas glared at Narcisa, venom evident in his eyes. "I'm surprised your shadows are not doing your dirty work for you. If it's my life you want, then take it. Leave her out of it."

Narcisa howled with laughter. "Leave her out? Oh, honey, she is the reason this is all happening." She glanced down at William's dead body, her heel kicking the poor corpse several feet into the grass. "Leading this idiot to the gates all because he couldn't handle his little possession being used by another. But I have to hand it to him. He was able to pass through the barrier and essentially reduce it down to nothing."

The grounds that used to be covered in thick rolling banks of fog were, as she said, nonexistent. Shattering the soft quiet into the chaos of screams unfolding between the living and the dead.

The fog.

The fog kept people walking in circles, the last defense barrier for Silas and the ghost.

"The fog," I rasped, the words grating in my throat, "you are—talking about—the fog—aren't you?" I coughed, bloody ribbons in the night as crimson dancing in the midnight garden.

"Ding, ding, ding! *We* have a winner! Slow on the uptake, though." Narcisa grinned.

Coldness replaced the person I thought I knew. Ayla never existed. I was once more a pawn in someone else's game.

"What is it that you want, Narcisa? I did not think you would have the gall to stick around after that night," Silas growled.

"Tsk." Narcisa grimaced. "You should have died that night. How was I to expect that Cecilia had contacts that planned to derail my attempts to take the throne? I got rid of one piece of trash, only for it to get replaced." She pointed knife in our direction. "Won't you be a dear and die?" Narcisa lunged, disappearing in a flurry of movement descending upon us.

Silas countered Narcisa, struggling for control as I registered the knife missing my head by a few inches., their struggle blurring across the garden.

I clutched at my abdomen, scorching dulling in tides. Panting, I needed to move, to get help—mind raced as a pain shot upward, setting fire to my body.

Narcisa kicked Silas, throwing him several yards into the rose bushes. "I have had enough! One iteration of you was enough, but now twice, obscene."

I stumbled to my feet, adrenaline coursing through my veins.

Narcisa stepped forward, unhindered, toward me. "Goodbye, Val—"

Silas rammed into her, both of their bodies becoming a blur as they disappeared into the night.

I seized the opportunity, stumbling up the path into the castle.

If Narcisa was to kill me, then so be it, but I was not going to simply lay down to do so.

The scene in the castle interior was thrusted into chaos. Villagers against ghosts, shadows diving onto poor men to eat away at flesh. Ghosts wailed as they staved off exorcisms others from committing acts against the living.

I stumbled up the stairs, clutching at my stomach.

"Where do you think you are going?" one man sneered. He held a large wooden stake in hand with the other holding a gun.

I brandished the knife and smiled. "It would be best if you turned around."

The men did exactly that, flesh turning pale upon seeing Ebony. Blackened hair set free from her prim, proper bun, lips curled to gruesome sharp teeth and eyes red as a burning ember. Sinew and blood coated her apron, while she held a man's head. Eyes rolled back to reveal the whites.

The men both ran past, stumbling down to get away from the heinous ghost.

I leaned against the banister, the scent of blood rising higher and coating my nostrils. "Ebony . . . I need . . . I need—your help."

Ebony flickered back to the black coals and rushed to my side. "You're hurt. Oh my, we need to get you medical attention. So much blood, you've lost so much blood. Perhaps we need to find Si—"

"There's no time," I wheezed.

With the banister as support and Ebony's cold touch, I started to climb the steps up to the west wing clinging to life for as long as I could.

"Get me to the library."

The west wing was in chaos.

Ebony guided me down the converging hallways, stones falling and slamming into the red carpet.

Terrible shrill voices screamed out within, *LET US OUT! LET US OUT!*

Determined in my mission, I pressed onward, cradling the keys in my palm and prayed the library was intact.

I had no idea how long it would take Narcisa to track me down or how long Silas could hold them off.

"Hold on a little longer," Ebony cried in my ear. She held me upright with what little form she carried.

I used the wall as support, leaving a trail of blood smeared to the walls the closer we came to the familiar doors.

With haste, I unlocked the door.

The library was in ruins. A large stone had collapsed onto the piano and tore through many of the book cases. Books were scattered alongside chunks of stones embedded into the wood. The tall spiral was in shambles but still stood gallant.

I breathed a sigh of relief. "Quickly, we must find the key!" I limped to the stacks, begging my mind to remember where Silas had placed it.

Ebony worked through stacks of books scattered along the floor. I traced fingers against the shelves of the tower, leaning against them for support. Among the books, I found the volume and the silver key shivered with anticipation. "Ebony, the door."

She took a hold of me, guiding us up the long spiral stairs to the door, one I'd never thought I would come to again.

The dark voices urged from behind the door, *You're back, child! Come to free us now?*

They shrieked as I pressed the key into the lock and twisted it open. The door swung back to inky blackness and the curling of shadows.

"Gotcha." Narcisa's arms looped around me, and a knife pressed to my throat. "Out of places to hide, huh." The blade bit into my neck. "Surely, this was not the best you could come up with. I'm a little disappointed."

From the depths, the shadows watched with eyes pulled to the scene and heinous grins stretched wide. *Say the words . . . Say you release us from our prison, and we shall . . . assist you.*

Throat bobbing, I didn't spare another second. "I release you from your prison. Come forth, shadows."

"What?" The knife dropped out of Narcisa's palm, clattering to the ground. "No!"

Shadows bubbled and bulged, their form bursting forth from decaying wood and stones. The mass stood on four legs, crossing the threshold into the moonlight in heinous awful beauty. Shadows rose to the surface of its flesh, a mess of eyeballs flickering into our direction as its black body shifted in iridescent light.

I suggest you run, little child.

It lunged for Narcisa, clamping its maw around her arm and clawing at her. Shadows shot upward and meeting the mass's attack. Blood streamed down her arm, enticing the beast more. It came again, snapping onto her leg.

I did what it said and ran to the ladder connecting to the roof, not looking back at the terrible sound of ripping flesh and Narcisa's or the mass's hallowed screams.

Thirty-Four

I clung to the ladder, forcing myself to climb. The door to the roof was there as the cries of Narcisa died down, replaced by haunting wails. I threw open the door, cold wind gusting snowflakes into the blood moon's glow. The world turned into a haze, dipping in and out with dark spots clouding my vision. I broke out in convulsing shivers, fingers slowly turning icy blue.

The blood from my abdomen had slowed. Leaning against the tall spire, I noticed the trail of blood gave away where I was hiding. There was no masking and death breathing down my neck, kissing me softly.

I dug my fingers into the stone, preparing to climb again but, instead, collapsed. "No."

Legs shook as I attempted to stand. I shuffled one step at a time, refusing to raise an eye an inch above the ground before collapsing to my knees. I panted out clouds of air, the silver of the gown matching the moon's eerie glow as did the snow.

I clawed at the stones, vision blurring.

"There you are," Narcisa whispered in my ear. She held her arm tight with a sneer and limped forward on my leg. It appeared the shadows had taken a piece of her before scattering. "Nowhere left to run, I see. Once I put you out of your misery, he will succumb to this curse and do what he should have done all those centuries ago—die."

I tilted my head up, and Narcisa was bathed in the light, ash hair aglow in scarlet, painting blood onto her shredded dress. Cuts and scrapes were bleeding slowly, but she had suffered heavy losses with her limbs.

Shutting my eyes, I steadying the world in my mind as it tilted and spun. I heard everything in the heavens and on the Earth. The falling of a snowflake onto a warm stone, the soft whispers of the moon rays kissing the grounds, the cries of the battles of the living and dead with none of them knowing the implications. I heard the soft trickle of blood from Narcisa's wounds and knew she would also die tonight.

Did she kill Silas? Was he alright? I forced a breath into the burning storm building in my chest. I needed to stay alive a little longer, just a little longer.

"Isn't it enough that I will die? Why go through all the dramatics? Aren't you tired?" I rasped, the energy draining me as I cracked an eye open to Narcisa holding a knife limping closer in heavy clicks.

One, two, three. I counted each of her steps, trying to stay lucid.

She stopped, blood droplets streaming down her arm and leg with anger clouding icy blue eyes. The flat stone of the upper deck had a trail of blood leading to where we stood.

Perhaps Silas would find my body quickly if she managed to get this far.

I gripped the knife at my side. "You killed Cecilia and tried to kill Silas. You drank the same poison and had been cursed the same as he. Except you preyed on the villagers while he sat with his demons. For centuries, you have rotted in a village, waiting to kill Silas. Why? What for? Power? A throne? All of it is gone, so what does it matter anymore?"

Narcisa grinned from ear to ear, continuing her advance. "You make it seem so much more mundane than what it is." She laughed, baring my neck against the cool metal. "You see, I did all of this simply because I loved the man so much that I hate him. All I wanted was power—to rule, and he just tossed me aside. I became something for him only to be tossed aside for what—a woman from a country who was continually causing war. I saw how happy they were, and I hated it, so I killed her."

She traced the blade downward to the center of collarbone. "Little did I know Silas chose to heed the words of the same crazy witch, sending Amaris into chaos with a silly little curse. The difference between his curse and mine is that he chose his tomb. Mine was one crafted as long as he remained alive."

"And the villagers—the people in the ballroom that night."

"They hardly know they are fighting among ghosts. Forgotten people barely held together by flesh and bone. Trapped the same way he and I are. And all you had to do to free them was kill the monster, and this would have been dealt with. I could have gone on to much better things than to be trapped in this bubble with these ghosts."

Hot blood trickled down my chest, the knife biting into flesh and the black spots overtaking my vision.

"You are the monster, not him."

Blood and fear tasted heady upon my tongue.

I yelped as the knife plunged deeper into my chest. "Such a trivial matter now. Although I should have killed you well before now."

Head dropped to the side, I spied Ebony floating with an army of the resident ghosts and shadows at her feet. It appeared the ghosts had expounded, some of the villagers among the faces I had come to know so well. Narcisa had yet to acknowledge them, and Ebony nodded solemnly as if she was waiting—as if she knew we were both damned.

"Let me ask you," I gargled out, blood gushing through my teeth as the blade pierced deeper, "you preyed on the villagers . . ."

"Oh, them," she snarled. "So gullible. And I had to survive somehow until I breached the castle walls."

"How about the woman that used to be the apothecary—a nurse." I nodded to Ebony, fury radiating into pure hot white light.

"I had to blend in somehow, so she was the first to go," Narcisa replied as the rumbling began.

The grounds shook under us, jarring Narcisa onto the ground, sending the knife skittering out of reach.

Ebony and her ghost wailed, toppling stones and collapsing towers. Ghosts surrounded the small scene, with Narcisa backed into the corner. They laid their hands on Narcisa, flickering before she doubled over, screaming. One by one as one soul after the next disappeared into her.

"No. NO!" Narcisa cried.

The specters crept closer. The tower behind us creaked and swayed, the sharp sound of stones—the groan of the collapse imminent.

"Stay away from me. STAY AWAY."

One by one, the spiritual orbs disappeared, and Narcisa collapsed, screaming in agony. Bit by bit, she withered, smooth skin decaying into rotting flesh as the ghosts tore her apart.

Black orbs stared up for the last time as Ebony gave a sad smile before joining others—disappearing into a purple ball and silencing Narcisa's screams.

The castle was still shaking, the stones behind my back groaning as the tower finally succumbed to the rampage, littering the ground around me and striking Narcisa.

I gazed up to the sky, the stars glittering among white frost, and closed my eyes as the crumbling structure came down at last.

377

Thirty-Five

"Y ou can open your eyes now, Little Dove."

A pair of warm hands strung across my lap with another pressed gently to the wound, long tapered fingers covered in my blood. Golden eyes searched mine, fierce and electrifying against my fading body.

The crumbled mess of the tower laid inches from my feet. A single pale hand stretched from the rubble, and gray stones covered the rest of the body. The taste of blood hung on my lips, and my grip on life was fading quickly.

Far away, Silas urged me to drink, words cutting through the blur of darkness before I took the plunge. "Valeria, you need to drink. You need to—I can't—I can't lose you. I love you. Come back and chastise me.

Come back and throw harsh words at me. Play me like the fool that I am. Just, please—don't leave."

I pushed his wrist away, the strength I had earlier all but gone. I was slipping into the darkness and didn't know if I was going to return. Vision tilting and blurring, I cupped his hand. "Silas"—I choked down fire—"your name—Vi et animo—the dragon crest . . ."

Silas cupped my cheek. "Shush, save your strength."

"It can't—" Blood was everywhere, swallowing the night sky whole and staining the land. "Blood spilled . . . upon a name . . ."

With a hand stained in blood, I held him, held him as the expansive darkness beckoned. I held him despite the cost.

For the last time, I had to be selfish.

I kissed him, the taste of blood and salt stinging my throat. When I released him, tears streamed down my cheeks as I uttered, "I . . . release you . . . Maven Drogos . . ."

"Valeria, no—NO!"

The darkness exploded into a bright white light.

Expansive and deep, the darkness rippled in a smooth cascade upon the distorted vision before me. The further I moved through the scene, the more the light came into focus to a soft field covered in bright red tulips. A woman stood alone. Burnt copper mingled with the summer wind as bright green gleamed at me with softness and assurance.

She stood by the willow tree, surrounded by blue water and sweet grass. She reached for me, delicate fingers rough with callus shattered the dark space, taking a hold of my hand. The light shifted, a ball of illumination mutating into the glow of the setting evening sun. Rubble turned into waves as the willow tree's soft limbs swayed.

I was in the field I had seen so often before, walking among tulips in the summer heat. The woman's steady gaze never wavered and never shifted from the serenity ebbing from her.

"You saved him from the curse but at the cost of your life."

When she spoke, the open air fell into cavernous echoes, whispering into the void.

She placed a small object into my hand and closed my palm before I could tell what it was. "You released us, but in doing so, you doomed yourself. A path you now must walk alone."

A glow emitted from my palm, warmth and a sense of wholeness difficult to place as the pain and aches erased themselves. Skin stitched back together in a golden glow, pulsating beat by beat.

The woman's form faded as light beamed into the field. Mournful, she clasped her hands together and watched as the world enveloped. The more I forgot—I forgot what pain was, what suffering was, I forgot how I ended up here, and I forgot the man who waited for me.

In the distance, the boy with raven hair walked to the man with hair as pure as driven snow. Standing apart, their expressions were unreadable, but there was clarity in which they greeted another. They exchanged unheard words, the boy nodding with an innocent smile. It was as if they had been lost to each other, sharing in silence to an embrace as petals showered them.

Darkness licked at the edges of the meadow, and Cecilia's sad smile followed me as the scene disappeared into the folds. Silas—Maven's voice cut through with urgency and renewed energy, shaking the scenery to its core, distorting it further.

"Valeria, come back."

The earth cracked, swallowing the boy and the man, beams fracturing.

Cecilia squeezed my palm. "Tell Maven I shall wait even if eternity passes and the fields are all but gone—I will wait. And, Valeria"—she planted a warm kiss onto my forehead and exploded into silver butterflies—"take care of him, will you?"

I opened my eyes to the blue sky and beautiful sunlight. The smell of sweet incense tickled my nose, and the soft chirping of birds blared in my ears. The bed underneath did little for my body, racked in pain as if I had torn my limb off and had sewn it back on. The ache in the back of my throat was on fire. Harsh sunrays streamed through broken windows, burning my eyes as my senses overloaded to the sights and sounds.

"You're awake."

At the edge of the bed sat a tense man. His blood sang to mine, heart thundering with anticipation or fear—hard to deduce as it roared. It took me a moment to fully recognize the man sitting in front of me. His long snow hair was gone, replaced by locks dark as night. Bright golden eyes no longer stared back at me but instead were round, tear-rimmed midnight eyes. Jagged white scars were prominent on his face, but there was no doubt I had encountered him in visions before and had haunted me since.

I sat up, clutching my throat, "Sil—Maven, I thought—where are we—"

His name was strange on my lips yet still tasted as it had been before.

The room was small and dank. Petrichor smothered the room in the same way dust had settled over the wood. It was familiar as my gaze landed on a large table full of herbs that sat undisturbed.

"The castle is gone," Maven said as he rubbed at his knee. "The ghosts, the villagers, Narcisa—are all gone. And um . . ." His throat bobbed as he took my hand in his, rubbing at the inner part. "I carried you. I wasn't sure if you were dead, and I hardly knew what to do. All I could think about the entire way was that . . . you weren't breathing."

His words were laced in sheer agony.

He came closer, the scent of cloves and spice mingling with his blood. The thirst clouded my mind, and I gripped his arm, digging long nails into his blouse. Searing pain inflamed my gums, grazing his neck, and I sucked in a gasp.

"It's a wonder you didn't lose control. I'm so thirsty," I breathed, body burned with need, with want and desire.

Maven took my hand, opening my palm to an object pressed against cool skin. The bloodlust drained out of my body. In my hand was a single red tulip crinkled from being held so tight.

I shuffled to the head of the bed, creating distance between what was and what is. I cleared my throat, the thirst grating against my vocal chords. "Cecilia said she was waiting for you."

Maven plucked the flower gingerly from my hand. His expression was in disbelief as he glanced between us. Several long moments passed before he set the tulip down onto the nightstand and pulled me into an embrace.

"For whatever happened, I love you. That doesn't change anything. I will love you with whatever time I have left. My life is in the palm of your hands for you to do whatever with." He nuzzled my neck, and tears welled in my eyes as I struggled with the thirst.

"I love you." I shook against him.

In an instance, his lips captured mine and sated the thirst burning through my chest. I plunged my teeth into his neck, Maven letting out a soft moan as I drank deeply. The sweet elixir invaded my body at rapid speed, and I saw everything that there was to see.

His life—our life unfolding with such tender care. Tears fell in earnest, and I pulled away. Maven's heart beat roared in my ear, steady and strong. His arm slackened to my side, rubbing at the sheer fabric of the blood-soaked dress. He panted into my neck, and I held him—holding onto the last shred I had to this world.

"Valeria McCallister," he mumbled into my ear, raspy and humorous. He kissed my neck, slow and reserved. "Will you do me the honor and give me your life in exchange for mine?"

I laughed. "I thought we already had." I kissed him again, knowing that life was short and death so permanent.

Again and again, we devoured each other in that little cottage, reborn and no longer caged birds.

Acknowledgments

I started writing this book during a time where everything felt uncertain, so it feels weird to be writing this part after coming such a long way. Writing can be a lonely pursuit, but there are so many people I'd like to thank who brought this book from a dream to reality.

So, in no particular order, thank you to Joan for being the first person to read earlier drafts and providing me with your unhinged comments because, without them, I would have succumbed to madness during the editing process.

To my mother—yes, Mom, I'm thanking you for being excited to read the next book no matter what crazy ideas I tend to have and believing in them.

To Samantha, my fabulous editor and formatter. Without you, this book wouldn't be what it is today!

To Amanda, for being the first author friend I made in this community, who showed me the ropes and allowed me to talk at nauseum about this book— and my art addiction. As I said, writing can be lonely, but publishing can be isolating, so I'm glad I slid into your DMs!

To Angie, my wonderful agent at Lunar Literary Agency who believed in this project.

Without you guys, I wouldn't be leaning over my computer and crying while writing this! Thank you all!

About the Author

Holly Anne writes horror/thriller with a gothic flair or some such thing. Hailing from the Midwest, specifically from a corn maze in Iowa, Holly Anne grew up with a taste for the macabre and all things spooky inspired from works such as Edgar Allen Poe and Stephen King. Armed with her Masters in Social Work, a slight caffeine addiction, and her trusted familiar, Sebastian, Holly Anne crafts stories that rake into you. Stories that represent the harder parts of the human condition centering around themes of grief, longing, and pain.

When not contemplating her existence, she can be found consuming stories (spooky and non-spooky), giving herself emotional whiplash, enjoying long walks in the woods, and feeding the existential horror that persists. She is currently serving in the United States Army with her trusted companion Sebastian, who, unfortunately, is not a demon butler.

If you want to stay up to date with me,
check out my socials!

www.ingramcontent.com/pod-product-compliance
Lightning Source LLC
Chambersburg PA
CBHW030339120726
47901CB00007B/1839